A VERY DISASTROUS DARE

A FRIENDS-TO-LOVERS ROMANTIC COMEDY

CIDER COVE SWEET SOUTHERN ROMCOMS
BOOK 4

ELANA JOHNSON

feel good fiction

ELANA JOHNSON

ISBN-13: 978-1-63876-428-1

CHAPTER ONE

EMMA

THE BELL ABOVE THE FRONT DOOR AT PRETTY IN Petals chimes as I'm still fussing with a vase of cheerful daffodils and tulips. I wish I was as happy as their bright faces, but, "There's something just not...right...about this."

I move another pink tulip, but it immediately creates a hole that looks like a semi-truck could drive through it. Nope.

"Hello?" a woman calls, and I know exactly who it is. Regina Thompson. An older woman, probably a generation older than me, who orders fresh flowers for her monthly book club. I shudder just thinking about getting together with other people to discuss books. *Literature*, I'm sure Mrs. Thompson calls it.

My shiver continues, because it's freezing in the back room where I work with the flowers. I yell, "Be right out, Mrs. Thompson!" and pick up one more tulip. It irritates me that I'm going to give her extra flowers, but the centerpiece just isn't right yet, and more flowers is almost always the trick.

Sure enough, everything finally looks balanced between blooms, leaves, and garnishes, and I quickly sweep the bright pink ribbon around the vase and tie an expert bow in only seconds. I grab the beautiful amber vase and bustle out into the shop, where Mrs. Thompson waits at the counter.

"Sorry," I say breathlessly. "I've had a bunch of rush orders this week, and I've been running from dawn to dusk."

She gives me a closed-mouth smile, her credit card already out, ready to pay. I set her flowers on the counter and start to ring her up as she inspects them.

"What's the book tonight?" I ask her.

"*The Meaning of Everything*," she says, brightening like I'll have read that one. I've never dared to tell her that I only read floral magazines and the occasional domestic thriller novel.

"Sounds amazing," I lie right through my teeth, and I maintain my daffodil-bright smile until the chime above the door rings again, signaling her departure. Then my shoulders slump, and I look around the shop at all the carnage this week has brought.

Spring has officially sprung in Cider Cove, and my little flower shop is bursting with colorful blooms, which usually cheer me up. Today, though, it simply reminds me that everyone and their daughter is getting married. Hillary and Liam's nuptials are next week, and Ryanne and Elliott have set a date in May so as to give everyone a month to recover.

Then, Claudia and Beckett will be married in July— and I'm doing the flowers for all three events.

I swear, if I make it through the next three months, I should get a gold star, a tiara with real diamonds, and a special place in heaven.

I start cleaning up the shop, as I don't have any more orders being picked up today, and I should have a presentable retail space for anyone stopping by with the thought that their wife or girlfriend would like some flowers.

The door opens as I'm walking toward it, and Regina has returned in all her dark-haired sophistication. "I forgot to ask you," she says. "If you're coming to the small business meeting at the library tonight."

I'd completely forgotten about it, but I hitch my smile back into place and nod. "Yes, I usually do. What time is it again?"

"Six," she says with an air of importance. "I had them move it so I could still do book club at seven-thirty."

"Mm." I give her the closed-mouth smile now, because I'm open until six, and the small business meetings are usually later in the evening. But apparently not when Regina Thompson has book club. I mean, *book club*, you guys. It's gotta be the key to *the meaning of everything.*

I'm so glad others can't read my sarcastic thoughts, and Regina smiles at me. "I'll see you there." She leaves again, and though it's only four-ten, I want to go lock the door, pull the shades, and put out my "I'm sorry, we had to close early" sign. Who would it harm, really?

My stomach growls, a reminder that I haven't eaten since I grabbed a protein shake from the fridge at the Big House that morning. I keep tidying up, moving the bouquets and arrangements that didn't sell today to the refrigeration unit so I can preserve their freshness as much as possible.

There's nothing I like as much as sweeping up the shop, and I start to do that as I think about the business meeting. I did have it in my calendar, but I've just had such a busy day— "And this whole week," I say—that I'd forgotten. Now, with a little less to get done, my mind has more freedom to wander, and I remember that we're talking about the Summer Faire at the meeting tonight.

The town of Cider Cove is expected to open sign-ups for various things, from the parade entries, to vendors at the fair, to fair and boutique participants, and I've already determined that I'm going to apply for a booth this year. I didn't last year, because I was in the process of buying Pretty in Petals outright, and there was no time for anything else.

But as a local business owner, I want to make sure Pretty in Petals has a prime spot at the boutique and fair this year. Even if all I do is hand out business cards, it'll be a win. Cider Cove doesn't have another dedicated floral shop, but it's also one of several small communities that have glommed onto the bigger city of Charleston—and there are plenty of places to buy flowers in the metropolis that extends past the physical boundaries of the town.

In fact, most people who live in Cider Cove commute to work in the city. That's literally the definition of a suburb.

I mist the potted plants near the window, thinking about how much has changed since I bought this place last fall. It hasn't been easy, but every day I fall more in love with my little shop and the joy it brings to me, and to everyone who comes in to buy flowers for someone else.

That's the best part about flowers—they're usually given to someone else as a loving gesture. I love that about them, and I love providing that for people. No one ever buys me flowers, but I know how to take them home for myself or my roommates. With the thought of having my boyfriend come buy flowers from me, for me, I think of Aaron Stansfield.

We had a few "friend-dates" over Christmas and New Year's, but he started seeing someone else after that. "Anna," I mumble to myself. "Or Adrielle. Amy?" I don't remember her name, but I know it starts with the same letter as his. Aaron owns the hardware store right next door to my flower shop, and we're friends, but we're not like, call-each-other-and-talk-about-our-dates-with-other-people type of friends.

He took over the store from his father in January, and he's been going to the small business meetings for years. In fact, I learned about them from him.

For some reason, my heartbeat does a weird ping-pongy thing through my body, like someone's slamming it up to my skull and it's getting bounced around from left to right in unstructured ways.

I finish with the shop and finally return to my refrigerated room—Sir Chills-a-Lot—to check my phone. I've missed several texts on my roommates' thread, which isn't all that unusual. I swear, some of them can text by blinking and they have their phones with them and available all the time.

Hillary: *Final dress fitting tomorrow! You better be there, maid of honor!*

She's sent it to everyone, because all five of us in the Big House are her maids of honor. She moved back in about three weeks ago, but she's only got the essentials—clothes and toiletries—as if she's on an extended vacation. Everything else was moved into Liam's house next door, because that's where she'll live once they get married.

A sense of sadness looms over me for a moment, and

then I see Aaron has texted. I leave the confirmations of my roommates that they'll be at the dress fitting and go see what he has to say.

Are you going to the meeting at the library tonight?

The message came in twenty minutes ago, probably right when Mrs. Thompson had her toe tapping as she waited to pay for her flowers.

He's messaged again with, *My truck is having issues, and I need a ride if you're going.*

Then: *It's fine if you're not. Just let me know. I'll be at the store and can just walk over.*

He's been living in Liam's house while Liam and Hillary have been in LA, and in fact, I think Aaron is still there. He's been working on rebuilding and refinishing his grandfather's house closer to the center of town, but he hasn't moved in yet.

I'm going, I say. *In fact, I haven't eaten all day, so I'm going to close early and go grab dinner first. Do you want anything?*

I send the message before I even think or read over it. Only when my phone rings and Aaron's name sits there do I realize I've offered to buy the man dinner.

I'm obviously on my phone, so while I worry over what he might think of my offer, I swipe on the call and say, "Hey." So eloquent. A real masterful conversationalist, I am.

"Hey," he says in his semi-husky, all-sexy tone. He seems happy, and again, I start to stew over literally every single thing I've ever said to the man. Fortunately, I can't recall much, due to my faulty memory. Finally, one thing it's good for—saving me some humiliation.

"I'd love something to eat." Something scuffs on his end of the line, and his voice is lower and deeper when he adds, "Gill brought in lunch today, and it was disgusting. I don't think I'll ever get the heat out of my mouth."

I laugh, because while Aaron likes spicy food, he wants it to have flavor and not just fire. "Did his wife cook again?"

"I swear, it should be a crime for the woman to be in the kitchen." He sighs like he's really suffering. "Where are you going?"

"I don't know. I haven't decided."

"Maybe I'll just come over." He almost phrases it like a question and almost doesn't.

"Sure," I say airily. Just because I think Aaron is good-looking doesn't mean I have to start dating him. Besides a brief stint over the holidays, I've never thought he's liked me as more than a friend. He's Liam's best friend, so we've been at parties and events together for almost a year now. "We'll decide when you get here."

"On my way."

The call ends, and I hurry to go lock down the shop and put up my *We're Closed Early* sign. Aaron will come in the back door, and it too has a buzzer, so I'll know when he's there.

In my office, I start gathering my things to leave, and

my eyes land on the framed photo of Grams and me from last Christmas. Her proud smile as she stood in my shop for the first time still warms my heart. "I'm doing it, Grams," I whisper. "Just like you always said I could."

I take one last look around the office, breathing in the sweet floral scent that has become my signature. Lilacs, roses, and a hint of eucalyptus – a perfect spring blend scent, if I do say so myself—and turn to leave.

"Emma."

I yelp at the sound of a man's voice coming from the front of the shop, and I spin that way, holding up the only thing I'm carrying—which happens to be a black pen wrapped with floral tape with a fake white lily on top of it. Like that's going to do any damage at all.

Then I think of my spy novels, and the heroines in those books can definitely incapacitate a man with a lily pen.

And the man in front of me is definitely someone I need to incapacitate...because it's my former boyfriend.

"What are you doing here, Tucker?" My back is pressed into the wall behind me, and I don't lower the pen as he smiles. He's the reason I haven't dated in over a year. He's the reason every time I even start to think I could maybe go out with someone, I put myself in a boyfriend-free zone.

He shrugs like he just happened to be in the neighborhood, but I know that's so false. My heartbeat thrashes at me as the buzzer for the back door sounds, and I twist that way. "You need to leave," I say. "I know I locked that front door."

"It wasn't closed all the way," he says like it's no big deal that I just told him to leave.

As much as I don't want to put my back to him, I turn and stride down the hall toward the back door, because I know who'll be on the other side of it.

"I was thinking me and you were good together," Tucker says, and my whole world turns upside down.

I open the back door and find Aaron standing there. Well, kind of. It's an elvish version of the hot handyman, and I take a moment to blink at his robes, his pointy ears, and his goofy grin. "You're not dressed up," he says.

"Should I be?" I scan down to his shoes—also pointed—and back to his face. "Why are *you* dressed up?"

Some of his fun, flirty demeanor falls. "The invite for the small business meeting tonight said to come dressed as your favorite book character."

I can somehow sense Tucker behind me, maybe getting closer, maybe about to say something. I look right into Aaron's eyes and barely move my mouth as I say, "I need you to play along with me, okay?"

His eyes search mine, and at least he realizes how serious this situation is. "Okay?" He looks behind me, and I'm sure Tucker is there based on the way Aaron's expression changes in a split-second. "Oh, I thought you'd closed."

"I did," I say. "*Tucker* was just leaving too." I nod slightly and then turn to face Tucker, who has advanced down the hallway. He looks at me and Aaron, and oh, how I wish Aaron had on his dark-wash jeans and one of his hardware store tees—the ones with the tight sleeves because his biceps are so impressive.

"Who's this?" Aaron asks, and thank the stars above, he puts his arm around my waist.

"You remember him," I say sweetly. "Don't you, baby? I know I've told you about my exes." I've done no such thing with Aaron, but he doesn't miss a beat.

He kneads me closer as an entire fireworks show explodes through my hip from where he's touching me. "Oh sure," he says almost dismissively. "Tucker." He says his name with pure distaste, and we all hear it. Then Aaron takes a deep breath and looks at me. "We're still going to dinner before the meeting, right, sweetheart?"

"Mm, yes." I tip my head back and stretch up at the same time. Aaron realizes I'm going to kiss him point-five seconds before I do it, and I register the surprise coursing from him the moment my lips touch his.

After that, it's only an inferno of heat, the fizzing bubbling of a violent chemical reaction, and the musky, husky, manly, sexy scent of Aaron Stansfield. Everything else melts away, and he kisses me like I've never been kissed before.

CHAPTER TWO

AARON

I'M NOT SURE HOW LONG WE STAND THERE KISSING, but it's nowhere near long enough. When Emma finally pulls away, I have to force myself not to chase after her lips. My head spins as I go over every touch, every sensation, every pounding beat of my heart. The softness of her hair and skin—both of which I've obviously touched. At least my fingers have a memory of it, and I look down at my hands dumbly.

I've imagined kissing her so many times over the past few months, but the reality blows every fantasy out of the water.

I take a big breath, barely able to form coherent thoughts, and look up at her. More stupidity chases through me at her lack of costume, because it only reminds me that I'm dressed like Legolas from *Lord of the Rings*.

That invite one-hundred-percent said to come dressed as my favorite book character. I will go to my grave believing that, but I curse my fixation on certain things. My ADHD screams at me to get back to kissing Emma, that we'd like a lot more of that, please.

Emma's cheeks hold a gorgeous flush I haven't seen before, and dare I think she looks just as dazed as I feel? For a moment, I forget why we're even here, standing just outside the back door of her floral shop, until I notice movement behind her.

Right. Tucker. Emma's ex.

I clear my throat and make an attempt to regain my composure. "So, dinner?" I ask, hoping my voice doesn't betray how affected I am.

Emma nods quickly. "Yes, dinner. Let me just get cleaned up." She turns to give Tucker a dirty look. "And we'll go." She presses her purse into my chest. "Do you want to drive tonight? You can pick me up out front. I obviously need to make sure that door gets closed properly."

"Sure," I say, doing my best to sound like I'm not asking her a question. Or to act like I've driven Emma's car many times. I haven't. Or that I'm fine to leave her alone with her ex. I'm not. I give him a dry look. "You come on out this way with me."

"My car is—"

"Get out, Tucker," Emma says as she steps past him. "I'll see you out front, baby."

I love that pet name for me in her voice, even if it is fake. Tucker doesn't know that, and by the time I tear my gaze from Emma's retreating curves to look at him, he's cocked his eyebrows. He does exit the shop through the back door, which I then pull tightly closed and double-check to make sure it locked. It did.

"How long have you two been dating?" he asks.

"A few months," I say causally. My mouth sometimes runs away from me, getting me in trouble, and I vow to stitch my lips together before I tell this Tucker character another thing.

Thankfully, I know which SUV is Emma's, and I dig into her purse to find her keys like I've done so a million times before. The truth is, I don't think I've ever rifled through a woman's purse, and it almost feels wrong to be doing it. And with Tucker watching? And my cape billowing in the afternoon spring breeze?

A sweat breaks out across my forehead, and I feel like he might arrest me for A) lying about being Emma Newberry's boyfriend, and B) kissing her like I'm Emma Newberry's boyfriend.

Oh, how I want to be Emma Newberry's boyfriend.

But I clear my head and focus. It can't be that hard to find car keys in a bag. And yet, I've severely underestimated every woman who's ever walked the earth with a purse, because I cannot for the life of me find her keys. Frustrated, I look up to find Tucker standing there staring, his eyebrows raised.

"They're in here somewhere," I say, now kneading the bottom of the bag just to see if it'll produce a jangling sound. To my great relief, it does, and I dive back into her purse to pull out the keys. I hold them up like they're a Gold Medal I've just won in the Invasion of Privacy event in the Olympics.

"I gotta say," Tucker says. "You don't seem like Emma's type."

"I'll be sure and let her know," I throw back at him. "See you around." I'm not going to tell him it's great to meet him when it's not great to meet him. And Emma obviously doesn't like him, so I'm not sorry to walk away, get behind the wheel of her SUV—with several adjustments to the seat, because wow. Who needs to sit so close to the steering wheel?—and leave her back lot in favor of the street.

She's waiting on the sidewalk, her thumbnail against her teeth, and relief washes over her features as I come to a stop and she opens the door. She blows into the car with all the scents of fresh flowers and her fruity perfume, and I'm all smiles again.

I've really got to tone that down, so I'm not so obvious in how I feel about her. *Well, I think that kiss gave you away,* I think, but I say nothing.

Once we're rolling away from the flower shop, Emma lets out a long breath. "Thank you," she says softly. "I'm sorry I sprung that on you."

I want to tell her she can spring kisses on me

anytime, but I know this isn't the moment. "Don't worry about it," I say instead. "That's what friends are for, right?"

She gives me a grateful smile, and I simply keep driving toward the town square. It's so not the answer I wanted to give, nor is her silence what I want her to say in response. Somehow, an elephant got in the car with us, and he's making it very hard to breathe or speak.

Finally, when I'm faced with almost-end-of-day-traffic and nowhere to go, I ask, "Where do you want to go to dinner?"

"Bellyache's?" she suggests. "I'm craving a lot of bacon and cheese right now." She won't look at me and instead keeps her focus out the passenger window.

Bellyache's is an old diner that serves American fare, and I can eat a burger for any meal, any day of the week. So no problem for me there, and I make the turn that'll take us a little bit away from downtown—and right past my house.

"So," I say, gesturing to my ridiculous elf costume. "I guess I should explain this."

Emma laughs, the tension from earlier melting away. "Please do. I'm dying to know why you're dressed like you just stepped out of Middle Earth."

"The invite said to do so." I quirk my eyebrows at her, since she clearly knew which book character I'd dressed as. "The real question is why you didn't do it. Or what you would dress as if you had gotten the memo."

"I gotta be honest, Aaron," she says, too much glee in her tone. "You took the memo to a new dimension."

"I've read all of Tolkien's books," I say. "Four or five times. Love the movies. Play the video games. It's something I can do with my brother, and well, I don't have a lot in common with him."

And just like that, I've killed the fun, flirty, *I'll-kiss-you-again-later* vibe between us. I've done so at least fifty times in the past several months, because just when I think I'm getting close to blurting out my feelings for the gorgeous blonde in the passenger seat, I chicken out.

Or she says something that puts me in my place, that lets me know we're just friends.

I scoff right out loud. *Just friends.* Two of the worst words on the whole planet, in my opinion.

"You okay?" she asks.

"I'd love to hear all the stories of your exes," I say instead. Maybe wearing this elfin garb, I can say things the normal Aaron Stansfield wouldn't say. I can be someone else. Someone brave and ferocious and very, very good at what he does.

I drive by the huge corner lot that's been sitting dormant for the better part of three years now. Cider Cove's been in a legal battle with the construction firm, and the huge hole they built before a judge executed a stay order has been a stain on the town since. But Belly-ache's is just around the bend, and I swing the SUV that way while doing the same with my attention as it moves over to Emma.

"And, you know what?"

"What?" she asks, her eyes finally coming to meet mine.

I want to talk about that kiss, I think inside my head. I can even hear myself saying it in a movie-type setting. And Emma will confess her undying love for me, and I'll somehow rope a horse the way Legolas would, and we'll ride off into the Middle Earth sunset.

But in real life Cider Cove, I say, "Maybe I could stop by my house and change before we go to the meeting. It's just around the corner from Bellyache's."

And just like that, I'm back to being the cowardly Aaron Stansfield, the upstanding oldest son who runs his daddy's and granddaddy's hardware store, and who can't keep a girlfriend for longer than three months.

All women say they want a guy like me. A man with a good job. Nice house. A *nice* guy.

All women are lying.

———

I MANAGE NOT to make a fool of myself during our burger binge, and I leave Emma standing in the fully remodeled living room at my house while I hurry into my not-fully-remodeled bedroom to change out of the elf costume. I pull on jeans and a tee, grab my sneakers, and hurry back out to her.

"We're not going to be late," I promise her, though we probably are. I swear, every restaurant, cafe, and bistro in town has some Tuesday night special, as if people will only come out to get food if it's on sale, and traffic around the library is pretty insane this time of night.

They have a big parking garage that's used for a lot of the downtown business district, and I fear having our small business meeting so early will make it hard to find a place to park. So I pull my shoes on as fast as possible and jump back to my feet. "Ready."

Emma giggles and shakes her head. "No, you've got an extra ear still, Mister Stansfield."

I love it when she calls me by my last name in that flirty tone. I find it hard to believe she likes me as only a friend, though she's never, ever, *ever* given me an indication that I'm wrong about that.

Besides that kiss.

Now, she steps over to me and lifts her hand to my right ear. "This one looks a little otherworldly still." Her fingers gently brush up my neck, along the bottom of my beard, to my ear, and my word, I feel like a star that has exploded. I'm in a hundred million tiny pieces, everything shooting out at the speed of light plus sound.

Our eyes meet, and Emma's smile slowly drifts off her face. Her touch is light, careful almost, and oh-so-sexy as she sweeps her fingers around to the back of my ear and releases the costume piece. "There," she whispers. "I got it."

Her hand drops, and I immediately cover the ear in her palm with mine. Maybe if I want to get the girl, I have to act more like Tucker. *At least in the beginning*, I tell myself, because I'm not sure I can be a jerk long-term. My momma will cuff me upside the head and demand, "What are you thinking, Aaron?"

Right now, I'm really thinking I'd like to kiss Emma again, but I know Mister Nice Guy isn't going to get the job done. So I step back and toss the ear to the end table beside my couch. "Now I'm ready." Then I lead the way out of the house, not even bothering to hold the creaky front screen door for Emma.

In fact, it slams in her face, and I hear her grunt behind me as I go down the front steps. The man I really am wants to run back and make sure she avoids the rotting parts of the porch, since I replaced it and it immediately rained before I could preserve and protect the wood. The whole thing needs to be redone, but I'd already moved on to the interior of the house.

My best friend, whose house I've been living in, is back in town and has been for the past few weeks. He's marrying the love of his life—and one of Emma's best friends—next week, and I'll move out while they're on their honeymoon. It's another ten days, and I can do a lot in ten days' time.

Not when pining after Emma, I tell myself sternly, because I'm not going to do that anymore.

I drive her car and her over to the library, where sure enough, it seems the whole population of Cider Cove has converged. We're only ten minutes late to the small business meeting, and they haven't started yet, thankfully.

I act like I don't care as I take a seat in the back row. Emma pauses at the end of it and looks up front, then back to me. I pretend to be engrossed in something super amazing on my phone, and I even smile like a really beautiful woman has texted me back that she can't wait to see me for dinner later.

Emma walks away, and a tiny piece of my heart turns black and falls to the soles of my feet. Is this how the bad boys feel all the time? Because I feel like I'm going to throw up, and I think I'd have rather walked into this meeting wearing my elfin gear than sit on the back row alone while Emma finds a seat closer to the front next to a woman who owns a dog treat bakery.

The meeting starts, and I pay attention the way I normally do. I take the information packets for the upcoming Summer Faire, as it's something my family always participates in. We do simple household task demos, like fixing doorknobs, or painting a sunroom, or sealing a deck.

Then, the woman who's been running our meetings this year, Margaret Pajonas, who owns a daycare and preschool on the opposite of town from where Emma and I work, holds up a yellow folder. "And we just got something exciting from the City Council." Her eyes hold hope and excitement, and I sit up a little.

This meeting has gotten a little stale, but maybe just for people like me who've participated in the Summer Faire before. But this is something new.

"The City Council and the city of Cider Cove have finally resolved the issue on the corner of Sweetbriar and Salty Dog."

A murmur moves through the crowd, because this is big news. The hole I'd driven by earlier? That's the lot on the corner of Sweetbriar and Salty Dog, and it could be such a beautiful place for apartments, a hotel, or even just a park. Everything just got abandoned, and it's become a wasteland.

"And they're hosting a city-wide event specifically for small businesses to get involved in the community. We don't have a bunch of information yet, but the bottom line is, every small business has a chance to help beautify that twenty-four acre lot, and..." She holds out the word and surveys the whole room.

I'm holding my breath, because this feels important, and a few people a couple of rows ahead of me actually lean forward.

Margaret really has us all on the edge of our seats. She grins and flips open the folder. "And I quote, 'More information and rules and regulations will be coming within the next two weeks, emailed to all small business owners on record within the city boundaries of Cider Cove.'"

She looks up, just to make sure we're all still with her. And I am. I'm *so* with her, and I glance up to where Emma's sitting. She's practically drooling for more information.

Margaret returns to her folder. "And we'll be revealing an event where small businesses can show off what they provide to the community by participating in a contest that will have winners chosen based on voting from the general population of Cider Cove, government officials, and City Council members, with a proposed grant provided to the winning small business in the amount of twenty-five thousand dollars."

I suck in a breath, and it's like that action has vacuumed out all the oxygen in the room, because I'm not the only one who's just gasped like they've just met the most popular member of their favorite boy band.

Everyone has. People are murmuring the same thing running through my mind.

"Twenty-five thousand dollars?"

"Twenty-five thousand dollars!"

Emma turns around, and I stand up and look at her, completely forgetting that I'm going to play the bad boy and ignore her, act like I don't like her at all, and that that kiss didn't rock my world.

"Twenty-five *thousand* dollars," we say together, and

I can't *wait* to get the email about this community service project that could change my life.

She hurries toward me, the meeting obviously over, and I turn and leave the room ahead of her. "Can you believe that?" she asks. "That's so much money."

"Yeah," I say in a short, clipped word, my stride long so Emma has to jog to catch up to me.

"Can you slow down?" she grumps at me, and that only makes me want to go faster. Or slow down? I honestly don't know.

I slow down slightly, and I glance over to her.

"Why are you mad at me?" she asks.

"I'm not," I lie. Fine, it's only half a lie, because I am sort of mad at her, but I'm totally not at the same time.

"It's because I kissed you, isn't it?" She makes a sharp detour and pushes open the door to go into the stairwell instead of joining the throng of people queueing up at the elevator.

I follow her, annoyance singing through my veins. "You know what? Yeah, I'm mad about that. We agreed a few months ago that kissing was a very *unfriendly* thing to do."

"But helping a friend is a very *friendly* thing to do," she throws over her shoulder at me, then turns and practically flies down another flight of stairs. "And I needed help with Tucker."

We burst out into the parking garage on level two, where I'd managed to find a space, both of us huffing and puffing. I glance over to her, and oh, I am so losing this battle against her. In the end, I *will* lose. I know that in this moment.

But right now, I mentally dig my heels in and vow to myself to hold on for a little longer.

Her car is locked, and I have the keys, so when we get there, she stands outside the passenger door, waiting. I stand at the back bumper and glare at her. "You know what, Emma?" I have so many things I want to tell her, and none of them would come out of a not-nice guy's mouth.

I have to get out of here. Just leave.

"I'll find my own way home."

Her breath catches, and for a split second, our eyes lock, the air between us crackling with something electric. Something dangerous. Something half-alive and real, but also abstract at the same time. I'm pretty sure it's attraction, because that's all I can feel for her right now. But she might just be experiencing an extreme case of fury.

Without another word, I toss her the keys—which causes her to yelp, throw her hands up, and miss the keys. They jingle-jangle as they bounce on the concrete.

But I'm already walking away.

A point goes to Mister-Not-Nice-Aaron, and I do my best to hold my head up high as my heart wails at me like I've just done the worst thing possible.

CHAPTER THREE

EMMA

I'VE MANAGED TO STOP STRANGLING THE STEERING wheel by the time I park behind the Big House. Since it's mid-April, the sun stays out at night longer and longer, and it's not quite dark yet.

Twilighty, sure, but I need the full cover of darkness to sneak into the house and up to my bedroom on the second floor. The moment someone sees me, there will be questions galore, and I don't feel like telling them about Tucker's sudden reappearance at the flower shop, the fake kiss with Aaron, and then him throwing—legit, *throwing*—my keys at me and stalking away.

That was no underhand toss, let me tell you.

Of course, there's the pretty amazing dinner we shared too, along with the possibility that I could have twenty-five thousand dollars to invest into Pretty in Petals.

My mind feels like I've inhaled a whole quart of pollen, and nothing really makes sense. "I certainly don't want to tell anyone about it."

Lizzie will most likely come into my bedroom, as she lives right next door in the same hall, and we chit-chat every night before bed. Maybe I can just leave out the bits I don't want to talk about.

"Yeah, right." That would be like me denying that succulents are real plants. Of *course* they are, and of *course* I'm going to blurt out the fact that I kissed Aaron before my head hits the pillow tonight.

I get my fingers to release the steering wheel, and I flex and curl them, trying to get the ache out of my joints. I have wrist braces and fingerless gloves I wear at work, as I do so much with my hands, usually in cooler temperatures.

The back door opens, and a couple of dogs come bounding out. Super. Beckett's here with his hounds. I actually really like Duke and Rocky, but the appearance of the dogs means Beckett comes outside too. He migrates toward the corner of the back porch and watches his pups, and I figure maybe there'll be a disturbance in the Force, and I can somehow make it upstairs among the chaos of Claudia's boyfriend being over with the dogs.

I get out of the car and twist toward the back seat. I lift my crate out of the car, kick the door closed, and head for the house. Beckett smiles at me, waves his hand, and I nod at him.

I make it into the Big House without having a conversation, and I think maybe the madness of having five roommates—three of whom have boyfriends—might play to my favor. For once.

I stride through the kitchen and slide my crate on the top shelf of the extra racks at the back of the kitchen. I just have to go around the wall and dart up the steps, but that means I have to enter the living room.

Taking a deep breath, I listen to try to figure out what's going on out there. Beckett comes back inside, and Duke races toward me. "Hey, buddy," I say, because I can't resist a dog or a flowerbed.

"Duke, leave 'er alone," Beckett says. "Sorry, Em."

"It's fine."

He approaches, and he must see something in my face, because he slows. I swallow and ask, "What's going on out there tonight?"

"They released a mini round of shows to tease Shark Week." He glances toward the doorway leading to my freedom...and the living room. Beckett leans closer. "You should not get between Tahlia and Shark Week."

I grin at him. "Oh, I know."

"You want to go behind me and upstairs?"

"Can I?"

He moves over to the doorway and looks out. "It's a

commercial," he says out of the corner of his mouth. "Wait a second."

I rush over to the freezer and pull out a package of my toaster pancakes, then hurry back to him. "Okay," I say, almost breathless. "Tell me when."

He stands there for a few extra seconds, and then Claudia calls his name. I see this going badly for me, and my heart pounds as Beckett shifts in the doorway. My ears malfunction as Beckett says something back to her.

Then he hisses at me, "Move," as he steps out into the living room.

I flow with him, turning right and going up the steps as fast as I can. But since my form of exercise is floral arranging and sweeping, I can't maintain a fast pace for more than a few stairs. Thankfully, that's all it takes to get me far enough up the steps that I won't be seen.

Heard, however, is another issue, but thankfully, a round of shushing happens from the first floor as the show starts again. Tahlia refuses to miss even a moment of it, and I've sat through several rounds of Shark Week with her.

I duck into the first room on the left and close the door behind me. I need some of Ry's coveted M&Ms, and I suddenly remember the pancakes in my hand. They're apple cinnamon, and I move over to the toaster on my desk and set two in the slots.

My phone chimes in my back pocket, and I cringe.

Lizzie has said that she can hear my ringtone if my phone volume is up all the way—like it is right now.

I slip my phone out and turn it down all at the same time, my eyes quickly taking in who's messaged me. My pulse blips through me that it might be Aaron, but it's Lizzie herself.

I see your crate in the kitchen. How'd you get upstairs without anyone seeing you?

I'm a ninja, I send back to her, and I twirl my desk chair around and collapse into it. Exhaustion moves through me, a sense of tiredness that not even the scent of browning apple cinnamon pancakes can soothe.

I exhale and run my hands through my hair, freeing the last of it from its ponytail. Maybe I should just text Aaron. Apologize for kissing him the way I did.

My phone mocks me, but I can't make myself pick it up. My thumbs twitch as if I'm already typing an apology to Aaron. Just as I reach for my device, Lizzie taps on my door with her nails and then opens it.

"You're having pancakes up here?" she asks before I can even focus on the fact that she's wearing the cutest purple wrap shirt I've ever seen. Lizzie always has the best clothes, as she's a plus-size model, and she gets new shipments every week.

She runs a pretty amazing social media account, and she's actually a fashion influencer in addition to her job as a compliance officer at a chemical company. So as she cocks her hip and folds her arms, she's the perfect picture of honey-haired beauty.

"My evening was eventful," I say.

Lizzie actually dyes her hair a darker shade, so she'll get more respect at work, but she's blonde like me. I'm actually thinking of putting some red in my hair, but I haven't been able to get myself to do it yet.

"Didn't you have your small business meeting tonight?" she asks.

"Can you close the door?"

She does, then moves over to my bed just as my pancakes pop up. I open my top drawer and pull out a paper plate. "Want one?"

"Tahlia has a whole shark-themed party downstairs," Lizzie says, her blue eyes sparkling like sapphires. "I saved you some of her 'shark fin pizza,' and Ry insisted that we save you a 'shark's blood' Jell-O cup." She grins. "Tahlia took today off work and spent all day in the kitchen."

I hold up one of my apple cinnamon pancakes. "And I'm up here eating freezer pancakes."

"Yeah." Lizzie pins me with her sharp gaze that will pierce me and make me spill my guts in no time flat. I fill my mouth with pancake as she asks, "So why's that?"

I could tell her that I forgot about the Shark Week party, because I did. I could tell her that there's just a lot on my mind because of the upcoming weddings, which is totally true.

Instead, I swallow and say, "Tucker came into the shop wanting to get back together, and Aaron was there, and I kissed him."

Lizzie sucks in a breath, her eyes going wide. "Emma."

I spin away from her, my desk chair squeaking as I do. "I know, okay? And now he's mad at me, and I don't know what to do."

———

THE NEXT DAY, I key my way into the back of the flower shop while shooting the hardware store a furtive glance. There's always a lot of activity around the back of it, as they house their large pick-up orders off the dock there.

I've never seen Aaron there, but it'll be just my luck that he needs some air right as I'm glancing over. In fact, as a man wearing a gray-green tee steps outside, I suck in a breath and duck inside as fast as possible, the words, "Sweet snapdragons," coming out of my mouth.

I lock the back door, detour into my office to set down my crate and my purse, then I pull out the orange folder. These are my orders-due for today, and I need them done by lunchtime. The shop doesn't open for another couple of hours, and I expect to be able to complain to Sir Chills-a-Lot about everything that's happened in the past twenty-four hours.

I sigh as I walk into the cold room where I do all of my arrangements—and all of my confessions. After Lizzie persuaded me to come downstairs and have more for dinner than apple cinnamon pancakes, I'd spent some time on my laptop to make notes.

I like to name all of my arrangements something fun and festive, and I have a pretty good list for this weekend. I sell way more flowers later in the week, and the crowds will start to swell tomorrow evening, pick up on Friday as people head home for the weekend, and Saturdays are my best day of the week.

"Petal to the Metal," I mutter as I look at my idea list. "Bloom with a View. Ferntastic Friday."

Thistle Be the Day.

I smile at that one. I wish this would be the day that I could figure out what to do about Aaron. We've been on shaky, non-defined ground for so long. Maybe I just need to make a move.

He didn't text me last night either, and I don't know what that means. I've never seen him upset before, at least not with me, and I barely know what to do with the flash of frustration I saw in his eyes in the parking garage.

My phone zings, and I glance over to it. It's Margi from the Small Charleston Businesses Association, and I step over to my device as I pull on my fingerless gloves.

We need one more person to help with the Spring Fling Festival. I know you said you were too busy, but if I make it as easy as possible on you, will you do it? I have to submit the names by Friday, and if we don't have a solid five, we don't get the funding from the Conglomerate.

My pulse sinks into my stomach.

The Spring Fling Festival is a singles evening event. A dating event.

I don't want to do it on many levels. I do want the very best for Cider Cove, and I'm sure singles in town will find their One True Love.

I met Tucker there a couple of springs ago, so it's definitely something that holds a lot of bad memories for me.

A sigh tugs through my lungs, and I pick up my phone. *As easy as possible? Define that.*

I just need a name to put on the paperwork, Margi says. *And your name has come up to do the flowers for it anyway. You might have to go to a couple of meetings, but so much of it has already been organized. I mean, it's in three weeks.*

I don't know how to tell people no. It's definitely one of my biggest weaknesses, one that I've been working on in the past few months. But as I stand in the ultra-cool room with all my blooms, I look up to the ceiling.

"What do you think, Sir Chills-a-Lot? Say yes to the Spring Fling Festival? They probably just want me to do the roses the men hand out."

And I can do that.

"Then text Aaron?"

The refrigeration unit hums to life, and I pretend it's the best advice I can possibly get. "Fine," I grumble. My thumbs fly across the screen. *Okay,* I say. *Put my name on the list and put me in touch with who I need to talk to about the Spring Fling Thing.*

That's such a better name than Festival, and I smile at my text.

Oh, thank you, thank you! Margi says. *And here's your first easy task: the committee chair is Aaron, and I know you already have his number. Just let him know you're now on the committee, and he'll get you all up to speed.*

I drop my phone, and it clatters against the stainless steel counter in front of me. "Sir Chills," I say in a disgusted voice. "You could've told me the committee chair was Aaron *before* I texted and said yes."

CHAPTER FOUR

AARON

THERE'S A VERY SPECIFIC KIND OF CHAOS THAT happens when I hyper-fixate on a project. It's like time ceases to exist, the world around me dissolves into static, and all that remains is the one thing I *must* finish.

For me, that thing has been fixing the back porch and steps at my grandfather's house—my house now—all morning.

The man used more nails than a medieval blacksmith to hold pieces of wood together, and I've spent hours yanking them out, sanding down splinters, and muttering under my breath about "proper joint work" like some kind of wood-obsessed lunatic.

But oh, it's worth it.

Because when the fresh coat of sealant dries, that deck is going to look perfect and be the pristine place to sip my sweet tea after I finish work at the hardware store.

No one will be able to tell it's been through seventy years of wear and tear, not to mention the questionable design choices my granddad made in the seventies. Burnt orange wood stain, Grandpa? Really?

I'm running high on the satisfaction of a job well done when I get to the hardware store in the early afternoon. That high lasts exactly thirty seconds before the day decides to derail me completely.

"We got in the twelve-inch bits instead of the fourteen," Fonda tells me the moment I walk in. She's leaning over a magazine at the standing counter at the back of the store, and I'm still holding my dinner in my hand.

"Did you call Holy Holes?"

"I did not."

"Why not?"

"They won't take my calls." She only moves her eyes over to me. "You have to do it."

Fonda has a certain...way with people, and if things don't go her way, she lights a match on fire and bridges get burned.

"Fine." I glare at her as my phone vibrates in my pocket. I'm sure I have a million messages, because I usually do when I come down from a hyper-fixated high. A sense of being completely overwhelmed hits me, and I add, "Give me five minutes, and then connect me to Barry, okay?"

"Yes, sir," she says, flipping a page in her magazine.

It's full of boxes, so it's not like that can hold her attention for long. "And you have four consults this afternoon, starting in twenty minutes."

"Thanks," I say, knowing I laid out the folders for the consultations before I left early yesterday.

Ah, yesterday, I think as I duck into my tiny office. It smells like leather polish and candle wax, mixed with something metallic.

I ate lunch at home, so I tuck my dinner into the mini-fridge in the corner. It's got an assortment of tools on the top of it, and I swear I'm going to clean up my office soon. Soon-ish. And hey, if I could just fixate on that, it would be done to perfection.

I flip open the top folder to remind myself of who's coming in first—oh, boy. Jake Forrest, who insisted he could build a treehouse without looking at the instruction manual. Now he wants me to walk him through how to fix what he's done, and he's emailed in at least thirty pictures.

Honestly, it would be better if the whole structure got ripped down and rebuilt. Maybe I'll suggest that, and I slip his folder under the others.

My second appointment is a couple who wants me to help them build an addition over their garage, and this type of project excites me. I start into the blueprints, and I become a racehorse with blinders on, galloping straight toward the finish line.

It's why I'm good at what I do—why I can fix

anything in a house, build anything with wood, and spot structural weaknesses in two seconds flat.

But it's also why I completely miss Emma stomping into my office. "Aaron," she barks.

I blink, the white and blue lines of the blueprint imprinted on the backs of my eyelids. When I see her, I jump to my feet. "Emma."

"I've texted you a million times." Her voice cuts through the lingering haze in my mind like a bright, unexpected ray of sunshine. Or, you know, a thunder-clap. Because the moment I see her standing there in her honey-colored glory, her eyes doing that thing where they sparkle like the ocean on a clear day, I'm struck dumb.

I'm not even sure where my phone is at the moment, but I can't admit that. "What are you doing here?"

Her eyebrows go up, and she holds up her phone like it's a piece of evidence. "Margi told me to talk to you about the Spring Fling Festival. Apparently, you're the committee chair?"

Ah, yes. The Spring Fling Festival. The singles mixer that Cider Cove thinks is the crown jewel of its community events calendar. Otherwise known as my personal nightmare.

I agreed to chair the committee because then I won't have to do anything for the Summer Faire, and I won't have to chair another committee for at least a year.

But now that Emma's standing here, looking at me

like I might actually have my life together, I'm regretting every decision I've ever made.

And the fact that I haven't even *tried* to come in here with a garbage bag to clean up the empty Diet Mountain Dew bottles.

"I am." I look down at the folders on my desk, but none of them are for the Spring Fling Festival. I'm not sure why I can't look up at her. "I need to take a break."

"Aaron." She cocks one hip they way angry Southern mommas do when their children have disappointed them.

"Let's go for a walk." I squeeze past her and cast a covert look left and right, like no one can see the two of us exiting my office. It's then that I remind myself that the bad boy wouldn't care who saw him leaving his office with a gorgeous woman. So I hold my head high and head for the back door, marching right past Fonda, who does raise her eyebrows at me.

"You have eight minutes," she says. "Before Jake will be here."

"I'll be back," I say.

Outside, the wind has picked up, and I glance up into the sky to find foaming gray clouds. "Looks like rain," I say.

"Aaron," Emma says again, and she half-jogs to catch up to me.

"I only have a few minutes," I say, making my voice hard and tight, like she's irritating me. "The Spring

Fling Festival is nearly done. We're just working on refreshments and last-minute details now." I can already see the glint in her eye that says she's ready to spar, and I'm not sure I have the energy to keep up with her today.

The air is thick and humid, the kind of weather that promises a storm but doesn't deliver right away. I shove my hands in my pockets, trying not to focus on how close she's walking next to me—or how good she smells, like flowers and sunshine and a little bit of citrus.

"When are the meetings?" she asks. "I need to get everything in my calendar. You're aware Liam and Hillary are getting married *next week*, right?"

"I'm aware," I say crossly. "I'll check my calendar right now." I slow my step and pull out my phone. Of course I didn't schedule a meeting over my best friend's wedding. "I wasn't aware we needed another committee member."

"Margi said she needed me for the funding."

"Just my luck," I say. Total bad boy move.

"Hey." She swats at my shoulder. "Why are you being like this?"

"Like what?"

Thunder rolls through the sky, and it echoes in Emma's eyes.

I should just tell her. *I want that kiss to be real. I don't want to be "just friends" with you. Will you be my date to Liam's wedding, because I still don't have one, because I've been hoping against hope that I can take you.*

The words are there, tickling the back of my throat. I don't know why I can't say them.

"Aaron," she says. "You're acting really weird."

"Maybe this is how I am," I say.

She tilts her head and studies me. "This is *not* how you are."

"It's a new me." I shove my phone back into my pocket and start walking again. "We have a meeting on Thursday at three at the hardware store. And one Friday night before the event to finalize everything. That's not for another couple of weeks. I'll send you the info."

"There's no way I can make a middle-of-the-day meeting on Thursday—that's tomorrow, Aaron."

"I'm sure Gentry just wants you to do the roses for the men." Besides, we've planned the whole thing without her, so what's one more missed meeting?

The first raindrop hits my forearm. I take a deep breath. "Listen, Emma." The rain quickens. "I don't want that kiss to be fake."

She squeals as the sky opens up, and I'm not sure if she heard me or not. I actually slow down and look up, and the sky has gone from hazy gray to full-on ominous in a matter of seconds. "Uh-oh."

Emma takes off at a run. "Uh-oh? That's all you've got?"

The heavens have opened, and water comes down in

torrents. I'm drenched in seconds, the kind of wet that makes me think I've walked into a car wash. I start running too, grabbing her hand and yelling, "Over here!" over the pounding sound of the rain.

I haul her toward the gazebo at the edge of the park, though it needs to be rebuilt. By the time I reach it, there's no point. We might as well stand out in the elements, because my clothes are stuck to my skin and my hair is plastered to my forehead. I fling my hands to get the water off, dripping from everywhere and trying to catch my breath.

Emma pants beside me as she wrings out her hair, muttering something about how she should've stayed in her flower shop, and I can't help but laugh.

"Glad you're finding this amusing." She glares at me.

I grin at her, the kind that stretches my face so much it probably looks ridiculous. "Oh, come on. It's just rain. You're not gonna melt."

She glares harder, but then her lips twitch, and I know I'm getting in there somehow. "I might," she says. "I'm like a sugar cube of stress right now. One drop of water, and poof—I'm gone."

I bark out a laugh. "That's a new one."

"I'm glad my unraveling is so entertaining for you," she says, but now she's fighting a smile too, and a little thrill of victory squirrels through me.

She huffs and crosses her arms, looking out at the rain. "This is your fault, you know."

"My fault? How is this my fault?"

"You're the one who wanted to talk outside."

"I needed to breathe."

She rolls her eyes. "Seriously, Aaron, why didn't you answer my texts earlier? I thought we were friends."

"You *thought* we were friends?" I lean against one of the wooden posts holding up the gazebo's roof. Water drips steadily from the edge, splattering into the puddles that have formed on the ground. "Here's the thing: I'd like to be something else entirely."

Her brows knit together, and for a second, her eyes soften, like she's trying to figure out what I mean. But then she shakes her head, brushing it off like she doesn't have time to untangle whatever nonsense I just said. The rain is loud on the roof of the gazebo, despite the many leaks in it.

"Okay, well, *friend* or not, you've been acting weird since last night," she practically yells, poking me in the chest before she retreats again. "First, you kiss me like—like *that*—and then you're Mister Grumpy Pants in the parking garage, and now you're avoiding my texts and acting like giving me calendar dates is akin to revealing a national secret."

I scoff. "Mister Grumpy Pants?"

"Yes," she says, crossing her arms over her chest and cocking that sexy hip. "You've been a total grump. And don't even get me started on the whole 'bad boy' thing you're trying. It's weird—it's—it's like watching a golden retriever try to be a Doberman."

I snort, irritated that she saw right through my bad boy act. "A golden retriever? You realize that's a dog, right? You just called me *a dog*."

"You're the human equivalent of one," she says. "All loyal and sweet and—" She cuts off, her cheeks turning pink as she realizes what she's just said.

The rain only intensifies, and I wonder if I can cancel my whole afternoon. I certainly can't sit in wet denim for four consultations.

"Anyway," she continues, her tone sharper now. "You're not fooling anyone with the bad-boy act."

I don't know whether to laugh, run, or kiss her again. Instead, I slide a hand through my rain-soaked hair and say, "Maybe I'm just trying to figure out how to be someone you'd actually notice."

Her jaw drops, and for a second, she just stares at me, the rain dripping from her nose and chin. I can see the wheels turning in her head, but before she can respond, I push off the post and start pacing.

"Look, Emma," I say, gesturing wildly with my hands. "I'm not good at this. The whole...feelings thing. Or the...what-do-you-call-it? Emotional vulnerability. Whatever. But I can't keep pretending like that kiss was no big deal. Because it was. To me, at least."

Her mouth fishes open and closed, and she looks like

she's trying to process what I'm saying. I don't give her the chance. If I stop now, I'll never get it all out.

"I've liked you for a long time," I say, my voice rising over the sound of the rain. "Probably since the first time you walked into the hardware store and started talking to the potted plants in aisle three like they were your friends."

She blinks, her expression unreadable, and my stomach twists into a knot. This is the moment where she either tells me she feels the same way or crushes my heart into a million tiny pieces.

The rain slows, the world holding its breath as I wait for her to say something—anything.

CHAPTER FIVE

EMMA

"Who's at the store?" Aaron asks while I'm still reeling from the other things he's said. I'm soaking wet, but it's not cold, which is somehow worse. Everything feels hot and drippy, and that's good for plants, but not so much for humans.

I blink. "Uh, Tahlia came by after school for a few minutes."

And she can't stay forever, I remind myself. I glance over to the row of shops that line the back of the park, and my floral shop is a couple down. The rain has slowed into a misty drizzle, and I just want to go home, shower, put on my fluffiest set of joggers, and curl into bed with my phone.

Aaron's face darkens, and I'm sure he's about to go into Venus Fly Trap mode again. "What are you doing tonight?" I blurt out.

He lifts his chin slightly, those brown eyes so pretty. "You are not asking me out on a date."

"I..." I trail off, because I was going to suggest dinner. But the way his eyes shoot lasers at me makes my throat dry right up.

"I'm stuck in consults all afternoon," he says. Then he looks down at his sopping clothes. "Maybe I should reschedule." He only lifts his eyes, those eyebrows also cocking up. "I only have a few more days—well, nine—until I have to be out of Liam's hair, and my house isn't exactly ready for me to live in full-time."

"But you're living there," I say.

"Partially, yes," he says. "I don't shower there, because I'm not quite done with the bathroom." He slicks his hands through his hair again, and then down his beard. And holy vines and cherries, he should be arrested for what he's done to my pulse.

And thinking about him showering?

Puppies, I practically shriek to myself. *One if by land, two if by sea.*

M-I-S-S-I-S-S-I-P-P-I.

"So I need to spend all my spare moments at my house," he says. "But I can order whatever you want for dinner, and maybe you could just come...hang out."

"No," pops out of my mouth before I can think too hard. Or at all.

Aaron's cheeks turn a brilliant shade of red. "Sure,

no. Okay." He's been stuck over against the far railing of the gazebo, and he starts toward me.

I realize what I've said, and I dart in front of him. "I mean—I don't mean no." I flatten my palm against his chest, feeling the ridges of his muscles that his wet tee shows me.

His eyes meet mine. "What do you mean then?"

"I meant, I'm too old to hang out with men. We're not fourteen."

"I'd like to see you," he says.

I give him a coy, flirty grin. "We're seeing each other right now."

"Are you going to respond to what I said at all?"

I swallow my smile. So many things blitz through my head, and it's hard to seize onto just one thing so I can say it. "I don't want to be friends either."

Pure hope enters his expression, and he searches my face, his eyes darting left-right to each of mine. "You don't?"

I shake my head. "But, Aaron, I'm..." I sigh, because how does one sum up all of their dating failures in just a few words?

His fingers slide between mine. "If I can arrange it, maybe you could come by the house after you close up, and I'll stop working to have dinner with you."

"I don't want to cause you a delay."

Aaron leans closer, his eyes falling closed as he takes

a deep breath. "You're worth it." He straightens and ducks his head again. So not a bad boy.

I squeeze his fingers. "Are you going to be the golden retriever or the Doberman?"

A slow, sexy grin slides across his lips. Oh-so-kissable lips, and I rip my eyes away from them. "Depends on how my consultations go."

I return his smile. "So you're a *moody* canine." As I stand there in this leaky gazebo, the rain petering to nothing, holding hands with Aaron, I realize I'll rearrange anything to drop by his house that evening.

"I'll text you about what time tonight," he murmurs as he releases my hand. "I have to get back and get things rescheduled."

"I need to get back too," I say.

"I can catch you up on the Spring Fling tonight too."

"So it'll be a working date," I say as I fall into step beside him, he takes my hand again, and we go down the steps to the path.

"It'll be a talking date," he corrects me. "And we'll talk about the Spring Fling and the weddings and...whatever else you want."

Whatever else I want.

A kissing date?

I shove the thought away, because the fear threading through both chambers of my heart tells me it might not be healed enough to start kissing hot and handsome handymen for real.

We reach the gate that leads to the back of our shops, and Aaron slows. He still wears a slightly Doberman-like look in his eye as he glances over to me. He pulls his hand away, and says, "I'll text you back."

"Mm-hm," I say. "You better." I give him a spicy look of my own, and then head for the back door of the floral shop. I don't need to make a fool of myself more than I already have, and I feel like the whole world has grown eyes and is watching me as I walk back to the shop.

When I reach the back door and open it, I glance over to the hardware store bay. Aaron's not there, so not watching. Still, my lungs still feel like they can't get enough air, and there's no way I can keep working in my wet clothes. I'll be frozen to the bone in a matter of minutes inside Sir Chills.

Tahlia is perched on the stool behind the cash register, and she drops her phone as her eyes widen when she sees me. "What on earth happened?"

I look down at myself, horror moving through me when I see the color of my bra through my cream-colored shirt. "Yes, I'm wearing a pink bra," I say.

And surely Aaron saw it.

Then I ask, "How long can you stay? Long enough for me to run to the Big House and change?"

Tahlia cocks her head. "Why were you outside?"

She's going to have so many more questions, and part of me just wants to vomit up everything, call an emergency roommate meeting where Tahlia will get out the pink fake-mic, and everyone will help me riddle through the past twenty-four hours.

Another part of me wants to figure things out on my own, and a third part of me shouts about how much work I have to do, not only for the shop, but for the upcoming weddings.

And now, I'm going to have to put in an extra rose order and prep those for the singles event I don't want to do.

"Aaron needed some air," I say, and I turn to go back to my office to get my keys. "I'll be back in forty-five minutes," I say, since I have to drive twenty to the Big House, and then twenty back.

"Get ready to talk," Tahlia calls after me. "Lizzie's going to stop by with pizza so we can help you get caught up on orders."

My stomach drops to the soles of my feet, and I want to rage at Sir-Chills-a-Lot for forgetting to remind me I'd asked my roommates to come in for a couple of hours tonight. I won't be able to go to Aaron's after that, not without a major to-do. And not if Lizzie's stopping for pizza.

"Okay," I say as I duck into my office. It's not until I'm halfway to the Big House that I realize what I agreed to.

Get ready to talk.

"Great," I mutter, but maybe it is great. Maybe I don't need to keep everything bottled up, only confessing to my walk-in refrigerator, and wishing That Special Someone will come into my own flower shop and buy me the arrangement of my dreams.

When I get back to the shop, Lizzie's car is parked against the fence, and I jump out and hurry inside. I didn't eat lunch, and the scent of marinara and extra cheese greets me the moment I pull open the back door.

Lizzie and Tahlia are laughing, and that also lifts my spirits. "Hey," I say breathlessly as I arrive in the front of the shop. Lizzie and Tahlia both sober, and they exchange a glance with one another that makes my throat close.

"What?" I look from Lizzie to Tahlia and back.

A long moment of silence fills the shop, wherein I move over to the box of pan pepperoni pizza and take a piece. "Someone better say something."

"Aaron came over," Lizzie says like she's saying it rained earlier.

I freeze with my favorite food only a couple of inches from my mouth. My heartbeat crashes against my ribs, and I force myself to take a bite. Cheesy and herby goodness meets my taste buds, and I moan.

Tahlia smiles and hands me a napkin.

"Okay," I say. "So Aaron came over. So what?"

"He seemed a little put out that I'd brought dinner." Lizzie raises her eyebrows.

"Seemed surprised to see us here at all," Tahlia says,

and she's the worst at nonchalance. Everything is chalant for sure.

"I, uh, didn't have time to text him." I take another big bite of pizza to buy myself some time, but Lizzie is well-versed with this tactic, and Tahlia teaches junior high. They so have me beat.

"Yes, he barked something about how he'd forget about dinner, and he'll text you something about the dates for a meeting?" Lizzie steps over to me and takes the half-slice of pizza in my hand. "Emma. Stop eating and tell us what's going on."

I swallow and wipe my face very deliberately. Then I say, "What's going on is that dealing with Aaron is like riding a roller coaster."

"That man likes you," Tahlia says.

"Yes, he told me this afternoon," I say, lifting my chin and tossing my hair over my shoulder.

"Oh," Tahlia says. "I wasn't expecting you to acknowledge it." She looks over to Lizzie, who takes a bite of my pizza, the traitor.

I sigh, deciding I better just get everything out. I take my pizza back from Lizzie, glare at her, and say, "Fine, Aaron and I had planned a little date tonight after work, and I just forgot I'd asked you guys to come help."

"We can reschedule," Tahlia says.

Lizzie nods, still chewing her pizza.

"No," I say. "I have to get all the arrangements done for tomorrow and Friday, so I can spend my time here working on the wedding." I look around at my cozy shop, my safe space, everything I've ever wanted.

"Hey," I say. "Someone got the 'You're Succulent' arrangement." I smile, pure happiness moving through me. I step over to the empty spot on the shelf and move the other arrangements so it doesn't look like there's an empty space there.

"Who got it?"

"Just some guy," Tahlia says over the top of Lizzie, and I turn in time to see them exchange another glance. I don't even care at this point.

I finish my pizza and say, "Let's get going, because maybe I can still make it to Aaron's for dinner."

"Take two minutes to check your phone," Tahlia says. "He muttered something about that on his way out too."

My throat tightens as we all move toward the back room where I make the blooming magic happen, because I did storm next door today and demand Aaron pay more attention to his device.

I pull my phone out, and my mouth goes dry as I see how many times Aaron has texted. Eleven.

"For the love of lavender," I mutter as I start to read through them. Dates of the meeting. That he's rescheduled his last two consultations. That he'll order my favorite Thai for takeout that night. I just need to text him when I'm leaving the shop.

All the sweetness I'd expect from Mister Nice Guy Aaron.

After that, the texts turn Doberman-like as Aaron morphs into a thorny rose. I sigh, because while Aaron and I are friends and we've known each other for a while, he clearly doesn't know me as well as he thinks he does.

So I let my fingers fly, telling him something I don't tell very many people. I send that text, and then more, finally telling him I'm going to silence my phone so I can get my work done while my friends are here, and then I do exactly that.

"Sir Chills," I murmur as I head for the cold room to work. "It would be great if you could get us out of here in time for dinner."

CHAPTER SIX

AARON

THERE'S SOMETHING YOU DON'T KNOW ABOUT ME, Emma has said. *I'm really forgetful, okay? I've tried fifteen different planners, I keep multiple calendars—paper and digital—and I set alarms on my phone, and no matter what I do, I can't seem to keep very many details in my head at the same time.*

So I just forgot I'd asked for help tonight, okay? We're going to try to work super fast, so I can still come over by six-thirty-ish.

My ire calms with every sentence I read. Then the foolishness starts to creep in. I glance over to the cute arrangement of succulents I'd bought from her shop, and I hope Tahlia and Lizzie haven't told her it was me who did.

Unless you're going to be Grumpy Gus, she continues. *Then I'll just go home and eat popcorn and pancakes for dinner, and we can reschedule. I've got the dates on my calendar for the Spring Fling meetings. Thanks for those, but I don't think I can make it tomorrow. We'll see how tomorrow goes—and if I remember.*

I'm going to silence my phone now, so I can focus and get these flowers done, so I can come "hang out" with you tonight.

Okay, I send her. *I'm sorry.* I stare at the words, wondering if they make me pathetic. My momma wouldn't think so. She taught me it's always okay to apologize and clear the air, so I leave the words and send them before I let the Doberman back in.

Man, opening the door to the bad boy sure is dangerous, and I sigh as I look up to the ceiling in my office.

Let me know when you leave the shop if you're coming, and I'll still get the Thai. You can have it for breakfast, at the very least.

Someone understands the assignment, Emma sends back, and I can just hear it in her flirty voice. I smile, because I hope this means I'm not in the moody doghouse anymore. I can't be if she's text-flirting with me like that, right?

"Aaron," Fonda says as she opens my office door. "Your next appointment is here, baby."

I flip my phone over and get to my feet. "Thank you, Fonda," I say as formally as I can. After all, she just called me "baby" in front of a client. It's a curse of the

South, for sure. I smile as a tall gentleman gestures his wife into my office.

I so should've cleaned up, as this woman is wearing a pencil skirt in the middle of the afternoon on a Wednesday. She screams money, and I remind myself *they're* interested in working with *me*.

"Mrs. Lindsey," I say smoothly as I extend my hand toward her. "It's great to meet you."

"You too," she drawls out, and we shake hands before I indicate one of the chairs in front of my desk. I go left as she dodges right, and I grin at her husband, Clark.

"Thanks so much for coming in," I say. "Sorry about the mess; I've got a lot of projects on my plate right now."

And that's putting it mildly.

I shuffle my folders around to get the right one as everyone settles in. My desk chair squeaks in an embarrassing way as I finally find the Lindsey's folder and flip it open.

"We hope ours will be one of them," Sara says, her smile positioned just-so on her face.

I have this file memorized, so I don't need to look at it. I meet her eyes. "An above-the-garage addition is one of my absolute favorite things to do."

Her face lights up, and Clark's smile settles into one of satisfaction. "Is that right?"

"Your blueprints look pretty good," I say, sliding a

page from one side of the folder to the other. "But these pictures have me concerned..."

The Lindseys both lean forward, obviously anxious to explain to me why I should take on their project. I let them give their spiel, and I take several notes. Those I will need later, and when Mrs. Lindsey starts repeating herself, she reminds me so much of my momma.

"All right," I say as she takes a breath. "I think I have enough to give you a quote."

She reaches for her husband's hand, and I wonder what my life would be like if getting a bid on the addition for my already-big house was the thing worrying me the most.

I take a deep breath. "I can take this on in about a month," I say, making it sound like I'll have to reschedule several other projects. I do have to finish my house first and get through Liam's wedding.

"It'll take me about ten weeks." Which puts me really close to the Summer Faire, and I reconsider everything. I clear my throat and move my hand so it covers the number I'd written on my notepad. I'll have to print out an official quote to add them to my building schedule anyway, and they won't know the difference.

"And be in the mid-two-fifty range," I say. It's a lot of money, and I do love acting as a general contractor. But I'm almost hoping they say no.

They exchange a glance, and the tension in the room simply sits on my lungs. But I rescheduled my other two consults today, and I'm semi-anxious to get out of here so I can work on my own house.

————

I'M COVERED in fine dust when I hear someone enter my house. "Howdy-ho," my momma calls, and my stomach tightens into a dense ball.

It takes me another moment to blink my way out of the drywall in the master bathroom. Once this is done, I can texture, put the baseboards back on, paint, and this room will be remodeled.

"In the bathroom," I call. I should've expected to see my momma soon, because it's been a few days.

"There you are," she says just as I get the last piece of sheetrock in place. The nail gun goes *pop-pop-pop* as I get the nails locked in the right position. "The back deck looks stunning, sweetie."

I smile over to her and lean toward her so she can kiss my cheek. "Thanks, Momma."

"Daddy is sliding dinner in your oven."

I hold my tongue about the Thai—and Emma. "Thanks, Momma. You guys staying?"

Please say no, please say no, please say no.

"Maybe for a minute," Momma says. "We're waiting for Thomas to get done with his community class, and then I think we're gonna go get cheesy fries."

My stomach growls, and of course my mother hears

it. "You should take a break," she says. "Come eat. I made you chicken and biscuits, and everything's hot."

"I want to finish this up," I say. "You guys relax on the back deck, and I'll be out when I get this wall done." I wanted to tape and mud it too, and now I might not be able to.

I don't tell any of that to Momma, nor do I mention that I can't have Emma come "hang out" in my private master bathroom tonight, so I need this done before I move on to removing the popcorn ceiling in my office.

That's the place I was hoping I could hang out with the pretty blonde tonight, while we flirt and eat Thai. Of course, my momma's cooking might be a good meal to win Emma over with too.

You're not trying to win her over, I tell myself. But I so am.

"Okay?" Momma asks.

"Okay," I say, though I have no idea what I just agreed to. It gets my mother to leave, and I keep working, faster than before. See, now I have to get rid of my parents in the next...I glance over to my phone.

Twenty minutes until six-thirty-ish.

"Great."

I tape and mud like I've never taped and mudded before. With everything where it needs to be for tonight, I leave the bathroom and pull the bedroom door closed behind me just as someone knocks.

"Come in, Tommy," I call as I duck into the guest

bath to clean up. No one comes in, which is a little weird. As I reach for a hand towel, I realize it's weird for Tommy to ring the doorbell at all.

"Tommy?" I toss the towel on the counter and leave the bathroom. The house is open now, and I cast a glance through the kitchen to the back deck, where I catch sight of my parent's heads.

I swivel my attention to the front door just as it opens, and there's Tommy. But he's not looking at me or watching where he's going. He enters my house walking backward, with the fabulous, curvy Emma following him.

Was I so focused on finishing the bathroom that I didn't hear her text come in? I don't even remember my phone chiming, and I've assigned her a special one, so I can make my pulse go crazy without even seeing what she's said.

No matter what, Tommy says, "Yeah, that's why they had to go all the way into Mordor to destroy the Ring of Power, you know?" and I lurch toward the front door to rescue Emma from my younger brother.

But there will be no saving her from my parents, and to my great dismay, the squeaking of the back screen door fills the air as I say, "Hey, you made it."

I have no idea who I'm talking to, as Emma wears a plastic smile and Tommy adds, "It could only be destroyed from the fires from whence it was forged, and only the hobbits could do it."

CHAPTER SEVEN

EMMA

AARON WEARS A FINE WHITE POWDER IN HIS BEARD. It rides on his eyebrows too, and the best part is that he has no idea. He grabs onto his brother, his eyes locked onto mine. "Momma and Daddy are waiting for you," he practically yells.

"He's here," another woman says, and that gets me to look past the two Stansfield men in front of me.

"And you're leaving," Aaron says, stepping away from his brother and turning his back on me. He actually backs up a step, almost smashing me into the closed front door. "They were just leaving."

So many people start talking, and it's like the Stansfields haven't seen each other in years and all need to say everything that's happened in that time.

"I'm hungry," Thomas says.

"Oh, we've got chicken and biscuits right here," Aaron's momma says. "He's hungry too."

"No," Aaron shouts. "Y'all are going for cheesy fries, remember?"

I don't detect the scent of Thai food, and I wonder if Aaron has missed my texts again. *Of course he has*, I tell myself. *Have you seen his eyebrows?*

I have, and they make me smile.

"Oh, you're all covered in powder, baby," his momma says, and she starts brushing at his face.

"Momma, stop it," he gripes at her.

"I know you're hiding someone back there," his momma says, dropping her arm. "Why can't I meet her?"

Aaron heaves the sigh of the century, and he falls to the side. He waves his hand toward me. "Momma, this is Emma Newberry. She owns the flower shop right next door to the hardware store now."

His mother seems to drink me up in less than a second. "Oh, honey." She presses one hand to her throat. "You're gorgeous."

I glance at Aaron, who rolls his eyes. "Thank you?" I guess, because she sounds truly surprised to find a pretty woman at Aaron's house.

"Okay, you guys have fries to get," Aaron says, and he practically pushes me past the front door and into his living room so he can open the door. "Bye now. Buh-bye. Good of you to drop by."

His momma starts to protest, and his daddy seems to

want to stay too, but Aaron talks over both of them and manages to get all three members of his family out the door. "Don't dawdle on the porch," he calls. "It's not structurally sound and needs to be redone. Okay, bye! Love you!"

He closes the door behind them in a near-slam, breathes out, and then presses his forehead against the wood as he inhales.

Then, as if nothing has happened, he straightens, his shoulders box up as he breathes, and he faces me with a big smile on his face. "I missed your text, but I can order the Thai right now." He pats his pockets and comes up empty. "Just as soon as I find my phone."

He turns and rushes away, which makes me giggle. "Check your beard too," I call after him, because his momma hasn't gotten rid of all the powder there.

While he's gone, I take in the interior of his house. I've only been here for three minutes before, and the whole thing testifies of Aaron's skill. Built-in bookcases line the wall on either side of the fireplace, which has a beautiful wood mantel holding trinkets and framed photographs.

The living room holds comfortable furniture, polished wood floors covered by understated rugs, and it flows easily into the back of the house, where the kitchen and open dining room wait for Aaron to host an amazing party.

I smile at the thought, because Aaron is not the party

type. Sure, he's come to a few things my roommates have put on, but he hovers on the outside edge, sipping a drink and putting in the minimum effort.

He's exactly the type of party-goer I aim to be, and I first started getting to know him more personally several months ago at a Halloween party at Liam's house.

I wander into the kitchen, where more original pieces take center stage. A unique butcher block island nods to the handcrafted dining room table, and the amount of wood here is stunning.

Aaron is not the neatest man in the world, but I like the way his house is lived-in. It feels warm and welcoming, like I can kick my shoes off and not get in trouble, and that I could spill something and we'd simply clean it up.

Something clicks, and I turn toward the sound. I realize it's his oven, and I move over to it. I pull open the oven door, as my memory zings at me about the chicken and biscuits his momma said she'd brought over.

Sure enough, a creamy sauce with chicken and veggies bubbles away in the oven, with a foil-covered tray that must have the biscuits on it.

"I just ordered the Thai," Aaron says as he comes down the hall, and I close the oven door.

I've just tucked my hands in my back pockets when he arrives. "Okay," I say. "But this should probably be turned off if we're not going to eat it."

Aaron reaches past me and presses the button to

turn off the oven. "Okay." He looks at me, his eyes harboring edges and ledges of anxiety. "I'm sorry I missed your text, but I wouldn't have been able to get rid of my parents any faster."

"It was great to meet them," I say, though I didn't really meet them at all. "What were their names again?"

A rush of horror crosses his features. "Oh, I've done myself dirty."

I giggle, because he really has. I may not have had the best mother in the world, but my Grams is as Southern as they come, and there's no way she'd let me get away with an introduction like the one Aaron gave his parents.

"It was a non-troduction," I say. "I'm surprised your momma hasn't called yet."

His eyes darken. "She has."

I burst out into full laughter as his phone rings again. He slides on the call and turns away from me as he says, "Momma, it's not a date, and no, we're *not* dating, and if you call me one more time tonight, I will never let you into my house again. Okay, goodbye." He delivers all of that in a single breath, and I've managed to stop chuckling by the time he faces me again.

"Thai is fifteen minutes out," he says as if I dropped by as planned and his family wasn't here. "Tell me what my brother said to you on the porch." He reaches for me, and I give my hand to him. Then he leads me over to the couch, where we sit together.

"You aren't going to work?"

"I need a break," he says with another sigh. "I just finished up in the bathroom, and I'm hungry like a wolf."

"Hungry like a wolf?" I stifle another laugh. "That's a song lyric, Mister Stansfield."

He turns toward me, something playful and glinting in his eyes. "You confessed something to me earlier, so... here goes."

"Mm, I'm nervous," I say when he doesn't go.

"I love eighties music," he says.

I grin at him. "So much that you quote it sometimes."

He smiles back, his fingers in mine tightening for a split second. "I'm just livin' on a prayer."

I tip my head back and laugh, and the sound is so much better when his deeper one joins it. "Okay, okay." I wave my free hand to get myself to stop acting so hyena-like. "Tell me what I need to know about the Spring Fling Thing, so we can enjoy dinner when it arrives."

"Ah, the Spring Fling...Thing." He smiles at me, and that thing should be illegal for what it does to my pulse. The feelings I have for him are so *un*friendly, and I'm not sure what to do with them. I haven't had the best of luck with men, that's for sure.

My smile falters as Aaron quickly goes through what he and his committee have already planned for the singles dating event. Light hors d'oeuvres from Crisp

Catering, with decorations from Angela at Pretty Parties.

"Oh, that'll be nice then," I say. "Angie does beautiful work."

"She's doing something classic," Aaron says. "We wanted it to be less cutesy than in the past. See if we can't attract some older singles."

"Are you going?"

Aaron snorts, and I have my answer. His face flushes, and he quickly says, "I've been in the past, but no, I'm not going as a participant this year." He rolls one shoulder. "I have to go as the organizer, but it'll be just to make sure everything goes off without a hitch."

"Why'd you volunteer for this?" I ask.

"Because then I won't have to serve on a committee for another year." He kicks up that lopsided grin again. "I've got Margi figured out, and out of all the things she wants to committee, putting on a couple hours of speed dating is pretty easy."

"Smart," I say. "Is it still at the Lion's Den?"

"Sure is. Venue: easy. Utilizing all the small business owners to get their products in front of hundreds of people: easy." He puffs his chest out and exhales. "Trust me, Em, the Spring Fling *Thing* is the easiest one to do."

I relax into the couch beside him, all of my muscles finally melting enough to be comfortable. "So you want me to do roses for the men."

"Yes, ma'am," he says. "We have seventy-four registered so far, and sign-ups close this weekend. It'll be a fixed number, and they can be any color."

"All right," I say.

"And you can give out any literature, coupons, cards, stuff like that you want at the event. And flowers? With singles? It should help at least a little."

"Thank you, Aaron." We've spent some time together, and he knows I'm always working to get Pretty in Petals out in front of people. I turn my head toward him, and he looks at me too. The moment sobers and electrifies, and holy hydrangeas, all I can think about is that kiss in my flower shop.

My eyes even drop to his mouth, where my heart plants itself in thick soil and takes root. That is so not good, but I can't seem to rip myself away from him. Aaron smells like something woodsy and something alive and something very much like he's been doing construction, and it tickles me in just the right way.

I lean toward him and tip my head back at the same time he moves closer to me too. Before he can kiss me, his doorbell peals, and I jump as he swears under his breath.

"Thai Palace," a man yells, and Aaron groans as he gets to his feet.

I exhale the trapped air in my lungs and stand too. I run my fingers through my hair, my heartbeat hammering a hundred miles an hour as I move into the kitchen while he answers the door. I get out forks and plates, and Aaron puts the food on the counter.

"Will you be my date for Liam and Hillary's wedding?" he asks above the rustle of the plastic bag.

Our eyes meet again, but lightning doesn't strike the same place twice, I guess, because I keep my gaze locked on his.

"I mean, if you don't already have a date." He ducks his head though all the containers have been unpacked.

"Yes," I say simply. "I mean, no, I don't already have a date, and I'd love to go with you." I do the duck and tuck too, pushing my hair behind my ear as a hint of embarrassment floods me.

"Great," Aaron says easily. "I'm sure you'll be busy with the flowers, but I can help if you need me."

"Ooh, you're going to regret that," I tease. "And you know, *this* could be a date." I shrug one shoulder, wishing I wasn't wearing the same clothes from work, even if I did run home to change that afternoon. "You bought dinner. We're eating and talking." I pinch up a piece of chicken and pop it into my mouth.

"If that's what counts as a date, then last night could've been our first date."

"We went out for Christmas," I say, wondering why I need this defined. I'm not sure, but I do.

Aaron watches me for a moment. "Yeah, but that was like, a formal thing. Fancy dresses and makeup and stuff."

"Did you wear makeup, Aaron?" I grin at him as I tip my favorite, Pad Thai, onto my plate and then snag a spring roll.

"I'm not wearing makeup right now, no," he says without missing a beat.

"So it's not a requirement for dates."

"I would say no."

"Good, because I'm not wearing makeup right now."

He peers at me. "You're not?"

I blink at him, the spring roll pinched between two fingers. "Can you seriously not tell?"

"Can this please not be our first date?" He snatches the spring roll from my hand and takes a bite. "I don't want it to be our first date."

"Why not?" I pick up another spring roll, though I want to grab mine back from him.

He swallows and turns away from me to open the fridge. "Because, Emma, when we go out for real for the first time, I don't want it to be you coming over after I missed a text."

He pulls out a couple of cans of soda and a few bottles of water. Setting them all on the counter, he pins me with another sultry look. "I want our first date to be magical."

I don't know what to say, so I twirl up a forkful of noodles and put them in my mouth.

"I at least want us both to know it's happening," he says. "That's a low bar, right?"

"Aaron, I don't think you can do anything low bar."

"Yeah, tell that to the front porch, which I have to rip out and redo."

I round the counter and sit at his butcher block island and reach for a can of Cherry Sprite. "Did you buy this just for me?"

"No," he said. "It's my favorite non-cola soda." He takes a seat too. "The only thing I know to buy for you that you love is pancakes." He grins over to me, and I sure do like the pops and twizzles that move through me.

"Will you go out with me tomorrow night?" he asks, his voice low and set somewhere between Mr. Nice Guy and the Doberman.

"Maybe," I say coyly, already trying to remember my schedule. Trying, and failing. "I'm busy on Thursday afternoons, and I'm expecting a big shipment of flowers for the wedding on Sunday."

"Okay, yeah, sure," he says.

"If you're willing to have a late dinner—or whatever magical thing you have planned—I'd be thrilled to go out with you."

"You tell me when to come pick you up at the Big House, and I'll be there." Aaron gives me a look out of the side of his eye and focuses on his food again. "No makeup necessary."

CHAPTER EIGHT

AARON

I PULL UP TO LIAM'S WORKSITE AND REACH FOR THE Styrofoam containers sitting on the passenger seat of my truck. "Wings," I yell to Liam, who's up on the roof.

"Be right down," he calls back.

I go around to the back of my truck and lower the tailgate. Liam probably eats in the air-conditioned cab of his truck most days, and I hope the wings are enough to make up for the open-air lunch.

He joins me a few minutes later, an enormous jug of water in his hand. He sighs as he pushes himself up onto the tailgate with me. "What brings you by?"

I hand him a container. "Gotta eat."

Liam wears a skeptical expression, but he doesn't deny the food. Seriously, the man loves chicken wings with his whole heart.

I've been out with women before, and I've never run my plans past Liam. I don't know why I need this reassurance for tonight's date with Emma, but I only manage to eat one wing before I can't get even my saliva down my throat.

"Listen, so, I, uh, asked Emma to dinner for tonight, and I'm not sure—" I cut off when Liam starts coughing.

"You—asked—Emma—to—dinner?" He wipes his mouth and peers at me over the top of the napkins. "When?"

"Last night." I glare at him. "I also don't like the wide-eyed surprise. What? I can't ask Emma out?"

Liam recovers quickly. "Of course you can. I didn't know you wanted to."

"Really?" I roll my eyes. "All the sighing and pining hasn't clued you in?"

He chuckles and shakes his head. "I just moved back here, brother."

I take another bite and look across the piles of lumber Liam's laid out on the front lawn. "I'm worried that what I have planned for tonight isn't good enough."

"What've you got planned?"

I knew he'd ask that, and I can't bring myself to say it. "It's dinner," I say.

"Your details astound me," he says dryly.

"I don't want to say."

"Then I can't comment on whether it's good

enough," Liam says. "Though I'm sure it's absolutely fine. Hill and I went to the bowling alley for our first date, for crying out loud."

"Yeah, but the bowling alley's fun."

"Have you planned somewhere not-fun?" Liam asks.

"I don't think so."

"Then it'll be great. Em's real easy-going."

That's not an adjective I would've used for Emma, but I know her in a different capacity than Liam. She's not uppity, though, and I've never seen her all put together like Claudia. Not that she isn't put together at all—she is. In a different way.

She's a jeans-and-tee-shirt type of woman who arranges flowers into masterful works of art, and I stifle a groan. Will a florist want to go see more flowers?

Maybe everything I have planned in a few hours is all wrong.

"I really like her," I say in a near-whisper. "Emma. I've had a crush on her for months."

Liam does me the courtesy of staying silent for several moments, probably absorbing what I've said. "I didn't know," he finally says.

"Well, you've been gone."

"And you never talk about the women you like."

I give him a wry smile. "That too." I point a chicken wing at him. "But you wouldn't even tell me who your first date was with when you went out with Hillary."

Liam grins at me. "Just give me a hint about dinner tonight."

"Forget it." I think of the succulents I bought yesterday, and I remind myself that Emma loves flowers and plants, and she's going to love a date centered around them. Now all I can do is hope and pray that flowers and plants possess enough magic to make this first date unforgettable.

———

I'VE DRIVEN over to Cherry Lane thousands of times. After all, my best friend has lived at the end of the lane for years. I've never been as nervous as I am now.

Emma asked what the dress code for tonight was, and I'd texted her, *Casual. Easy. Whatever you're comfortable in.*

I'm secretly hoping she's wearing those dark wash jeans that cling to her every curve. She lives with five other women, one of whom is a model, so she's always got something super-amazing to wear, and I lose right turns and have to wonder if the last light I went through was actually green just thinking about her.

I didn't kiss her last night when she left my house, because it felt lame to do it on my own front porch, or next to her car in my driveway, or in my office—which now has the popcorn ceiling removed.

After lunch, Liam sent me a bunch of texts, and by

three p.m., Beckett and Elliott had chimed in to the group text. As I near the last turn I need to make before I'll be on Cherry Lane, their texts are all I can think about.

Everyone will be there when she comes to the door, Beckett had said. *Don't say anything you don't want all six of them to hear.*

I recommend kissing on the first date, Elliott said. *But they have a front porch camera, so you've got to plan around that.*

You guys are freaking him out, Liam told them. *He wanted advice for a first date, not all of this.*

He's wrong and right—I want it all.

No matter what, compliment what she's wearing, Beckett said. *It's probably not all hers, and you need the roommate points.*

Does he, though? Liam had asked. *They all know him.*

They know him as Aaron-the-hardware-guy, Elliott said. *The friend who goes to small business meetings with Emma. Not as her boyfriend, and take it from someone who's had to bridge that gap and reinvent himself, he needs the roommates on his side.*

At least Emma likes you already, Beckett said.

Total uphill battle for us, right, Becks? Liam had added a laughing emoji to that text.

I need a checklist of things to do and things not to do, and before I know it, I'm walking up to the front door of the Big House. The siding is this pretty butter-yellow color, and Tahlia makes everyone do jobs every spring and autumn—I know, because I gave her four hours of excavator use to move some rocks last year.

So I'm not surprised that the pillars, the railing, and the shutters look like they've been freshly painted a bright white. I reach to ring the doorbell, telling myself not to fiddle with my collar or check for my phone and wallet.

I pocket my hands and actually look over my shoulder and toward Liam's, as if I'm just here to try to sell solar panels. It takes for-freaking-ever for someone to come to the door, and I stand still, remembering that Beckett said it would take them a long time.

They like to line up and take a look at you first, he'd said. *Wear something nice.*

I'm suddenly sure my own jeans, cowboy boots, and dark gray polo aren't enough. I should've grabbed a hat or chosen a shirt that had stripes on it. Something.

Finally, the bright blue door opens, and Tahlia herself stands there. "Hello, Aaron," she says pleasantly. "Emma's having a bit of a footwear crisis, so come on in." She backs up as she says it, and I step up and into the house.

"Evening, Tahlia," I say, finally remembering my manners. "I didn't know someone could have a footwear crisis."

"Oh, you don't know much about women, then."

Tahlia gives me a knowing smile, and all it does is make me feel like a complete fool.

"I just have one brother," I say. "I don't think he's gotten a new pair of shoes in five years." I manage a tight-lipped smile.

"Aaron, hey."

I turn toward the familiar voice and find Beckett almost on top of me. He takes me into a fast man-hug and steps back. "I like this shirt." He grins at me like he knows a secret I don't.

"You like his shirt?" Claudia asks as she joins the greet-Aaron party in the foyer. "Have you guys rehearsed this?" She pins me with her dark-eyed gaze, and she really is a bit terrifying.

She's just so polished and so sophisticated, and now that I see her loop her arm through Beckett's, I realize he is too. The man is wearing black slacks, shiny dress shoes, and a pale blue shirt open at the throat at nearly seven-thirty at night.

"No," Beckett says easily, but I have my doubts.

Claudia's sculpted left eyebrow goes up. "Sure, I believe you guys."

"You think I'm trying to make him look better than he already is?" Beckett scoffs. "Look at him, sweetheart. *I'd* go out with him in that shirt."

"It's a *gray polo*." Claudia rolls her eyes. "No offense, Aaron."

I lift one hand in a wave of whatever-acceptance. If a

polo isn't good enough for Emma, then that's that. I don't even own a dress shirt like what Beckett's wearing.

"Are you guys going out tonight?" I ask Beckett and Claudia.

"No," Claudia says while Beckett says, "We're taking dinner to my aunt." They look at one another, and oh, boy, I've started something there. Hex nuts and screwdrivers.

They bicker as they go back into the living room, and I wonder who else I'm going to have to impress tonight.

"He's standing in the foyer?"

Relief paints through me at the sound of Emma's voice. I turn away from the living room to see her exiting the mouth of the hallway on the left, something I didn't expect.

"You couldn't have offered him a seat?" She throws Tahlia a look, but Tahlia simply smiles at her.

"He was talking to Claude and Beckett literally five seconds ago."

I stand there and stare at the gorgeous blonde I've somehow conned into going out with me. I can't believe we're getting together for the third night in a row, even if the previous two evenings weren't technically dates.

Emma's hair falls in soft curls over her shoulders, where it rests on a bright blue, short-sleeved sweater that makes me want to touch the fabric. Or maybe just her.

And she's got those dark-wash jeans on, with a pair

of bright blue ankle boots that swallow the hem of those pants. And they look like they're velvet.

Emma is made of sapphires and gold, and I can't wait to be alone with her. I don't think I'll be able to stop myself from kissing her tonight.

"Wow," I say. "It looks like you solved your footwear emergency in the best way possible."

Emma smiles at me, and I lose my ever-loving mind, because the next thing I know, I've dropped to my knees. "Are these things velvet?" I reach out and touch the boots, feeling the soft, furriness of what is definitely velvet.

I pet her shoe until I feel like I've gone insane. And Lizzie says, "What are you doing, Aaron?"

Humiliating myself completely, I think as I look up and find her, Emma, Thalia, and Ryanne staring at me with various levels of incredulity on their faces. Or horror. Disdain? Disgust?

Before I can move, the front door opens, and Liam and Hillary walk in. "Is he proposing already?" Hillary asks at the same time Liam goes, "Why are you on the floor?"

"I'm not proposing," I bark at them, and I wave off Liam's hand as he offers it to me to help me stand. I get up and down all day long, and I can get up myself. I do, every cell in my body burning hotly.

I can't even look at Emma as I say, "Are you finally ready?"

The moment the words leave my mouth, I know I've made a mistake. One of the roommates gasps, and that clues me in too.

"The Doberman has arrived," Emma says.

"Don't act like you don't like the bad boy," Ryanne says, and that makes me gasp. She nudges Emma away from her side, and I extend my hand toward her.

"I didn't know it would take ten minutes to get you. We might be late."

"Factor in the pick-up time next time," Lizzie says. "Because now we'll need to hear Claude's and Beckett's commentary on your clothes every time you come over." She grins at me, and adds, "*Fifteen* extra minutes, Aaron."

"Let's go, Grumpy." Emma takes my hand and looks up at me with plenty of teasing in her expression.

"After you, Snow White," I say, and that causes more gasping. Emma opens the door and steps out onto the porch as some slight snickering comes from behind us too.

"Where are you two off to tonight?" Liam asks.

"Nice try," I throw back to him, and then I pull the door closed behind me. "Wow." I look at Emma, who waited for me at the top of the steps. "That was intense."

The doorbell beeps, and someone says, "We can hear you. Take your fancy polo and go."

Claudia.

Emma grins and grins, then starts to laugh as I hurry

past her and down the steps. And I was even warned about the doorbell cam.

"Aaron, wait." She rushes after me, catching me near the end of the sidewalk. "I didn't mean to be late."

"Whose shoes are those?"

"Can you curb your tone?" She shoots me a look, and I come to a full stop.

I grab her hand as she tries to go by me. "I'm sorry."

"You're like riding a roller coaster." She blows out her breath. "The good thing is, I know what ride I'm getting on, because everything shows on your face."

"You're gorgeous," I say, tugging her closer. "Sorry about that—whack-whatever I did in there." I lean into her and take a deep breath of her hair. I get peaches and cream and so much floral goodness.

"The shoes are stunning, and I just wanted to touch them."

"You're a very tactile man," she whispers.

"I'm not sure if that's a good thing or not."

"Maybe not in front of everyone," she says, leaning her head back. "You said we might be late, and now you're just standing here."

"Right." My visions of kissing her out here in the graveled parking area in front of the Big House evaporate. "Let's go." I walk her to the passenger side of my truck and hold the door for her.

Once I'm behind the wheel, I say, "Now, I have rules for my truck."

"Rules?"

"One, I don't want any screaming inside the vehicle."

"Screaming?"

"I have a private kitchen reservation at Stack Shack."

Emma sucks in a breath, and I'm reminded of the calm before a storm. Or that time between when a baby sucks in a big breath and is about to let a mighty wail loose. She starts to squeal, and I hold up my hand.

"Rule one," I say.

She sucks her shriek back inside somehow and blinks at me as I back out of the parking area. "Stack Shack, Aaron? How did you do that? It takes weeks to get in there."

"I know the owner," I say casually. "He opened up a table in their kitchen, so you can see the chefs work their magic on your beloved pancakes." I smile over to her, thrilled when she reaches for my hand. "And I have tickets to the Bloom Bonanza, but I'm realizing now that we might not have time to go tonight."

I glance at the clock. "The chef's table experience takes a couple of hours." I look over to her. "I maybe over-planned."

"You forgot I had to work late." She beams at me. "It's okay to admit it."

A sense of happiness like I haven't felt in a long time clears away my earlier humiliation of kneeling down to pet Emma's boots. "Yeah, all right," I say with a genuine smile. "I forgot we wouldn't be going to dinner until eight."

"I love it when other people forget things," she says, and she seems a little too happy about it.

I chuckle. "It just means we'll have to go out again."

"Can you get the tickets transferred to another night?"

"I'll call Misty," I say.

"Oh, right," she says. "I forget sometimes that you know everyone everywhere."

"Everyone, everywhere?" I scoff. "Come on."

"How did you get the tickets to the Bonanza?" She stares at me, and not in the *he's-so-hot-I-can't-look-away* type of way. But a confrontational way.

I squirm slightly in my seat. "I don't want to say."

She giggles in that sexy, womanly way she has. "You don't need to say. I already know you called in a favor."

"What are you doing tomorrow night?" I ask.

"It's the rehearsal dinner," she says.

"Will you be my date?" I shoot a look over to her.

"I think that's obvious by now," she says.

My whole chest warms, and I squeeze her hand. "Tell me what you need help with on Saturday for the flowers, and I'll be there."

"Really, Aaron?"

"Yes," I say simply. "Just boss me, Emma."

"You're going to be sorry you ever said that," she says.

"Maybe," I say, but I don't really believe that. I've been helping Emma at her flower shop for months now out of sheer desperation to be with her, and I don't see that changing any time soon.

I just have to keep the Doberman at bay—and not get down on the ground and pet Emma's shoes ever again.

CHAPTER NINE

EMMA

"I CAN'T BELIEVE WE'RE HERE." I GLANCE AROUND the nearly-five-star restaurant that serves pancakes, pancakes, and more pancakes. They have a variety of items on their menu—even hamburgers with pancakes as buns—but every item includes pancakes in some way, in some variety.

It's basically a restaurant made of my love language.

And Aaron got us a chef's table.

He stands at my side, his hands loosely in his pockets, and I lace my arm through his. "Do you see the ceiling?" I can't look away from it, and Aaron moves his head to look.

"Wow," he says. "It's like the Sistine Chapel, but with a pancake God."

I smile and can't stop. "Do you see the blueberry

pancakes?" I whisper, like we really are in the Vatican City, in the Sistine Chapel, and need to show reverence.

"Aaron," a man says, and I look at him. "You've got the chef's table tonight." He's got dark red hair, a smattering of freckles across his nose and cheeks, and the hugest smile ever. He and Aaron laugh as they shake hands and bump shoulders, and then Aaron returns to my side.

He slides his fingers between mine as he says, "This is my girlfriend, Emma. She's a pancake-lover."

"Ah, a soul-sister." He grins at me and says, "I'm Jeremy. You guys follow me. I know Ron has your appetizer pancakes ready to go."

"Appetizer pancakes?" I repeat as Jeremy leads us over to a red carpet—yes, a legit red carpet—that goes past all the tables in the main dining room. I feel like someone has put a heavy crown of jewels on my head, and I have to hold it extra-high under all that weight.

Jeremy says a few quiet words to servers and someone who has to be a manager, and then he pushes open a swinging door and indicates we should enter the kitchen first. Aaron switches his hand from mine to the small of my back, guiding me inside first, where there are two tables set up for guests.

Neither of them have people, and I stall far enough inside the kitchen that Aaron and Jeremy can enter behind me. The salty scent of bacon mixes with the sweet scent of maple syrup, and I watch with giddy excitement parading through my stomach as a chef only a few yards from me pours a pale yellow batter with shreds of cheddar cheese and bright green chives onto a hot griddle.

"He's making the chicken and cornmeal pancakes." I bounce on the balls of my feet. "I've always wanted to try those."

"This way," Jeremy says, and I have to tear my eyes from the cooking stations to go with him and Aaron to our table against the far wall. The view here is magnificent, as it sits up on a platform I have to climb three steps in Claudia's ankle boots to reach.

I freeze behind my chair, my eyes glued to the flower arrangement in the center of the table. "Is that my...?" I reach out and pick up the pretty succulent garden. "You're Succulent," I read from the side of the aluminum tray.

I turn toward Aaron. "You bought You're Succulent?"

He leans down, and I think he's going to kiss me here on this platform where all the chefs at Stack Shack can see. Instead, he puts his mouth right at my ear, his breath tickling my lobe as he whispers, "Well, you are succulent."

Then he straightens and pulls out my chair for me. I sit, still marveling over the succulents being here, and I put them right in front of me as Aaron takes the spot beside me.

Now we can both see the action in the kitchen. We've been sitting at the table for four for maybe ten seconds when a waitress and a waiter arrive with orange juice, sparkling cider, and water.

"Can I have a mimosa?" I ask, and one is brought in mere moments.

The moment the drink staff leaves, the chef who'd been pouring the cornmeal pancakes picks up two plates and heads our way.

"I'm so excited, I can barely breathe." I grab onto Aaron's arm with both of my hands, and he chuckles. "Did you pick a menu?"

"You don't pick a menu for the chef's table," he says.

"This is our Corn Cheddar Chive Stackwich," the chef says. "It's yellow cornmeal pancake based, with sharp cheddar cheese and fresh chives, with crispy fried chicken nuggets, a dollop of whipped honey butter, and a hot honey drizzle."

He puts one tea-sized plate in front of me, then one in front of Aaron. I've never seen anything so beautiful in my whole life, with that three-inch cheesy-cornmeal pancake on the bottom, a delectable piece of chicken dripping with hot honey, and then another pancake and another piece of chicken.

There's no toothpick or anything holding it together, and yet, it's stacked precisely right and hasn't moved.

Aaron nudges me with his elbow. "Are we eating or...?"

"I need to document every bite of this culinary journey," I say. So I pull out my phone and snap a picture of the best appetizer I've ever had the chance to meet.

Then Aaron says, "Look here, sweetheart," and I turn toward him. He's holding up his camera, and I make a face that says, *Can you believe this chicken stackwich?* and he laughs as he taps to take the picture.

Once that's done, I pick up my knife and fork, holding one in each hand, like I'm about to tuck into a truly exceptional meal. Because I am.

I move the top pancake to the side and slice the bottom one with its accompanying chicken nugget in half. I swipe it all through the hot honey, make sure I have plenty of honey butter, and put the whole bite in my mouth.

I cannot control the sounds my body makes after that. There's some moaning, I know that, what with that savory pancake with the mealy texture. It goes great with the creamy honey butter and the crispy chicken.

Everything that should be hot is, with the honey butter and the honey actually cold in temperature. I'm not a super-fan of spicy things, but with the chicken and the cornmeal pancake, the hotness of the honey is appreciated and actually a bit subtle.

"This is amazing," I breathe out as I fork up my second bite.

"I've never been here before," Aaron says. "Now I'm

wondering why." He puts his second pancake in his mouth, whole, and I grin at him.

"You've got a little something in your beard," I say.

He doesn't even reach for his napkin, so I pick up mine. He turns toward me and juts his chin out, and I giggle as I wipe the hot honey that's drizzled into the wrong spot from his beard. He finishes his bite and says, "Thanks, *honey*."

I shake my head, though every cell in my body is warm. That has to be because of the spicy honey, and not because touching Aaron's face so intimately has me fired up.

"Is the spice okay for you?" he asks.

"Yeah," I say just before putting my final bite of the chicken and cornmeal pancake in my mouth.

"Now *this* is good spicy stuff," he says.

"Mm." Yes, it is.

The moment I swallow and set my knife and fork on the plate, two people appear, one taking Aaron's plate and one taking mine. I reach for my mimosa as I say, "Tell me something about you I might not know."

He sits still for a minute, and then he picks up his napkin from his lap and resettles it as he shifts in his seat. "I play the saxophone."

"You do?"

"You don't have to screech it out like that." He smiles at me, and then we both look out into the kitchen. "I love jazz music. I sometimes put it on while I'm working around the house."

"You didn't last night."

"That's because I was talking to you."

"I thought you were into eighties music."

He cuts me a look out of the corner of his eye. "A person can like more than one genre of music."

"I didn't even know they were called genres," I say. "Who do you think is making our next course?"

All the chefs in the kitchen have jobs to do, and they're doing them. Griddles line three of the counters, with other stations behind them, like the fryers and condiment containers.

"Will you play the saxophone for me?"

"Absolutely not."

I turn toward him again. "No? Why not?"

"I'm no good."

"So you're bad."

He looks at me, his dark eyes searching mine. I give a micro-shrug. "You seem like you want to be the bad boy."

Aaron scoffs. "Being a bad boy and being bad at playing the saxophone are two entirely different things."

"Yeah, someone who plays a woodwind can't be bad." I laugh again, and he shakes his head.

"Tell me something about you I don't know."

So many things come to mind, and while I want to tease and flirt with Aaron, I also want things to be real.

We've been friends for several months now, and he knows a few of the major things about me.

But he doesn't know a single thing about my family.

I immediately reject the idea of telling him, and instead, I say, "I have a toaster in my bedroom, so I can have pancakes even when I don't want to deal with my roommates."

"You guys seem close," Aaron says, a hint of coolness in his voice. "There are times when you don't want to deal with them?"

"Sure," I say casually. "I love them, of course, but of course. Don't you ever just want to be alone?"

"Everything I do is alone," Aaron says, and I can't get a read on how he feels about that. Usually he's such an open book, but the Doberman is better at concealing what he's thinking and feeling.

I bump him with my shoulder. "Lucky you."

"Your next course is a sampler of three of our most popular main dish pancakes," a woman says. She's brought two more chefs with her, and I turn my attention to them as she places an enormous plate in front of us with a trio of pancakes.

"The Loaded Baked Potato Pancake," she says. "Savory potato pancakes topped with melty cheddar cheese, broccoli crowns, crispy bacon crumbles, and a homemade ranch dressing."

And not just one, but a stack of three latkes with all

the deliciousness layered between them. My mouth waters just looking at it.

"This one is a Sausage Breakfast Pancake Taco," a man says, pointing to the one closest to me. "Our savory herbed pancake with sausage, scrambled eggs, avocado, and a fennel crema."

"And the last one is our Spicy Mediterranean Roll-Up," the third chef says. "Buckwheat pancakes filled with a fire-roasted hummus, roasted veggies, feta cheese, and a drizzle of tahini sauce, rolled up. You just pick it up with your hand and eat it."

They nod at us, all smiles, and turn to go back to their stations. There are two of each type of pancake on the platter in front of us, and I drink them all in.

More pictures, from loads of angles, and then Aaron says, "What are you starting with?"

"I don't know."

"Dare you to try the Spicy Mediterranean Roll-Up." He wears a smug smile too, and I exhale out my breath in a puff of air.

"You think you'll get to eat mine if I don't like it," I say. "But I'll just take your potato awesomeness."

He bursts out laughing. "Potato awesomeness?"

"I forgot the name of it." Grinning, I pick up the Spicy Mediterranean Roll-Up and turn toward Aaron. "All right, Mister Stansfield," I say in a flirty voice. "Open up. You're going to try this one first and tell me if my delicate taste buds can handle it."

His eyes blaze with desire as he opens his mouth, and I feed him the first bite of the Roll-Up. "Mm, yes," he says around the mouthful of food. "It's good, but I'm not sure you'll like it."

"No?" I look at the beautiful food. "Is it really that spicy?"

"Fire-roasted isn't tame." He nods to me. "Go on. Taste it." His expression blazes with the unvocalized dare. Again.

Committing, because I've never turned down a dare when it's been issued twice, I put the other half of the Roll-Up in my mouth.

And fire explodes across my tongue.

CHAPTER TEN

AARON

I CHUCKLE AT MY PHONE AS I STRIP OUT OF MY work clothes and step into the shower, Emma's text burned into my retinas.

I still can't believe you laughed at me about that Roll-Up and then ate all of the Pineapple Upside Down Pancake Delight.

"There was no *delight* in the name of that dessert," I murmur to myself as I start to scrub my hair clean. "And I didn't eat it all."

No, she didn't like the Spicy Mediterranean Roll-Up, but she adored everything else. Seemingly even me, as she hung all over my arm and pressed in close to me as we wandered down the street on the way back to my truck.

I've never wanted a date to continue more than the one last night, and I wasn't as savvy as Elliott and couldn't come up with a plan to avoid the doorbell camera. So I didn't kiss Emma last night.

It's fine.

We're new.

And going to our best friends' rehearsal dinner tonight, thus, why I'm in the shower for the second time today. Good thing I got my bathroom finished this morning. Now, all I need to redo is the front porch, and my house will be pretty livable. I have a few projects still to do, but nothing that prevents me from living well.

The darkness that comes every time I think about Liam getting married hovers over me, despite my attempts to push it away. I'm happy for him—and Hillary. I am.

I just wish I didn't feel so lost. So replaceable.

My phone rings just as I'm wiping conditioner through my hair, so of course, I can't answer it. I should've put it out in the bedroom, because I hate hearing it chime and zing at me while I'm showering. It makes the usually calming experience a frenzy.

And I use showering to calm myself, so when my phone rings again only ten seconds after it stopped, irritation fires through me hotly.

Thankfully, it doesn't ring again, but it bleeps out a chime every second or two. Great. They've gone to texting.

"It's probably Momma." That's so her MO. Call

Aaron and if he doesn't answer, fire off a million texts at him.

I'd given myself plenty of time to shower before I have to get to Liam's house for the dinner. He and Hillary are getting married in his orchard, and the dinner tonight, and on Sunday after the wedding, will be in his backyard.

But I rush through my shower so I can get to my phone faster, and that leaves me unsettled and hyper-focused on my device when I needed to be hyper-focused on clearing my head.

Momma has called, yes. But so did Emma, and all the texts that came in were from her too.

We got the packets for the Summer Faire!

Emailed, Aaron. Go check right now!

Holy cow, I can't believe this.

It's going to be so great.

The twenty-five thousand dollars is really real!

We have to submit a proposal for part of the park and be responsible for cleaning up that space. Then, they'll choose someone to win the prize money and base their complete park redo on their design.

This is so exciting!!!

Oh, roots and shoots. I'm never going to have time to do a proper proposal. It's due the same weekend as Ry and Elliott's wedding.

My mind buzzes, and yes, I want to run to my email

and comb through the packet myself. I smile at Emma's plant-swears.

Don't stop believin', I send to her, hoping it'll make her smile. I get dressed in my only pair of pants besides jeans—a pair of navy blue slacks I got just for this wedding. Liam's as Southern country as they come, and he said I didn't have to wear a white shirt, tie, and jacket, so I bought a blue, yellow, and black plaid shirt—hey, it has a collar and buttons—for the wedding.

I pull on my cowboy boots again, this time pairing it with my hat, because I know Liam will be wearing his. The man loves hats of all shapes and styles, and I sure hope we can still meet up at the sports bar and watch rodeo re-runs.

My phone rings again, and this time I swipe on the call from Emma. "Go for Aaron."

"I—" She cuts off, and I chuckle into the stunned silence. "That's a terrible way to answer the phone," she says.

"I knew you wouldn't say hello."

"You did? How?"

"You used three exclamation points in one of your texts."

She huffs, and then says, "How fast can you get here? Maybe we'll have a few minutes to go over the packet before we have to go to the rehearsal dinner."

I don't tell her I usually take thirty minutes in the

shower to calm myself at the end of a day, and instead say, "I'm almost ready to leave the house."

"Great, I'll see you soon." She hangs up without saying good-bye either, and I shake my head.

"The things I'm willing to put up with." But for some of Emma's sapphire and gold, I am. I totally am.

My mind revolves and stews on the way to the Big House, and by the time I pull into the gravel parking lot out front, a fully-fledged idea has formed.

So when Emma answers the door, a sheaf of papers in her hand, I blurt out, "We should submit a proposal together."

She opens her mouth, then closes it. Then asks, "What?"

"What?" I lean in the doorway with all the swagger of a bad boy cowboy. Or at least what I assume bad boy cowboys swagger like. "You think you can do better than me at a park clean-up? Sweetheart, I have every tool at my disposal, and I've actually done landscaping designs from concept to implementation."

"I—well—you." She swats me with her printed packet.

"In fact, I dare you to try to put something together that'll beat me." I chuckle. "Won't happen."

She shakes her head, but her hair is all pinned up on her head, so it doesn't sway back and forth. "Down, you bad boy. Come in and talk to me like a human." She turns and walks through the foyer and into the living room, her hips swaying in a way that's very, very dangerous to my pulse.

She's wearing a dark blue dress about the same color as my slacks with plenty of glittery gems on it. The back dips low enough to show me her sexy shoulder blades, and I blink as she disappears from view completely.

"Don't just stand there staring," Claudia barks over the doorbell cam speaker, and I swear under my breath and hurry inside the Big House as she adds, "Nice shirt, Aaron."

"Be nice to him," I hear one of the roommates say as I close the door, swipe my hands down my sides to dry my palms, and then I commit to entering the living room.

I've been here before for parties and such, but it's completely different now that I'm Emma's boyfriend. She stands near the corner of the couch, and she's holding Claudia's phone away from her as her friend says, "I meant it. It's a nice shirt."

Claudia's eyes come to mine. "Look at it. He's like a perfect Southern gentleman."

Every eye comes to me, so now I'm shouldering five pairs of female eyes, and let me tell you, they're looking at more than just my shirt.

They're all wearing a dress in navy, and they're all beautiful in their own way. None as much as Emma, and my eyes gravitate back to hers. "Ignore them, Aaron," she says with her nose in the air. "Come into the kitchen, and let's talk for a few minutes."

I nod my cowboy hat at her friends, the Doberman coming to the surface, as I follow her through the living room and toward the kitchen. "Ry," I say. "Love the shoes. Claudia, your hair is exquisite. Tahlia, lovely as always." I actually reach up and touch the brim of my hat with that one. Just one more to go.

"Lizzie, you're always the best-dressed in the room."

Thankfully, Emma has already entered the kitchen, so I'm not technically lying.

"Oh, you're a charmer," Lizzie says, and the doorbell rings over her light laugh.

"That'll be Ell," Ry says just as I duck into the kitchen after Emma.

She's standing over a few pages she's spread over the table, and she glances at me as I join her. "Look here."

"Can I just look at you for a minute?" I slide my hand along her waist and pull her close. "Because you in this dress is somethin' special."

She straightens, the surprise on her face melting into something else entirely. "Oh, you think you're a cowboy because you're wearing the hat. Is that it?" She reaches up and flicks the brim.

"No, really," I say. "Heaven is a place on earth when I'm with you." I grin at her, hoping she'll get the song reference.

She leans into me. "You've used two in one day."

"Is that against the rules?"

"Yes," she says as if she just decided.

"You can't make them up as we go. You know that, right?"

"You have rules for your truck."

"*Established* rules," I say.

"Well, this is my house, and I say you can't use two eighties song lyric references in the same day." She leans over the table again. "The same hour."

"I only used one here, sweetheart." I move up beside her and look at the pages. "And since you called, I didn't have time to check my email."

"They're being menaces, sending this out on a Friday night," she says crossly. She points to the page again. "Proposals have to have pictures of some kind. Diagrams. Pictures from other projects that the applicant has done. Blueprints. They can be real or mocked up."

"Hmm."

"I don't have anything like that." She straightens with a huff. "How hard can it be?"

I say nothing, because using mockup software can be a tad difficult if she's never done it. I tear my eyes from the papers, because I'm not reading the print on them anyway. I can't seem to focus on it right now.

Now with Emma's body heat so close to mine, and with the flowery scent of her skin and hair…I can barely remember my own name or why I came here tonight.

"You've surely got loads of pictures of your floral arrangements," I tell her. "I've seen your social media."

She turns those glinting sapphire eyes on me, and I dive in deep. Too deep. So deep, I miss what she's said until she swats my chest and asks, "Are you even listening to me?"

"Yes." I blink to get myself back to normal. "A collage is an interesting idea." I have no idea if she's said that, but my words appease her. "I still don't think you can beat me, sweetheart."

I grin at her displeasure, and feel very Doberman-like as I do.

"You want to bet?" she asks. Then her eyes widen. "Wait. Forget I said that." She shakes her head. "Claude bet Beckett something, and it was a very bad idea."

"I already issued you a challenge," I say. "I dared you to try to do a proposal better than mine while standing in your doorway." I hook my thumb over my shoulder, as if she's forgotten where the door is. "Just now. When I got here."

Her eyes search mine, and I kick up my Doberman smile.

"Well?"

She shakes her head again. "No, I can't do it."

"Then I dare you to join forces with me. Let's submit something together."

"Aaron, you're making me tired."

I've heard that before, but I don't tell her that. "A)

You've already said you won't have time to put together a proposal," I say. "And B) you've never done a blueprint or a mock-up. If we work together, I can shoulder the bulk of it."

She gathers her papers back together and turns to face me fully, cocking one curvy hip away from the table. "And who gets the money if we win?"

I stall, because I hadn't thought of that.

"Yeah," she says dryly. "Exactly. Where's your eighties lyric for that?"

"You said I only get one per day," I shoot back at her. "I'm just following your rules."

"It's time to go," Tahlia yells from the living room. "Em, we're going."

"Okay," she calls back, and she steps over to her crate and tucks the papers away. She breathes in deep and blows it out as she faces me. "Ready?"

"To go have dinner outside in the evening heat and humidity?" I offer her my arm. "Lead on, my good lady. Lead on."

———

I'M PUTTING on a good show of joviality, laughing and chatting and holding my flute of champagne without actually drinking any. I do have to drive home after this wedding, after all. I notice that Elliott doesn't drink either, and he never goes anywhere without his adorable, tawny dog.

The rehearsal dinner a couple of nights ago went off without a hitch. Yesterday, I spent all afternoon and evening with Emma and "Sir Chills-a-Lot" to finish the flowers for this event, and now we've been mingling for a half-hour, waiting for this wedding to start.

But when Liam says, "I need the wedding party to come into the house," my stomach drops all the way to the ground.

Emma kisses her grandmother's cheek and comes my way. We're not walking down the aisle together, because I'm the best man, and I have to walk by myself. My blood already vibrates through my veins because of it.

She loops her arm through mine, and we turn to go up the back steps to the deck. "Will you introduce me to your grandmother later?"

Emma looks over to me, obviously wary. "Maybe."

"What does it depend on?"

She grins at me outside the established bride's room where her friends are ducking inside. I have to keep going through the kitchen to Liam's bedroom, and I'm dreading every step.

"If I have a total eclipse of the heart," she says with a smile. "Or not."

CHAPTER ELEVEN

EMMA

I can't believe I quoted an eighties song to Aaron, but seeing the look on his face makes me giggle. I leave him standing in the kitchen as I duck into the bride's room, where Hillary has been getting ready with her mother.

Oh, her mother.

Just seeing Mrs. Mays, with her gold, glittery mother-of-the-bride dress, makes me a touch happier that my mother probably won't come to my wedding. And that I haven't had to deal with her for almost twenty years now.

Of course, I'm not really happy about that, and a thread of guilt tugs through my gut for even thinking it.

"Emma's here," Ryanne says. "That's everyone."

I join everyone around Hillary, crowding in close on her left side with Tahlia. We make the perfect halo, with her the bright white center in her gorgeous mermaid wedding gown. I sigh, so much happiness parading through me.

"You're gorgeous," Claudia says, her voice as soft as angel wings. Hillary's twisted and pinned her hair up in ringlets, and her strapless dress has a beaded and glittering bodice that gives way to shiny satin as it clings to her hips and upper thighs, then billows out.

If she's wearing shoes, I can't see them, and they're not needed to complete the picture of a perfect bride.

"I'm really doing this," Hillary says. "I can't believe it."

"Of course you are, dear," Her mother waves her hand almost dismissively, as if Hillary hasn't been engaged twice but never married. Her eyes meet mine, and I give her my best reassuring, encouraging smile. After all, I have a mother who says cruel things too, whether intentional or not.

"Is Daddy ready?" Hillary asks.

"Yes, of course," her mother says.

Hillary turns from the mirror, and we bloom out to give her room, and then the five of us close in again, creating a six-way hug. "This is going to be amazing," Tahlia says.

"You're beautiful, and he's so lucky," Ryanne whispers.

"The wedding of the year," Lizzie tells her.

I hug my arm around her waist tightly, smiling

around at everyone. Claudia sniffles and says, "I love you guys."

"I can't wait for all of you to get married," I say, barely holding back my own emotions. We separate, and I flit around to check all the wrist corsages I made.

They haven't suffered any damage from our squeeze-fest, and Hillary's mother says, "It's time to line up, ladies. The groomsmen are in the kitchen."

That means Liam is at the altar, and I see Hill's eyes move to the window. It's curtained, so we can't see out, but I look too. "He's there," I tell her, and then I go to line up.

Liam owns his own business, and he works a one-man construction operation. Aaron is his only grooms-man, and he'll walk down the aisle alone. That leaves the five of us, as Hillary's roommates to walk down the aisle together, and we've decided on a V-formation, with the tallest of us in the middle.

That's Claudia, and she's the perfect cornerstone for us, and I link my arm through hers, and Lizzie connects herself to the V on my left side. Ry and Tahlia take up their position on Claude's other side, and we stand behind Aaron as Hillary's mom slips outside while her daddy goes into the bride's room.

I take a deep breath, suddenly able to feel the nerves pouring off of Aaron only a few paces in front of me. He's nervous about this wedding, because Liam is his best friend, and everyone knows so many things change when two people get married.

At his side, his fingers tap, tap, tap against his leg, and as I stand there and wait for the cue to go out the door and get to the orchard, I realize I've seen Aaron's nerves manifest themselves this way before.

Or maybe he can just never stand still.

No matter what, he holds us all in place until someone opens the door and nods to him, and then his shoulders rise with a breath, and he leads us outside.

We go down the steps and sidewalk and past Liam's garage. I'm starting to think we should've staged closer to the actual event, but then I see the chairs and decorations in the trees. They've just started to blossom, and everything inside me sighs at the sight of those flowers.

And Liam at the altar.

Music lilts through the trees, and Aaron pauses at the end of the aisle so the guests can get to their feet.

Then he takes the first step, and I admire him so much for being able to walk down the aisle all by himself. His shoulders are boxy and tense, but he practically glides down the aisle in his plaid shirt and cowboy hat.

We follow several paces behind him, and I can't help feeling shiny and magical. I can't stop smiling, and when we reach Liam, all five of us crowd into him and hug him tightly as he laughs.

Claudia will stand slightly behind Hillary, and I

throw a supportive smile to Aaron before I go to take my spot in the front row.

I turn to see Hillary standing at the end of the aisle, her arm delicately placed in her father's, both of them perfectly framed by the tree limbs and blossoms. I'm sure Liam trimmed them exactly right for her, because one quick glance at him shows his face shining with so much love.

I press my hand to my heartbeat, not even caring that I'm semi-smashing my corsage against my chest. The bouquet is exquisite, if I do say so myself, and I absolutely love weddings.

And the wedding of one of my best friends? All of the work I put into the flowers for this event has been totally worth it.

———

"AND I just don't know, Grams." I take another bite of her chocolate raspberry trifle, wishing I could bake half as well as I can arrange flowers.

"What do you have to lose?" she asks in her weathered, eighty-year-old voice. She covers my hand with hers. "Do you have time to do your own proposal?"

"No." I sigh out the word, because it's true and I wish it wasn't. Sir Chills-a-Lot told me to swallow my pride and accept Aaron's dare to submit a dual proposal to the city of Cider Cove. Because if I don't, I won't be able to participate in the clean-up project at the park at all.

"He just—you know what? He dared me to try to do something better than him, and that annoys me." I scoop up another spoonful of delicious, dark chocolate cake and that layer of raspberry crème. "I mean, what goes better with a park clean-up and renovation than flowers?"

"A handyman who knows how to build anything he wants," Grams says, no question mark in sight.

I give her a salty look and eat my dessert, because she's not wrong. In fact, no one in town can beat Aaron. We'll all just look pathetic trying.

In that moment, I realize that he's essentially given me half of his money by offering—daring—me to go in on a proposal with him. My heartbeat thrashes for a moment, and I tell myself it's because of all the sugar I've eaten this evening.

But I'm wrong, and I know it.

"When will I get to meet him?" Grams asks.

I look up and into her eyes. So much like mine, they shine with a blueness that all the women in our family have. "I don't know," I say.

"You don't have to hide him from me." She gives me a smile and stands. "You want some milk with your cake?"

"Yes, please," I say like I'm six years old, eating cookies and milk. "And I don't think I'm hiding him from you." My words slow as I try to put them in the right order. "I think I'm hiding you from him."

"What? Why would you need to do that?"

I sigh again. "Because, Grams, I haven't told him about our family."

She says nothing, which is her way of saying so much. "I'm not embarrassed of you," I say. "It's not that. It's just...I don't want to explain it all again."

"Well, that's just silly," Grams says in that old-lady way she has. She doesn't mean to hurt me, but she told me a decade ago that she doesn't have any sugar-coating left in her. So she just says what she means now.

"You want to fall in love, right?" she asks, plunking the glass of milk down in front of me.

"So aggressive," I say. She cocks her eyebrow at me. "Yes, of course, Grams."

She sits and folds her arms, those blue eyes so cold and calculating now. Yikes. "So you're going to wait until I die, is that it? Then you won't have to explain about your family. You'll just say—'I don't have anyone.' And that'll be it."

"No, Grams. I'm not waiting for you to die." I take a sip of the milk, really wishing I could have whole milk all the time. It's all Grams drinks, and I love her for it.

"The man you marry will want to know all about your family, whether I'm alive or not." She unclenches her arms and leans into me again, giving me a side-hug.

"If you're not embarrassed, then what's holding you back?"

"I'm not embarrassed of you," I say again. "But that doesn't mean this situation isn't...hard for me." I look right at her, knowing I can tell her. I just never have. "I'm worried about how it'll make *me* look, Grams."

Confusion riddles her brow. "I don't understand."

"My parents abandoned me here when I was fifteen," I say. "Because why? Because I'm so horrible they couldn't stand me? Because I came along so far after Seth and Paul, they ran out of patience?"

I swallow, the truth right there on my tongue. And it won't go away. "Because I'm so unlovable?"

"Of course not," Grams barks out. "Emma, none of that is true."

"For you." I swirl my spoon through the trifle, but I don't take another bite. "Sometimes...sometimes I wonder if all of the above is true, and you've simply been too kind to say it all these years."

"I say what I want," Grams says. "And it's not true." She points one wrinkled finger at me. "And any man— *any man* on this planet, Em—who would even think that for *one second* is not worth your time."

I smile, though tears prick my eyes. "Okay, Grams."

"So are you hiding him from me because you think he'll think that? Because if so, you should be glad he didn't kiss you at the wedding. Hasta la vista to this hot handyman. We don't need 'im."

"Grams, calm down." I laugh and shake my head. "No, I don't think Aaron will think that. Sometimes, I'm just a little irrational."

"So no more hiding."

I swallow, and it takes an extra second to nod. "All right," I say. "No more hiding."

Grams beams like she's just won a year's worth of Christmas Days. "Great. Then I'll have you two for dinner this weekend."

"Grams—"

"Don't argue with me, young lady." Grams pins me with a pointed look. "I know you're busy, but you can spare two hours with me next Sunday. You'll be here anyway."

And she's, once again, not wrong, so I say, "Okay. Aaron and I will come to dinner next Sunday."

CHAPTER TWELVE

AARON

I WORK AROUND MY BEARD, CLEANING IT UP SO THAT every hair is in place. I shouldn't be so nervous, at least according to Emma. But meeting her grandmother is a big deal.

I know, because she didn't introduce us at the wedding a couple of weeks ago, and Emma is taking time out of her ultra-busy schedule, where she's got ninety-one roses to prune, wrap, and ribbon this week, with Ry and Elliott's wedding only a few days after that.

They're getting married on a Tuesday, because apparently, that's the slowest day at the office supply store they co-manage.

I finish shaving and step over to my new, expanded master closet. I had to steal some square footage from the bathroom and the bedroom to make it, but it's worth it. I have three walls of shelves and rods, and I flip through my choices for shirts with the speed of a seasoned shopper.

"I'm here," Emma calls from the front of the house, and I spin around. I'd seen her text when she was leaving the Big House, and that was only ten minutes ago. There's no way she got here that fast.

"I'm back here," I call, and then I face my clothes again. "I could use your help."

Her footsteps come closer, really causing my pulse to ricochet through my body. I mean, I'm standing in my closet, shirtless, and I haven't kissed the delectable blonde who enters my closet with the tentative words, "My help?"

"With a shirt." I indicate the row of hanging garments in front of me.

Emma says nothing, and she doesn't move closer to the rack to sift through the shirts. I look over to her. "What's—?"

Her eyes are glued to my chest, and a certain measure of pride flows through me. I work constantly most days, with heavy objects and building materials, unloading and loading trucks, with a little paper pushing in there too.

I know I have muscles—and now Emma does too.

"I wish I had a doorbell camera to yell into," I say. "To tell you to stop staring and help me find a shirt."

Emma startles and blinks rapidly. "I—wasn't expecting this."

"I'm meeting your grandmother," I say. "I need something better than a gray polo. Claudia will never let me live it down."

She and Beckett comment on every shirt I wear now, and I have to say, it doesn't bother me.

"You look great in gray," she says.

"Just what every man wants to hear."

"Oh, come on." Emma finally starts to leaf through my clothing. "It is a compliment."

She's wearing blue, because she knows it's her heavenly color—a term I learned from her this past week. She claims that everyone has a "heavenly color" that simply brings out their best features, and that she can match any floral arrangement to it.

To my horror, she pulls a gray shirt from the hanger. "This one."

"That's gray." I refuse to take it, and instead, back up a step.

She shakes it toward me. "It has faint yellow stripes, and that'll bring out the highlights in your hair."

"I have highlights in my hair?"

"Can you just put this on, so I can stop being so distracted?" She tosses me the shirt, and I flinch like she's thrown a load of bricks at me. "We're going to be late, and if there's one thing Grams can't abide, it's tardiness."

She nods, sweeps her eyes down my torso again, and turns smartly on her heel to leave the closet.

"You didn't text from the Big House," I call after her. "There's no way. You'd still be over by Salty Dog if you had." I glare at the shirt in my hands, sigh, and pull it over my head. I tuck it in as I leave my bedroom, adjusting my belt as I go down the hall.

Emma paces in front of my fireplace, and I pause to watch her. "I forgot to text," she says when she sees me. "So yes, I texted from a stoplight a bit away."

"I thought you said I didn't need to be nervous."

"You don't." She throws me a look I can't decipher, turns, and paces toward the front window. Her hair falls in straight layers down her back, and she's clearly used a flat iron on that. It's shiny and silky, and I can't wait to run my fingers through it.

Of course, I've never touched her hair, so that would be a major accomplishment in our relationship.

Something is afoot here, and I shelve my hormones as I move over to intercept her at the end of the hearth. "Emma." I take her shoulders and force her to stop. "Tell me what's going on."

Her eyes meet mine, filled with horrible anxiety. I want to take it from her and ease it into oblivion. "I'm close with my grams, right?"

"Yes," I say slowly.

She swallows. "It's because she—well—she raised me. I mean, she didn't. My parents were here until I was fifteen. She—she didn't abandon me when she was done with me."

I don't know what to say, and I search her face for more of the story. It's not written there, of course. My heart thumps painfully against my breastbone as I try to figure out what to say.

"I'm sorry," comes out of my mouth, and I fold her into my arms and hold her against my chest. My cheek meets the silky quality of her hair, and I breathe in all of the floral goodness Emma has to offer. "I don't know why anyone would...abandon you. You're fantastic."

"I'm fifteen years younger than my next oldest brother," she whispers against my bicep. "My parents weren't expecting me, and well, Grams said they hung in there as long as they could."

I stroke one hand down the back of her head and through her hair, sighing internally in a blissful way. "Where are they now?"

Emma exhales heavily and steps out of my arms. She studies her shoes—a pair of wedges I've seen her wear before—and says, "They got divorced and left the Charleston area. My dad got remarried and lives in Florida now. My mom is up in Minnesota, of all places."

"How many brothers?"

"Two," she says. "One is in Atlanta. He and his wife have three kids. One is in Baltimore. They have two kids."

I gently guide her chin up, so she'll look at me. "And you're here, in the best small town in South Carolina." I give her a soft smile. "With your grandmother and all your best friends."

Tears fill her eyes. "Yeah."

"And you own an amazing florist shop," I add as her eyelids drift closed. "And you're beautiful, and kind, and hardworking, and if your parents can't see that, well, that sounds like a them-problem."

A soft sob spills from her mouth, and I haul her back into my chest. "I'm sorry," she says. "I didn't mean to cry." She sniffles, but I sure like the way she's holding onto me like she needs me to stand.

"You can cry about this—about anything—any time you want."

She pulls away and turns her back on me. I stand there helplessly, wishing I knew more what to do or say. She draws in a big breath. "I'm okay. Really. I've had a long time to get over this, and I am. I swear."

"But it's okay if you're not."

"I just hate explaining it to people." She faces me again, and all evidence of her tears is gone. "Can we go? I really don't want Grams to passive-aggressively text me that the rolls are getting cold." She puts a smile on her face, and all I can think about it kissing it off.

I move into her personal space and curl my fingers around the back of her neck. "We can go," I whisper. "Because you're amazing, and I want you to be happy, okay?"

She nods, her eyes falling closed again. "Do you have

anything hard you don't like telling your girlfriends?" She opens her eyes and looks at me, almost an edge of hope in her eyes.

My stomach turns hard, and I nod. "Sure, of course." I take her hand and lead her toward the front door. When I don't have to look at her, it's easier to get confessions out. "I, uh, have ADHD. The kind where you hyper-focus on something to the point of not being able to think about anything else."

We leave the house, the screen door crashing closed behind us. The new front porch is phenomenal, if I do say so myself, and I had to employ my ADHD to get it done as quickly as I did.

"It can come in handy sometimes," I say. "Like when I need to finish a project or pay attention to fine details." I glance over to her as we go down my front steps. "Other times, it's a curse. It makes me miss texts and ignore some projects that don't interest me as much."

I go around to the passenger side of my truck and open the door for her. We finally come face-to-face again, and I think of the lack of cameras on my property. Emma came to pick me up for this Sunday dinner date with her grandmother, because she said it didn't make sense for me to drive twenty minutes to the Big House to get her, then drive twenty-five minutes back to the center of town where her grams lives.

She smiles at me. "So many things are making sense now."

"Are they?"

"You fidget when you're nervous too."

"I fidget because I exist," I say. "I have a hard time sitting still. It's like my body...it doesn't match my mind, and I feel out of equilibrium." I shrug one shoulder. "I mean, that's how one of my doctors described it, and it made sense to me. So."

Emma puts both hands on my chest and leans into me, her smile curving up those pretty pink lips in such a slow, tantalizing way.

"How long until your grandmother calls?"

"Could be any second."

"Dare we risk it...for a kiss?"

Everything about Emma softens, and she nods. I don't need a verbal affirmation, and since I've been dying to kiss Emma for real for months, I lower my head and do exactly that.

An explosion fires through my brain, and I probably kiss her a little too roughly for the first few strokes. Then I settle down, get my mind and body in sync, and really enjoy kissing this woman I've liked for so, so long.

CHAPTER THIRTEEN

EMMA

THIS SECOND FIRST KISS WITH AARON CARRIES EVEN more heat than before. More passion. More hope. More of everything, and I thought I'd never be kissed the way he'd fake-kissed me in the back doorway of my shop.

But this one beside his truck?

Incredible.

The soft brush of his beard against my face sends delight through me, and I have no idea how long we stand outside his house, kissing. Long enough for me to feel like I might combust, and long enough for my lips to feel a bit puffy and bruised when he finally pulls away.

I keep my eyes closed, trying to commit every sensation to memory. I forget a lot of things, but I really don't want to forget how Aaron makes me feel when he holds me close.

"Let's—" he starts, but the shrill ringing of my phone cuts him off.

My pulse knocks through my body painfully. "Grams," I gasp out.

"I was just going to say, let's go."

I let the phone ring as I climb in Aaron's truck, and he makes the quick drive from his house to Grams's. She only lives a few streets over and across the bridge, and we arrive only five minutes later.

She hasn't called again, thankfully, but as Aaron puts the truck in park, I see her framed in the front window. Watching.

"Let's not dawdle," I say.

Aaron snickers, then clears his throat, and says, "No, ma'am," before dropping out of the truck and jogging— legit jogging—around the front of the truck to get my door. I can open my own door, of course, but I let Aaron do it, because Grams is watching, and it'll make her like him more.

I smile at him as he takes my hand. "Everything is fine."

"You'd tell me if I was walking into a landmine, right?" His smile stays etched on his face too, our steps slow as we go down the sidewalk.

"Of course," I say. "Grams is a good cook, and she'll probably have you fixing her kitchen sink before we leave." I squeeze his hand and trot up the steps just as Grams opens the front door.

"Grams," I say, releasing Aaron's hand and taking her into a hug. "Sorry, we're a little late."

"I called."

"Just once." I step back and smile at her. "Don't be mad, okay?" I whisper. "Aaron finally kissed me, so it was worth being late for."

Grams's eyes widen, and she looks over my shoulder to where Aaron stands. I turn to face him too and reach for his hand. "Aaron, this is my grandmother, Greta. Grams, this is my boyfriend, Aaron."

Something warm and wonderful moves through me at my use of the word *boyfriend*, because it's been a long time since I had one of those. I feel like sunlight beams from me, lighting Aaron's face as it does.

"Ma'am." He nods at Grams, steps forward, and hugs her, sweeping his lips across her papery cheek as he does. "Emma has told me so many good things about you."

"I'm sure she has." Grams smile at Aaron, then shoots me a look before turning to go inside the house. "Come in, y'all. We don't want the rolls to get too cold."

I grin and grin as Aaron watches Grams for a moment, then turns to face me. "Told you about the rolls."

"She likes me, right?"

I look at the open front door. "Well, she left the door open, so she doesn't *dis*like you."

He smiles at me, and we go inside the house. "So,

Greta," he says. "Em said you might have something amiss with your kitchen sink." He joins her effortlessly in the kitchen, and I stay back by the couch, watching the two of them.

And I know I always fall too fast—something I haven't forgotten, unfortunately—but that ooey-gooey goodness fills me, and I fall a little bit in love with Aaron as he takes the wrench Grams hands him and looks at it like she's torn off his arm and given it to him to hold.

———

THE BUZZER on the back door sounds, and I exhale and push my hair out of my face. "He's here," I say to Sir Chills-a-Lot. "You be nice to him this time."

Aaron's come to help me several times since I bought the florist shop, so this late-night meet-up isn't all that special. Except it is, because we've been dating for a couple of weeks now.

Three weeks, my mind shouts at me. And he survived dinner with Grams. In fact, she's texted me several times about how "wonderful," and "handsome," and "sweet" Aaron is.

A level of exhaustion pulls through me as I step toward the back door. I've been really busy lately, what with this Spring Fling Festival and Ry's wedding all within a few days of each other.

Aaron has been too, as he's taken on a new build

now that his house is finished. I can't even begin to understand how to make another level to a house, so I let Aaron sleep if he needs to, and I sweep my lips across his forehead before I drive back to the Big House.

I unlock the door and say, "Hey," immediately turning to go back to my cold room.

"I brought dinner," he says, coming in behind me and closing the door. "You want this locked?"

"Yes, please." I head back toward the cold room, where a hundred roses wait to be clipped, taped, and ribboned for tomorrow night's Spring Fling Festival.

"I have a draft of our proposal too," he says from behind me. "And I didn't get my hello kiss."

I turn to face him just outside Sir Chills-a-Lot and give him a smile. "Thank you for bringing dinner." I tip my head back to receive his kiss. His lips taste like chocolate and mint, and I hope he brought some of the milk chocolate sandwich mints he loves so much.

Because I love them too.

"Mm, better," he says as he pulls away. "So what are we doing first?"

"Flowers," I say, indicating the walk-in cooler. "Then dinner, while we go over the proposal?" I cradle his face in one hand and gaze at him. "Thank you for doing it, Aaron. Really. I know you're as busy as I am."

"I just took the pieces you provided and put them together." Aaron doesn't take compliments super well, and I tilt my head to the side. He blinks a couple of times. "You're welcome, Em."

He rubs his hands together and enters the cold room. "Let's get these flowers done."

"I'm going to grab an extra pair of scissors," I say. "You can cut the flyers after the ribbons."

"Yep."

After a quick detour to my check-out counter, I return to Sir Chills and hand the scissors to Aaron. "Do them long enough, so I don't have to try to tie them with hardly any clearance."

"Ten inches?"

"Don't confuse me with numbers, Aaron." I shoot him a smile. "Just cut them long enough, because my fingers are already going to be cold and tired." I pick up the thorn stripper and start cleaning the stem on a blood red rose.

I'll cut the stems down and wrap them with floral tape to preserve them until tomorrow night, when every man who checks in for the Spring Fling will get a rose. The first woman he gives it to is the one who'll go out on at least one date with him, and hopefully many love connections will be made tomorrow.

Aaron cuts ribbon, and I strip roses, and when I start taping, he starts cutting apart the flyers I picked up at the print shop down the street earlier this morning. I finish the taping and reach for the first ribbon.

"Done," he says. "I can help tie ribbons." He picks up a white one, and I quickly take it from him.

"No."

"No?"

"Aaron, you have amazing hands when it comes to building a deck or mudding a wall. But tying ribbons?" I shake my head. "I don't want to have to redo them."

A beat of silence echoes through the cold room, and then he bear hugs me, making it impossible to tie anything. "I have a delicate touch, I'll have you know." He rubs his beard against my cheek, which makes me laugh.

"Stop it," I squeal, and my shoe catches on the rubber mat that cushions the hard floor. "Aaron." I laugh even as I start to fall, and I grab tight to him, pulling him with me.

I land with a thud on my hip, my giggles turning into a groan as Aaron collapses next to me. He rolls onto his back while I'm still trying to deal with the smarting zing in my hip and leg.

Then he starts to laugh, and he tugs on my hand, pulling me back until we're both lying on the mats. "Sir Chills has done us dirty," I say, smiling up to the ceiling.

That makes Aaron laugh harder, and I join my laughter to his, not even caring about the delay in getting the roses done for tomorrow night's event.

———

THE FOLLOWING EVENING, I stand at the check-in table, wearing one of Lizzie's wrap sweater dresses, despite the fact that the calendar has just flipped to May. "Flowers here," I say, holding out the basket with the red roses.

Behind me, Pixie and Piper hand out the swag bags, where my shop flyers went. All men are going in on my side of the Lion's Club, and the women are going in the east doors. They then converge in the lobby, where there's a single table that Aaron's manning by himself.

This gives everyone a chance to mingle and talk before the organized events take place, and the dull roar of chatter and elevator music combine behind me into a low buzzing headache in the back of my skull.

I just want to go home, get out of this dress, and lay in Aaron's arms while I snack on a pancake. A couple more hours, and I'll be able to do that.

Oh, wait, I have an entire wedding's worth of flowers to organize and arrange in the next three days. And a shop to run.

"Sir," I say as a man walks by me without taking a rose. "You'll need a flower if you want to..." I trail off as I come face-to-face with Stewart Lipski, the chemist who broke Lizzie's heart last Halloween.

"Are the flowers mandatory?"

I glare at him, remembering how he ghosted Lizzie, how she said he only wanted to be a casual dater. "Yes," I clip out at him. "If you're not interested in setting something up with someone, then just leave."

"Hey, I paid to be here."

"This isn't a way to meet women," I say.

Stewart's perfectly plucked eyebrows go up. "Really? I thought that's exactly what this is."

"Stewart," I say with plenty of disdain in my voice. "You have to take a flower and at least pretend like you want a girlfriend for longer than a weekend." I cock one eyebrow at him. "Or a Halloween party."

I see the moment he realizes I know what went down between him and Lizzie. He must not have known her well at all if he thought she wouldn't tell her roommates. Then Stewart's arrogance slides back across his face, and he really is a Doberman bad boy that breaks women's hearts.

Like Tucker.

"If you don't take a flower, I can't let you in."

"Is there a problem here?" Aaron's smooth customer service voice makes me turn and look at him.

"This *gentleman* doesn't want a rose," I say, my teeth practically glued together.

Aaron frowns. "If you don't present a rose to a woman, then you don't get her name or number."

"No names or numbers?" Stewart sighs and reaches his horrible, chemically hand into the basket and takes a rose. "Fine."

"Hey," I say as a petal sheds from one of the roses still in the basket. "You don't need to be so grabby."

Stewart doesn't even answer me as he continues through the doorway leading into the foyer.

"Former boyfriend of yours?" Aaron asks, his hand heavy on my hip.

I hold out the basket for the next man who approaches. Once he's gone, I shake my head. "No, he went out with Lizzie once. Well, that's a generous way of putting it. They snuck off from the Halloween party last year. Remember that?"

"The party? Sure." Aaron steps back and then leans in close, his lips practically tickling the soft skin on my neck. "Have I told you how amazing you look in that dress?"

I smile and hold out the basket for the next gentleman who comes past. Once he's gone, I duck my head and whisper, "And yet, I can't wait to get out of it."

Aaron chuckles and asks, "Are we still on for a late dinner and falling asleep after we pretend like we'll stay awake and watch a movie?"

"Absolutely," I say. "And don't forget. You said you could help me tomorrow night after you get done at the store."

"Em, you're the forgetful one," he says. "I count down the minutes every day until I can see you in the evening." Then he goes through the door and into the foyer too, leaving me feeling warm and strong and sexy in this non-summer sweater dress.

CHAPTER FOURTEEN

ELLIOTT

"Momma." I brush her hand away from my bow tie, but she just lifts it back. "Momma." I glare at her and step back. "It's fine. Can you go out now? The wedding's about to start."

"Okay, okay," she says. "You look so handsome."

I look at myself in the mirror, and I just got a new pair of glasses. "I can see myself, Momma."

My brother joins us and links his arm through Momma's. "Momma," Brandon says. "It's time for us to go out." He looks at me. "You ready, Ell?"

"So ready," I say.

"I can't believe you're getting married before me." Brandon grins, though, and everyone understands why Ry and I have fast-tracked this wedding.

I want to *see* her walking down the aisle toward me.

I want to roll over in bed and *see* her sleeping next to me.

I want to memorize every detail of her face, the way her lips curve when she smiles, the way her eyes light up when she's happy—because someday, those memories might be all I have left.

Someone knocks on the door, and we all turn toward it. Momma hasn't left as I asked her to, and she marches smartly over to the tall wooden door and opens it. "Hello," a man says. "My mother says we're ready for Elliott."

I hurry over to the door too, and I crowd in next to my mom. "Hey, Danny. We're ready." I shake Ryanne's brother's hand, and he smiles at all of us.

"All right, guys," I say as he turns to go back down the hall. "He's our cue. Let's get going." I take Luna's leash from Brandon and lead the way out of the groom's room, but my brother and momma come to my side quickly in the hallway.

We walk without hurry toward the chapel in this grand wedding venue, where the sound of pretty piano music pipes back to me. My pulse increases with every step I take, and I'm actually semi-glad I'm going blind when I reach the doorway that leads to the staircase that goes down to the chapel. Then I won't be able to see the multitude of people here to witness this wedding.

I tell myself it'll only take me and Luna, Brandon, and Momma thirty seconds to go down the steps and then the aisle, and then I'll be in position for Ry.

Her whole family has come from New York, and everyone who works at Paper Trail is here too. The store will be closed for two hours today for our wedding, and we chose Tuesday, since it's our lightest time of the week.

I manage not to trip down the stairs, and all the work Ryanne, her sisters, and her mother did for the wedding shines back at me. Tall, waist-high pillars stand at the end of every row of chairs, which have been draped in white fabric. Bright pink bows have been tied around the backs of the chairs, and Luna and I pause at the bottom of the steps to wait for the guests to stand, though I'm not the bride.

I try to take in their smiling faces, commit them to memory. I tug down the vest of my tuxedo, look at Luna, and start toward the stained-glass window at the end of the aisle. An arch has been set up there, and it looks like it's floating above the ground, dripping with flowers in dusty rose, punch pink, and all shades and tints of red in between those.

I make it to the altar, which is a thick podium of stacked reams of paper with a huge, clear bowl holding every type of M&M known to mankind. I hug my mother and my brother, and then we each take a handful of candy and eat it.

They take seats in the front row, and I stand next to the stack of paper and the M&Ms, my eyes trained on the staircase across from me. I don't even dare blink, because I don't want to miss a moment of Ryanne walking toward me.

Her father enters the chapel from my right, and he parks himself at the bottom of the steps and looks up them. The arched doorway there remains empty, and that only makes my heart rate continue to climb.

Her mother comes down the aisle, and I grin and grin at her. "Grace," I whisper as I hug her.

"She's ready," she says. "They're lining up now."

I nod, swallowing hard as she moves to the end seat on the front row. She hugs my mother too, and my cells might burst with the kindness and love present in this chapel today.

Then, the music changes, and the wedding party starts down the aisle. I clasp my hands in front of me as Ryanne's siblings and their significant others come first, then each of her roommates, all of the women wearing pale pink dresses and flowers in their hair.

"You look sensational," Claudia says as she hugs me. She grins as she steps back, the bridesmaids fanning out to the right of the arch and altar-podium.

A collective gasp goes up from the crowd, and I yank my attention back to the stairs. Ryanne stands at the top of them now, absolutely angelic in her wedding gown.

It's bright white, with a similar bow to the chairs wrapped around her waist. It's satiny and bright pink, and I grin as wide as I ever have. Because I can see it.

I see her.

She puts one gloved hand delicately on the railing, looks down, and takes the first step toward her father.

Toward me.

Her dress shimmers in the early afternoon sunlight, and I can't tell if there's any lace or not. Wide straps go up and over her shoulders, and she wears a crown of pink roses and baby's breath on her head.

She reaches the bottom of the steps, looks up, and our eyes meet. I lift my hand and cover my heart with it. Ry smiles at me, and nothing will ever be as beautiful as her in that gown, smiling at me with a crown on her head.

She is my queen.

I thought about making my vows out of the things the Mars Rovers have said, but I decided against it.

Ry takes her bouquet from her daddy, then links her arm through his, and they start the march toward me. I memorize every step, every moment the sunlight glints on the gems on her dress, and as she gets closer, I see the bodice is covered in lace, beads, and gems, and I can't wait to touch it.

She arrives, and I loop one arm around her and hold her right next to me. "Mm, I love you, Kitty-Cat" I whisper.

I feel her smile against my cheek, and we separate as her father takes his spot in the first row. She smiles at me, and she reaches up and brushes her fingers across my forehead, sweeping my hair out of the way.

"I love your new glasses," she says. "I love *you*, Elliott."

Luna barks, and that makes me grin and a chuckle to ripple through the crowd.

"Yes," Ry says to my guide dog. "And now, it's time to get married."

CHAPTER FIFTEEN

LIZZIE

THE FIRST THING I LEARN ABOUT BEING PROMOTED to the Regulatory Affairs Department Chair is that everyone has their own interpretation of what being "safe" means.

For instance, Jessie from HR thought it was "safe" to surprise me with a small celebratory party in the cafeteria.

Somewhere between the paper hats and the sheet cake that said "Congrats Lizzie!" in bright pink icing, I nearly tripped over my own feet and face-planted in front of the entire room when someone yelled, "Speech!"

See, surprise parties—and speeches—are not my definition of safe.

They're my definition of an ambush.

What's safe?

Safe is wearing heels low enough to walk like a confident woman and not a newborn deer. Safe is visiting my new office during lunch hours when most people are busy debating whether to get an extra brownie or eat the salad. Safe is then returning to my old office, packing up my solitary cardboard box of personal belongings, and going with Marty, the Interdepartmental Secretary, and over to my new promotion.

Those are things I can plan. Things I can dress for, so when I walk in and meet the other department heads at yet another group gathering, I don't feel like I'm going to lose my lunch. Or, in this case, breakfast, as I skipped lunch in favor of stalking out my new digs.

Four walls.

I work not to squee, because ChemTech is not the place for squeeing. Honestly, the fact that there are two parties on a Tuesday is the most exciting thing I've ever seen a bunch of chemists do.

"Ken," Marty says. "This is Lizzie Trenton. She's our new Regulatory Affairs Chair." He beams at me like I've cured cancer.

"Hey." I extend my hand and shake Ken's. "What do you do?"

"I'm Sustainability," Ken says, and I wonder if I'm going to have to start introducing myself like that.

Not I'm Lizzie, but *I'm Regulatory Affairs*.

Hey, it could be worse. I could be Process Engineering or Supply Chain.

I used to work in the Environment, Health, and

Safety Department as a compliance officer, and that department chair would be EHS.

Like, eh, no one knows what I do for a living. Just keep smiling and let's move the topic to something else.

Yes, meeting men and telling them I work for Chem-Tech is a real mood-killer.

I meet a parade of men, from Sam in Sales and Marketing to Phillip in that Supply Chain Management role to Jeff in Legal and Compliance.

I'll work with him a lot, and it sure does seem like there are a lot of safety, regulation, and compliance departments at this company.

That's because there are.

And as I look around at this stale-cake party, I realize I'm the only female in the room. I'm wearing the cutest black pencil skirt ever, as it has a rippling fabric called crêpe.

I don't feel unsafe here, but I can't wait to simply unpack my stapler, the framed photograph of me and my roommates sitting on the porch at the Big House one day last summer, licking ice cream cones, and go fill my water bottle from the Department-Chair-Only lounge.

Oh, that lounge. I've coveted it since the moment I heard about it from a friend. See, Matt got promoted to the Process Engineering Department Chair a couple of years ago, and we stayed in touch for a while there. Then, as all good things do, the texts slowed and Matt had other friends here at ChemTech.

I suffer through the boring party—only chemists can make frosting un-fun—and finally escape to my office after thirty minutes.

"I'll let you get settled in," Marty says as he leads me into my office. It has a window, and while the view isn't super spectacular, it does give me a fifth-floor view that lets me see out past the western edge of Cider Cove, where our company is located.

"Oh, look, Jessie brought over the cake from EHS." Marty beams at the messy dessert, claps his hands, and turns to leave. Over his shoulder, he adds, "Jaden from IT will be in to help you get your computer set up." He's like a golden retriever on Xanax, and I'm not sad to see him go.

In fact, after I set my box next to the cake I'll be trashing as soon as I can find an acceptable bin, I hurry over to the door and lock it. I rest my back against it and let the grin I've been holding back for three weeks finally surface.

And fine, I squee a little as I dance over to the window and stand there, looking out to the west, where I imagine the best sunsets in the world will take place.

But I can't stand there all day, and I turn to go check out the Chair lounge. Surely the trashcans in there will be able to hold half of a sheet cake that looks like some hungry wolverines got into it. Seriously, who cuts a cake on the diagonal, and why can't people just take a whole piece, even if they only eat half of it?

I pick up the cardboard tray holding the cake and head for the door. But I can't unlock it with my sensible heels, so I have to return to my desk, put down the cake, and go unlock the door first. I prop it open, then return to get the dessert.

I don't know where this magical lounge is—and just the fact that I'm excited about an ice and water machine in a lounge tells me I might be as dry as some of the other chemists around here—but it's not that hard to find.

The giant lettering that spells out LOUNGE on the door helps too.

This door is also closed, but I can toe my way through it, which I do. Sure enough, there's a pretty significant garbage can across the room, near a sink, a long counter top, and two fridges.

Two fridges.

I feel like I've died and gone to heaven.

This lounge also has carpet, even if it's the industrial kind that I grew up with in my church. My knees sting just thinking about how many times I fell and skinned my knees. Rug burns on industrial carpet are the absolute worst.

I shouldn't be thinking about my childhood, old churches, or how many fridges this lounge has. Not when I'm walking with a large cardboard tray of mangled cake, which now reads, "Rats, Zie!"

That's not safe.

And you know what else isn't safe?

The speed at which the brown-haired man enters the lounge. Or the volume of his laughter. Or walking with his cell phone pressed to his ear, so he doesn't even see the best-dressed, new Department Chair—or my cake—in this amazing lounge.

"Whoa," I say, as if he's a horse. Or I am.

He does turn toward me then, but it's too late. I can't slow my roll, and the only thing I can do is try to make the cardboard tray smaller.

I tip it up so it won't hit him, and that blocks my view.

And then I slam into his very solid body anyway.

That smashes the cake into my jewel-toned teal blouse, a garment I'd chosen specifically to make my blue-green eyes pop on this very special day.

And let me tell you, icing is cold as it touches cleavage. Maybe that's why they call it icing.

I drop the cardboard tray and hold my arms out to my sides, my irritation combining with pure humiliation and horror as I look down at myself...and the vanilla cake now heaped on the floor.

"Why'd you stop?" I ask, of all things. "You were flying just a second ago, not even watching where you're going, and—" I cut off when my eyes meet his.

He's dropped his phone, and he's staring at me wide-eyed, blinking far too fast for someone who doesn't have a dry-eye condition.

"Matt?"

Matthew Giles.

Owner of the most impractical laugh, purveyor of mismatched socks, and one-time lunch buddy when we were both working on the EHS team.

I haven't seen him in months. Fine, years, which explains why I'm not prepared for the way he fills out the striped button-up and dark slacks. Or his perfect hair —a shaggy, chestnutty brown that looks like it belongs in a shampoo commercial.

My heart races.

His hazel eyes possess the precisely perfect combination of green and brown, and they crinkle into a mix of concern and amusement as his gaze drips down my body the same way that cake does.

"Lizzie." He's not asking, and how does anyone work for this man? His voice is made of melted, dark chocolate mixed with sunshine. He holds up his phone. "I'm so sorry. I was focused on my call."

"Obviously," I bite out, my tone the complete opposite of his. I look behind him to the counter. "Does this magical lounge have any paper towels?"

He laughs, which only ignites my attraction to him as much as it irritates me. "I'm sure we do," he says. "Let me get them." He starts banging through cupboards while I stand there, completely cake-i-fied and helpless. Again, my heart pounds in a strange way.

Not an embarrassed way.

Not an angry way.

In a totally unsafe way, for sure.

Because I want to know if Matt has a girlfriend, and if he doesn't, how I can get him to ask me to dinner. Perhaps he'll want to celebrate my new promotion.

"What are you doing over here?" he asks, finally turning with the prize—a roll of Brawny. Instead of handing it to me, he tears off a long string of paper towels and starts to dab at my chest.

"Matt," I say.

"I had some meetings in Lexington," he says, and I look at him to try to figure out what the devil is going on. He's staring at my torso, still dab-dab-dabbing away, hardly taking any frosting with him.

"Matt," I bark. He flinches, freezes, and I grab the roll of paper towels from him. "Maybe you could handle the mess on the floor."

He looks down at it as if seeing the two-foot square cardboard tray with more spattered cake on it for the first time. "Oh, sure."

I tear off a bunch of paper towels and just go all-in, smearing the icing as I try to claw it off my skin and blouse. I just have to get cleaned up enough to make it to the bathroom without flinging frosting everywhere as I walk.

"So..." he says. "You're over in the Department Chair lounge because... Did I miss a party? I feel like I got a text about it as I got off the plane."

"Yeah," I say. "You missed a real roof-raiser."

He reaches for the paper towels, grinning like a fool, and I hand them to him.

"We had a party—well, I had to attend two of them—because I got promoted to Regulatory Affairs."

His face lights up. "You did? That's fantastic, Lizzie." He stands, laughing again, and pulls me into a hug. He immediately releases me as if my chest has caught fire, and groans as he looks down at himself. He keeps his head down, but lifts his eyes to look at me.

"Oops."

I grin now, because he's just so fun. And for a chemist—and an engineering chemist to boot—that's something. "You caked yourself," I say.

"So did you," he points out.

"Because *someone* came out of nowhere." I step over to the sink, dropping my used paper towels in the trashcan as I do. Thankfully, the water works in this sink, but it is ice cold.

"Regulatory Affairs," he says, joining me at the sink. "That office is right next door to mine."

As if I hadn't noticed that during my lunchtime stake-out. "Is that right?" I ask. "I just got here an hour ago."

He nudges me with his hip. "I can't believe we're going to be neighbors again."

"Yeah," I say, my mind whirring as I scrub frosting from my fingers. "Neighbors." I hope my voice sounds calmer than I feel. "Tell me the truth now: Are you the kind of neighbor who borrows a cup of sugar and says thanks, or the obnoxious guy who thinks eight a.m. lawn mowing is acceptable on a weekend?"

Matt chuckles, deep and resonant, and I sink into it like relaxing into a hot tub on a cold night. "I'm more the guy who'd probably try to fix something, break it in the process, and then show up sheepishly asking to borrow your toolbox."

I close my eyes briefly, channeling every fiber of determination not to laugh. Because laughing will only encourage him. But then a mental image of Matt standing on my doorstep with mismatched socks, holding a broken lawn gnome, drifts into my head, and I make the grave mistake of snorting.

"I didn't know you had a penchant for breaking things, Mister Engineer." I raise an eyebrow at him as we stand at the sink together, the water running but neither of us using it.

"Engineers don't break things," he corrects me with a slight wag of his finger. "We create...opportunities for innovative solutions."

In that moment, I realize we're standing so close, I can smell his cologne. It's warm and woodsy, with a faint hint of something citrusy. Or maybe that's the frosting.

No matter what, it's in no way safe for my heart rate.

He's staring at me too, and he seems to notice about when I do. I take a breath and he startles away from me. "Well, welcome to the neighborhood—I mean, office. My door's always open if you need any...opportunities for innovative solutions."

And with that, he saunters out of the lounge, using a different door than the one he came in, or the one I came through.

"Innovative solutions," I murmur to myself, feeling both frazzled and flustered in equal measure. I can't believe I'm breathless, because there's no way a man like Matthew Giles is single.

It's just the surprise of smashing cake into myself. The chaos of today's parties and my move from a cubicle at EHS to a walled office in Department Chair Row.

So our quick exchange reminded me that I miss talking to him. He's fun and funny, and trust me, that's hard to find at ChemTech.

I finish cleaning up and return to my office, ready to get my space decorated for success. As I sit at my now-cake-less desk, I realize my pulse is still racing at an unsafe level.

I look to my right, where Matt's office sits just on the other side of the wall. Oh, no, it is definitely not safe for me to be thinking the things I am, and I'm going to have to put regulatory sanctions on myself if I have to work next door to Matt for any length of time.

CHAPTER SIXTEEN

AARON

WELL, MAY HAS COME IN WITH A VENGEANCE OF heat and humidity, and Mother Nature is not messing around. I wipe my forehead with the back of my forearm, ignoring the thin layer of sawdust that clings to my skin like a second skin. The Lindsey family's addition is coming along nicely, but I swear, if Mrs. Lindsey changes her mind one more time about the paint color, or the flooring she wants, or the window shape, I'm going to start charging extra for indecision.

I should've known this build would be easy, but the client would be hard. The money's good though, and I love my time outside of the hardware store. It was the one thing I told my daddy I absolutely had to be able to keep doing, and it hasn't been a problem yet.

Of course, I've only owned the hardware store since January.

I glance at my watch and curse under my breath. "Emma's going to kill me." Not gently either—she'll do it with a smile and a few clever words that will haunt me in the afterlife just before she jabs a thorny rose into my jugular.

I promised her I wouldn't be late for the park plot assignment meeting, and here I am, still atop a ladder, trying to shimmy a support beam into place. At this rate, I'm going to show up covered in sweat, sawdust, and regret.

"Hey, boss," Jake, my assistant, calls. He's young, a little too eager, and still hasn't figured out that the job isn't half as glamorous as he thinks. "You good up there?"

"I'm fine," I say, gritting my teeth as the beam finally slots into place. "Just praying this is the last revision." I can't keep putting in orders only to cancel them a few days later.

Jake laughs, but it's a nervous sound. He's still not sure when I'm joking and when I'm one moment away from losing it. "You heading out soon? You've been checking your watch every five seconds."

"Yeah." I climb down the ladder. "I've got somewhere to be." I look around, because maybe Jake can make sure I'm ready for tomorrow.

"Hot date?" Jake smirks, and I shoot him a look that shuts him up faster than a nail gun misfire.

"Can you make sure everything is cleaned up and under the tarp before you go?"

"Yes, sir."

"Thank you, Jake." Emma's my girlfriend, and we see each other every day, so no, I don't have a "hot date" tonight, though the thought of her waiting for me at the park does send a flicker of excitement through my chest.

And then, we're planning a "dare date"—her idea, and I actually can't wait for that.

I grab my water jug and chug a few swallows as I walk to my truck. I blast the AC the moment I start my vehicle, and the clock on the dashboard tells me I'm ten minutes late leaving the Lindsey site. The drive to the park on Salty Dog shouldn't take long, but with the way my luck's been today, I wouldn't be surprised if I hit every red light between here and there.

The engine rattles as I pull onto Main Street, and I grip the steering wheel. "Come on, girl. I'll get you fixed this weekend, okay? It's just a couple more blocks."

If I were Emma, I'd have named my truck, and I smile again. So maybe I've been falling for her a little bit. She's funny, and I like talking to her, and she makes me feel strong and smart when she compliments me on the quick dinners I make for the two of us.

I like holding her hand, and laying with her on the couch, and kissing her goodnight. She makes me feel less alone, especially now that Liam has Hillary—and his own construction projects—demanding all of his time.

I cross the bridge over the creek, and the park comes into view. It's a sad sight for sure. The big pit, the dirt, and more dirt, and more dirt. The grass trying to take over everything since it's unchecked. Thankfully, there's no structures—no playground equipment or pavilion or picnic tables.

But there's no structures—no playground equipment or pavilion or picnic tables. And people don't really want their kids to play in a pit.

As I pull into a parking spot way down on the end, I see it the way Emma does—a blank canvas waiting for someone to bring it to life. My mind darts to the application we submitted together.

I'd done most of the work on it, which was fine with me. Just listening to Emma talk about flowers, paths, benches, a family picnic area, and even "maybe a few pickleball courts, Aaron!" had been enough for me to get the ideas into words and diagrams.

Oh, and the pergolas. I teased her relentlessly about how she could've just used the word *gazebo*, and when she finally got irritated, I kissed her and begged her to forgive me until she couldn't stop giggling.

Yeah, things are going great between us.

Ahead of me, the group is already moving, and I pick up my step until I'm jogging. Emma's lingering near the back of the crowd, and she glances over her shoulder. I raise my hand, and I can see the relief paint its way across her face when she sees me.

"Sorry," I say as I reach her.

"You're late," she hisses. "You missed the whole

introduction, and Jean almost made me stay behind, since we have a joint application, and you weren't here."

I take her hand and immediately decide it's too humid to hold hands. "Sorry," I say again. "I lost track of time getting that beam in."

I pull my hand away before she finds me disgusting and gross and sweaty and wipe my forehead. "It's so hot."

Emma carries a clipboard, and she uses it as a fan as we catch up to the group.

Jean Hygrove is leading everyone, and she comes to a stop, which means we all do too. "All right," she calls in a loud voice. She used to be a high school principal, then retired and now volunteers for the city of Cider Cove. She's never been married, and I don't think she's even ever smiled.

I've only ever seen her hair pulled tightly into a bun, and today, she's added something I would've never imagined her wearing—a pair of sunglasses. So the South Carolina summer sun even gets to rigid Jean Hygrove.

"Every applicant will get a one-hundred by one-hundred-foot square. That's one thousand square feet to build your demonstrative plan for the park. You'll have the opportunity to have an artist expand your ideas, and we'll put up those displays before the public and City Council walk through."

She surveys the crowd, and Emma's hand finds mine

again. She squeezes while I lean toward her. "Are we still on for our dare date after this?"

"Seriously?" she hisses at me. "Focus, Aaron." She nods to Jean, who's consulting something in her binder. Yes, a legit binder, out in pit-park, in the mid-afternoon heat.

"This is me focused," I say. "I'm listening."

"This plot goes to Jimmy Kitchens," Jean calls. "Please step out of line when I call your name, and one of our other volunteers will help you mark off your plot. You can get a lay of the land before you leave this afternoon, and please make absolutely sure you check out with me, because I have more directions and instructions for you."

She somehow pierces each person in the park with her principal glare, and beside me, Emma nods. The Doberman wants to get his plot and leave without checking out with Jean, because I'm sure she could just as easily email me the further documentation I need.

Jean calls someone else's name a hundred feet down the path, and I wonder if people will be assigned any part of the pit. I really hope not.

Beside me, Emma's nerves continue to climb and climb and climb, though she looks simply stunning in a summer sundress with her hair pulled into a messy ponytail. My heartbeat skips around, and then I wonder what kind of dare she's come up with for our date tonight.

Man, my mind really is everywhere right now, and I take a deep breath and try to focus. Usually, I'm way too focused on something, but right now, I feel myself running in fifteen hundred different directions.

"When does this need to be done?" I ask her as someone else gets the next plot.

"The end of June," she says. "Which is great, because then I'll have a couple of weeks until Claude's wedding."

"When will we find out who wins?"

"They're letting the public vote for a month," she says. "Winners announced on August first." She presses her lips together as if she's on stage right now, the winner about to be announced.

"This plot goes to Aaron Stansfield and Emma Newberry," Jean calls, and I raise my hand again, as if she's called roll.

"Glad to see you made it, Mister Stansfield," she says. "Gerald will help you with your plot." She turns and continues down the path while Emma and I stay with the volunteer.

"This is perfect," she says, her voice breathless.

"Perfect?" I cross my arms as Gerald starts pounding a stake in the back corner of our lot. "Em, it's all dirt and weedy grass."

"It's going to be so beautiful." She turns to me. "Do you want to do the pergola? It would be such a good representation of what you can build." Such hope shines in her eyes, and I'll do anything she says.

I survey the thousand square feet like I'm really considering it. "We could do that, or a picnic area, benches. Covered benches, so they can see I could do a pavilion."

She sketches something on her clipboard, her pencil scratching against the paper. "I like the idea of a covered bench. That's quaint and cute."

"Is that what we're going for?"

"Think about who's going to come to the park, baby." Her eyes are stuck on her sketch, but I suddenly can't look away from her.

"You just called me baby."

Emma's head comes up, her eyes blinking fast. "You don't like it?"

I swallow and clear my throat. "I really like it."

She gives me a smile and a quick kiss and says, "All right, baby," in a super Southern twangy voice.

I chuckle and go help Gerald finish with our plot. There's not much else we need to do here, and since Emma is still drawing, I say, "I'll go check out with Jean."

"Don't die," Emma says, and that alone tells me how much danger my life is in.

———

NINETY MINUTES LATER, I've showered and Emma's finished her sketch. She leaves it behind as we go to the hardware store of all places. Giddiness romps through me as I lead her to aisle five, which is tools. "I dare you to make a bouquet fit for a king with only items from this aisle."

I grin down at the wrenches, the screwdrivers, the ratchet sets.

"You're kidding."

"I am not." I turn my smile on her. "You have one hour."

"One hour?"

"I want to eat at a decent hour," I say. "So take me next door and issue me my dare."

A devilish glint enters her eyes, and she takes my hand on the way back to the flower shop. She keys her way into the back door and then props her hands on her hips and grins as she gestures toward the cold room.

"All right, your next dare involves Sir Chills-a-Lot."

I blink. "The fridge?"

"Don't call him *the fridge*. He gets testy about that."

I glance toward the gleaming stainless steel door that leads into the room where she does her arrangements. I've been in there loads of times, but this is the first I'm hearing that he gets "testy" about his name.

"What's the dare?"

"You've got one hour to organize Sir Chills-a-Lot's shelves. Perfectly. Every stem and bloom and pampas grass in its proper place, every bucket filled with fresh water."

"Pampas grass? You just made that up."

"I would never," she says. "And, if Sir Chills-a-Lot starts humming weirdly while you're in there, you have to compliment him. Sincerely. He usually stops then."

"Compliment a fridge?"

"Sir Chills-a-Lot," she corrects. "And yes. You wouldn't want to hurt his feelings."

I stare at her, trying to keep a straight face. "How will you possibly judge how well I compliment a fridge?"

"I dare you to get Sir Chills cleaned up and complimented, so he won't break down on me. Do you accept?" She is so sassy and so beautiful, and I don't even care if I win the dare date or not.

"Emma," I say, laughing now. "You've officially lost it." And there's no way I can organize Sir Chills-a-Lot to Emma's standards, I know that.

"You have one hour," she says. "From when I text you after I get a basket and get back to aisle five."

"Don't forget the duct tape," I say as she heads for the back door. "Every good tool bouquet needs duct tape."

CHAPTER SEVENTEEN

EMMA

I FACE DOWN AISLE FIVE, SO MANY THINGS STICKING out to me. I'm going to have to edit my thoughts if I'm to win this dare at all. My heart does this funny little flip-flopping thing, especially when Aaron texts, *You're cheating, aren't you?*

No, I send back.

I'm sending Fonda to make sure you haven't started yet.

Sure enough, only ten seconds later, one of Aaron's managers, a petite woman with icy blonde hair—Fonda —appears at the other end of aisle five. I raise both hands, one of which still holds my phone. "I'm assessing."

She lifts her phone and says something into it. A look of distaste crosses her features, and she rolls her eyes as she says, "Aaron says that he's starting in five seconds, and you can stand there and assess all you want, but the clock is ticking."

"Fine," I call to her.

She relays the message to Aaron, turns, and leaves. I'm still staring down the wrenches, screwdrivers, socket sets, and other tools I don't even know the name of. "I can't believe he's charged me with arranging *tools*."

But being bitter about it isn't going to help me win. I start down the aisle, taking in the options for "blooms" and "stems" and "accents."

After one pass, I then go down the aisle and make the selections for my metal bouquet. The way they clank makes me cringe, and once I have everything, I take it all into Aaron's office. I thought he'd dare me to go through his desk and file everything.

As I take in the mess in his office, I realize that he's actually been kind to task me with this tool bouquet. "Still," I say as I peer down into the black shopping basket filled with silver metal. "I'm a florist, not MacGyver."

The familiar scent of fresh cotton, sawdust, and Aaron's cologne crowds into my nose, and it's the best smell in the whole world.

I reach for his water jug, which he's left behind, and it's semi-heavy, so he didn't drink all of his fluids today. "Naughty, naughty," I say before I hurry out to the drinking fountain to empty it.

Back in the office, I position the jug to be the vase for

my tool bouquet. I pick up the longest socket I could find, and that goes right in the middle. Of course, it doesn't stand up, but by the time I'm finished arranging the other tools around it, that'll be my center focus piece. And the cool thing about sockets is they have heads that poke out like a daffodil's corona.

Every bouquet needs a tall, central focus, and that socket is mine. I spy a roll of duct tape sitting on Aaron's desk, and I grab it. I hadn't seen any tape in aisle five, despite what Aaron said, and I wonder if he'll consider this cheating.

"Probably." I smile just thinking about him, because I don't really care if I win this dare. I just want him to come back and take me to dinner.

I rip off pieces of tape and fold them to make the petals of the daffodil. They're not yellow, but with the dark gray and the shiny silver, I actually think it's a new breed of daffodil.

My florist brain starts to kick in, and I imagine the wrenches as stems, the screwdrivers as filler accessories, especially the ones with thick handles, as they help keep all the other tools in place. I put duct tape "leaves" on the straight screwdriver tips, and before I know it, my bouquet is done.

Grinning, I snap a picture of it and send it to Aaron with the word, *Done!*

He calls, and I swipe it on. "I'm pretty sure I just won," I say.

He laughs, the sound rich and warm, and I can't help the way my smile widens. Being around Aaron is like standing in the sun—impossible not to feel a little brighter.

"I'm pretty sure Sir Chills-a-Lot has gone on strike," he says through his chuckles. "At this point, if you don't break-up with me for what's happened over here in the last half-hour, I'm going to call it good."

"Aaron," I say, my smile suddenly gone. "You're joking, right?"

"Let's go to dinner," he says. "I'll come pick you up."

"I need pictures of Sir Chills," I say very seriously. "If something's happened to him..."

"You need to chill, Em. He's fine."

At least he's not calling my walk-in fridge an "it" anymore.

"I'll send you some pics. Usually I bring you the bouquet, but you'll have to present me with yours." He ends the call, and a few seconds later, I get a picture of Sir Chills's shelves. He doesn't look much better than how I left him, so Aaron didn't do much. "He didn't make it worse, at least," I say.

Then I get another picture. Then another. The last one I get is a picture of the thermostat, and Aaron's said, *See? He's fine. I'll be there in two.*

And sure enough, two minutes later, he knocks on his own office door and waits for me to open it. I can't juggle the half-gallon water jug with all the tools in it and open the door, so I leave the arrangement and let my boyfriend into his own office.

He looks at me and then it, his whole face blooming to life. "You definitely win. This thing is *incredible*." He blinks at it a couple of times, then switches his gaze to me. "*You're* incredible."

A blush fills my whole body, and I'm not that great at taking compliments. "It's unique," I say.

Aaron slides his hand along my hip, pulling me against him. "I mean, it's not going to win any beauty contests, but it's creative. And it's very...you."

"Me?" I frown, because being me has never won me anything. "What's that supposed to mean?"

He shrugs, his smile softening. "You're creative and resourceful. You can take something ordinary and turn it into something special. That's what you did with this." He looks at me. "And gorgeous. I should've said gorgeous in there. Creative, resourceful, and gorgeous."

For a moment, I just stare at him, my heart doing that annoying flip-flop thing again. How does he always know exactly what to say to make me feel like I'm on top of the world? Then I smile just as he touches his lips to mine, and oh, I could lose a lot of time kissing this man.

"Where do you want to go to dinner?" he murmurs as he slides his mouth down to my jaw.

"You're not getting out of showing me what happened inside Sir Chills."

"Oh, he's fine." Aaron straightens and looks at me,

pure male desire swimming in those dark eyes. "Let's go to dinner and go over our designs. I need to know what you expect of me, Em. I'm busy this month with builds and stuff."

And he is. I know he is, and I also know the twenty-five thousand dollars will benefit me way more than him. A twist of guilt pirouettes through me. "We make a good team, though," I say. "I'll be able to help a lot, okay? Two weddings are done, and I've got ten weeks until the next one." I run both of my hands up his chest. "You're not mad about the partnership, are you?"

"No," he says. "We make a great team."

"Team EmRon." I grin at him, but he just blinks at me.

Then he shakes his head. "You'd tell me never to speak without checking with you if I said that."

I burst out laughing, because he's so right. "It feels like a Dad-joke," I say.

"Cringey." He leads me out of the office, his hand so warm, and big, and secure in mine.

"But we're not cringey," I say.

"Depends on who you ask." He nods to Fonda, who watches us with ice-blue eyes. I almost shy away from her, because she probably thinks we're totally cringey.

"Fonda," I say, pulling on Aaron's hand to get him to stop. He does, and he looks at me with wide, fear-filled eyes. I really have no idea what I'm doing, but I say,

"We're going to dinner. Do you want us to bring you something back?"

She blinks, clearly not expecting that. She casts a look toward Aaron, but he's turned into a fish—staring at me without blinking, his mouth slightly open.

"Where are we going, Aaron?" I ask—totally keeping it cringe-free by using his name and not *baby*.

"You were going to pick," he says.

"What are you feeling, Fonda?" I ask. "We'll go there, and I'll bring you back your favorite thing."

"I'm fine," she says at the same time Aaron says, "Archibald's artichoke pasta."

"Aaron," Fonda says, and if she said my name in that warning-filled voice, I'd curl up and cry.

"It's her favorite." He simply smiles at her, and I look back at her too.

"Okay, well, wherever we can get Archibald's artichoke pasta is where we'll go. You're working through close?"

"Yes." She swallows, a hint of nerves in her expression now.

I loop my arm through Aaron's, and we start toward the back exit again. "Where do we get that pasta, baby?"

"House of Flour," he says, and I light up.

"Perfect," I say. "I love their honey whole wheat bread, and everyone at the Big House will love me if I bring some home."

"You're a good person too," he says once we leave the hardware store.

"Fonda did seem surprised I spoke to her," I say, my voice pitching up slightly.

He scoffs. "I'm surprised she didn't rip your head off with her bare hands." He grins then and laughs. "And you think I'm a Doberman. She's like a pitbull on a forced diet."

I let him open the door for me, but I don't get in. "And you just stood there and let me do it."

"I wanted to see what would happen."

"What if she'd gone into pitbull mode?"

He wraps me up in his arms, and wow, I would love to stay right there, listening to the steady thump of his heartbeat and breathing in the cottony-woodsy-metally scent of his skin and cologne.

And I realize I'm falling really fast for Aaron Stansfield.

I tell myself it's because I didn't have to start at zero with him. We've been friends and have known each other for a while now. I have to tell myself that, or I'll start freaking out.

And I really don't want to do that when House of Flour is in play, because not only do they have the best bread in the whole of Charleston and all her suburbs, but they have the most delectable peach pie that Grams and I both adore.

So no freaking out, I tell myself as I step back and get in Aaron's truck.

He gets in the other side and says, "I put your clipboard with your plans and sketches right there on the dash, honeybee." He nods to it, and I reach out and pick it up.

I stare at the sketch I did a couple of hours ago at the park. I'd tossed this clipboard somewhere, and I can't even remember where right now.

But Aaron knew, and he got it for me.

Yep, he's definitely scoring a lot of points tonight even if he didn't win the dare and I'm a little afraid of what I might find when I walk into Sir Chills tomorrow.

CHAPTER EIGHTEEN

AARON

THE MOUNTAIN AIR FEELS DIFFERENT UP HERE. Cleaner. Lighter. It's still muggy because, well, South Carolina in May, but it's cooler in the shade of the towering oaks and pines that stretch up around us. I adjust my helmet and glance over at Liam, who's busy wrestling with the strap on his own.

"Need some help there?"

He glares at me, his hands fumbling with the plastic clasp. "No, I don't need help. This stupid thing is just... defective."

"Sure it is," I say, leaning casually against my bike. "Maybe being married has simply slowed you down."

Liam scoffs, rips off his helmet, and throws it at me. Good thing I have the reflexes of a ninja, and I catch it pretty easily. But I make a big show of staggering backward like he's just launched a boulder and I've caught it straight in the chest.

I laugh as I say, "Oh, yeah, domestic bliss has softened you."

"Domestic bliss?" His voice drips with sarcasm. "You realize Hillary makes me go to yoga with her every Thursday, right? *After* work. Bliss is not the word I'd use, Aaron."

"You're telling me you don't love a good downward dog?"

Liam bellows out a laugh so loud, a couple of birds squawk and take off from a nearby tree.

I chuckle with him as I hand back his helmet. "Come on." I climb onto my bike, which is really one of Liam's loaners. The man loves vehicles of all types, and he loves mountain biking on the weekends. Emma's doing a baking-fest-thing at a cupcakery in Sugar Grove with her roommates, so Liam and I have come up near Columbia to spend some time on the trails.

"Let's see if you can keep up with me," Liam said, a Cheshire cat grin on his face as he mounts his bike too. He takes off before I've even comprehended what he's said.

"There's no way I can keep up with you," I call after him, hurrying now to get my feet clipped in the pedals the right way. He's already down the path, and somehow, his laughter filters back to me. I get going, and the tires crunch against the dirt as the wind whips against my face as I follow-weave Liam through the trees.

I haven't done organized exercise in a while, but since I don't sit still well, I find my rhythm pretty easily. Liam and I don't have to talk when we're together, and I bask in the comfortable silence between us.

Only the sounds of the rustling of leaves and the steady hum of our tires fills my ears. Sometimes, when Liam rides alone, he listens to music, but I never do that. There's already too much noise in my head.

It's nice being away from everything. No customers asking for help finding the right size screws, no deadlines, no wedding plans or park proposals. Just the trail, the trees, and my best friend.

Eventually, Liam slows to a stop at the top of a hill, and I pull up beside him. He's breathing hard, his face flushed, but he's grinning like a kid. "It's been too long since I did this."

"Yeah," I say, taking a swig from my water bottle as he does from his. "Nothing like almost dying to remind you you're alive."

He swallows and grins at me. "So...how's it going with Emma?"

I glance at him, surprised. Liam doesn't usually ask about my love life—probably because it's been nonexistent for the better part of the last few years. "Did Hillary send us out here so you could get the details?"

"No." Liam blinks at me. "I mean, I'll probably tell

her whatever you say, but no. She didn't ask me to ask you."

I nod, my throat getting narrow. "Yeah, okay. Things are good." That feels like the understatement of the century. "Really good, actually."

Liam's eyebrows go up. "That's it? 'Good'?"

"I said *really* good."

Liam laughs and shakes his head. "I understand your momma's frustration so much better now."

I've told her absolutely nothing either, and yes, she's probably dying a slow death. "I should probably introduce Emma to my parents properly," I say. "Sometime soon." I sigh out and take in the view. Trees and sky and the brown of deep, rich earth. "It's just...we're really busy this summer."

"Summer is a busy time," he says. The fact that he doesn't ask me more about Emma means I've told him all he needs to know. Just the fact that I said I wanted to introduce her to my parents tells *me* a lot about how I feel about her, and it doesn't have to be said out loud.

"I feel like I can be myself around her," I say.

Liam nods, his expression softening. "That's how it's supposed to feel, man, and it's amazing."

"Yeah," I say, my chest tightening in that good way. "It feels easy with her. But also exciting. Like, I never know what she's going to say or do next, and I love that about her." I grin over to him. "She's hot and cold sometimes, and it's...interesting."

"Sounds like you're in deep." Liam nudges me, grinning. "Come on, let's get going. I'm hungry."

"You're always hungry," I say.

"So are you." He clips in and pushes off, and I let him get a bit ahead so I'm not breathing in his dust. The conversation bounces through my mind over the tree roots and rocks as we ride into the city, and I can't wait to see Emma that evening and see what kind of cupcakes she made with her friends.

———

"HEY, YOU."

I look up at the pretty sound of Emma's voice. She's carrying a pale pink box that makes my stomach roar though I've just eaten half an all-meat pizza.

I jump to my feet, my paperwork forgotten. "Hey, you," I say back, taking the cupcakes from her and setting them on my desk and pulling her closer to me with my other hand, all of it in one fluid movement. I take a breath of her and get sugared frosting and pretty petals just before I match my mouth to hers.

She kisses me for only a moment before she pulls away, her hand sliding out of my hair. "You have sawdust in your hair, baby." She brushes her hands together and looks up at me.

"Occupational hazard," I say, grinning at her.

"I thought you were going mountain biking." She takes in the pizza boxes on my desk. "No?"

"We went," I say. "Liam had to stop by one of his sites, and I helped him with the barn for a second." I pick up the top pizza box. "Then we got a second lunch. You want any?"

She puts one hand on her stomach. "No," she groans. "I ate so much at lunch."

"Are these cupcakes for me?" I reach over and pick up the pink box and flip it open. "There better be something chocolate in here, or I'm going Doberman."

"I decorated those in our class today."

I look at the delicate swirls and curls. "It was a class?"

She presses in next to me. "There's only one chocolate one."

I sure do like the heat of her beside me, the pressure of her at my side so needed and amazing. "Did you bake too, or just decorate?"

"We made the frostings today," she says, lifting out a cupcake with a tall, swooped hat of diamond-white icing on it. "This one is a white chocolate raspberry." It holds a silver-dusted star perched just-so in the frosting.

"White chocolate is not chocolate," I growl.

"Oh, calm down, Doberman. That one in the other corner is double-chocolate." She replaces the cupcake she removed.

I've just lifted the double-chocolate cupcake I want

from the box when Fonda pokes her head into my office. "He's here again, sir."

I blink, my mind whirring as I try to figure out who she means. She lifts her eyebrows. "Matthew, sir." Her eyes flit over to Emma. "Hello, dear. How did the cupcake decorating go?"

"Come see," Emma says, and I shouldn't be shocked that she's softened Fonda—who literally doesn't like anyone. Certainly never any of the other women I've dated. I'm not sure what's special about Emma, only that there's something.

"Matthew, right," I say as Fonda comes into the office to inspect the cupcakes. I don't dare leave the only chocolate one with the women, so I take it with me, sinking my teeth into creamy frosting. I eat the whole treat in only a few bites, and I dust my hands together as I approach the customer service desk.

"Matt." I extend my hand for him to shake.

He does, with a healthy smile. "I couldn't do it." He chuckles at himself. "So I need a new microwave, and I'm totally going to get the installation this time."

I can't even fathom not being able to install a microwave above the stove, but I don't make fun of him. "Couldn't do it? I sent you the instructional video."

"Yeah, I watched it."

"You're an engineer," I say.

"A *chemical* engineer," he says. "I don't hold screwdrivers and whatever."

I perch on the stool and click to get the computer to wake up. "Why do you need a new microwave?"

His face flushes slightly, and I lift my hand. "It's fine. I can send one with our installation team. When are you available?"

Matt pulls out his phone and starts to swipe and tap. "I've got so many meetings right now. Our fiscal year ends at the end of June."

"Mm hm," I say. Matt's moved into a house down the street from me, having inherited it from his daddy. To say it needs some upgrades is an understatement, and he's been coming in a lot, trying to do handyman projects in the evenings after his day job.

But the man is simply not super handy.

"Tell me when," he says.

"I have any day next week after four," I say. "And the week after that." I click again. "And the week after that." I look up, stifling the words that I'll probably be the one to come out and install his microwave. Several of my employees could do it, which is why we have so much availability.

"Thursday next week?" he guesses.

"Sure," I say as Emma joins me at the desk.

"I'm gonna go grab some more cupcakes," she says.

I pause halfway through putting in Matt's install, my eyes wide. "What? Why?"

"Well, Fonda really likes white chocolate," Emma says with a smile. Her eyes drift over to Matt too. "Oh, hello. I'm Emma." She shakes his hand too, and he might not have noticed the change in her tone, but I sure have.

"All right," I say to him. "You're set next Thursday at four-ten."

"Thanks," Matt says. He nods and then hooks his thumb over his shoulder. "What aisle might one find a socket set?"

"That would be aisle five," Emma says with a grin. "Tools. I can show you, because there's an amazing tool arrangement there I think you'll *really* like."

"Em," I say, but she waves me off as she goes with Matt.

Yeah, there's something going on there, but I'm not sure what it is. I stay at the customer service counter until Emma comes back, and I raise my eyebrows and fold my arms. "What is that about?"

She grins and comes around the counter and sits right on my lap, which makes me feel so dang good. She leans down and gives me a quick kiss. "He's Lizzie's latest crush," she says, looking out into the hardware store. "And I can see why. He's charming and handsome and personable."

"He's on his second microwave," I say dryly. "Because he couldn't install the first one himself."

She turns and faces me. "Are you jealous?"

"You just said he's charming and handsome and personable." Maybe I'm a little jealous.

"For Lizzie, he'd be great," she says. "Not for me, baby."

"Because I'm for you," I say, and I have no idea where the words come from. My throat suddenly feels like I've swallowed fire, but I can't look away from her.

Emma cradles my face in one palm, her eyes searching mine too. "Yeah," she says slowly. "You're for me." She kisses me, and wow, I've shared some hot kisses with her thus far. But this slow, sensual one is ten times better than any of those.

"Sir," Fonda barks in her not-so-subtle way, and Emma breaks the kiss and turns away from my back-of-house manager.

"Why am I the one in trouble?" I ask. "*She's* sitting on my lap, kissing *me*."

"Can I steal him, Fonda?" Emma stands up, smiles for miles on her face.

"He has to get payroll submitted by midnight," Fonda says, giving me the evil eye.

"Great." Emma reaches for my hand and pulls me, trying to get me to stand. "Come on, baby. Come buy yourself some more chocolate cupcakes."

And since I'd go to another planet just to be with her, I go.

CHAPTER NINETEEN

EMMA

Sir Chills-a-Lot hums in what I can only describe as a passive-aggressive tone. It's not quite the normal *clink-clink-hum* I'm used to. No, this one is slightly uneven, like he's annoyed with me, and honestly? He has every right to be.

"Okay, I get it," I mutter, brushing a strand of hair that's fallen out of my ponytail out of my face. "You're mad because you're overworked. But you're not the only one, buddy."

Sir Chills offers no response, just another grating *clink-a-link-cough-stutter.*

I exhale dramatically and glance at the mountain of orders stacked on my counter. Mother's Day decimated me—and every other florist, I'm sure. Not only that, but I've had a massive surge in bouquet orders from single men. And when they come in to pick-up, I recognize them from the Spring Fling Thing.

So that was helpful, and I've made at least four notes in various apps—and a paper calendar I cart back and forth to the shop every day in my crate—to make sure I sign up to do it again next year.

And now, I've got wedding season breathing down my neck and the park demo to cultivate. I planted a plethora of flowers and bushes that'll thrive in the South Carolina heat the very weekend Aaron and I got our thousand-square-foot plot. I have to go over there all the time—sometimes twice a day—to water everything, because there's no water in the pit-park.

So I'm hauling it in.

I wish I was kidding, and I feel like I'm clinking, and grating, and humming when I breathe too.

The bell out front chimes, and I look up from the bouquet I'm working on. "Sir Chills, be good," I say before I wipe my hands down the front of my apron, put a smile on my weary face, and exit the cold room.

To my surprise, Matt is milling about near my ready-to-go arrangements in the front refrigeration unit. "All of my cupcakes are gone," I say as I approach. "You have to reserve them or get here before noon."

He looks at me, his charming smile already in place. "Hey, Emma." He leans in for a Southern hug, and we quickly part.

I wasn't aware Lizzie had a date that night, and I hate the creepy-crawling feeling in my stomach that he's here for someone else. She hasn't said much about Matt, and I realize we need to have a midnight confessional or a roommate night where the pink mic makes its way around the room.

I've been so busy, and I spend almost every evening at Aaron's house, that I suddenly feel very disconnected from everyone I love in my life.

"You do cupcakes here?" he asks.

"I've partnered with Front Porch," I say. "Jaymie bakes, and I decorate—a skill I've been taking classes for. Then I arrange them with flowers, and they make a pretty amazing bouquet." I tuck my hands in my back pockets. "Can I help you find something?"

"Yeah," he says. "It's my mother's birthday, and I need something for dinner tonight."

Relief flows through me with the strength of a raging river. "Oh, sure," I say, eyeing the arrangements he's been looking at. "These are more for date night." I give him a smile. "I've got more motherly and grandmotherly stuff back here."

I lead him to the perfect arrangement for his mother, check him out, and greet my next customer. A man who's come in while I was helping Matt, and he has a call-in order for one of my date-night bouquets. I'd offered them for twenty percent off on my flyer at the

Spring Fling Thing, and boy, have the men in Cider Cove taken advantage of that.

The good thing is, they're simple and standard, and they only take me about twenty minutes to do. For twenty bucks, that's pretty good.

"There you go, Weston." I beam at him. "I hope you have a good date."

"Thanks, Emma." He lifts his red, pink, and white roses in good-bye and heads for the door.

I take a fortifying sip of my iced coffee and glance toward the front of the shop. The OPEN sign sways slightly in the breeze from the AC, and sunlight streams through the windows, illuminating the shelves of cheerful arrangements I've already completed. The shop smells like freesia and lilies, with just a hint of eucalyptus. It's my happy place, but today, it feels more like an overbearing boss who won't stop assigning me tasks.

Then I have to go back to the cold room and keep working. I have three more orders that will be picked up today, and I only have one and a half of them completed.

Daisies, lilies, baby's breath, pampas grass. Ribbon. Plastic pick. Card. I write the customer's name on a piece of floral tape and stick it to the front of the vase, then move to the next order. Whatever I can get done today is something I won't have to do tomorrow.

"You are in here."

I yelp and my reflexes have me bringing up the long-stemmed rose in my hand. One of the thorns I haven't stripped yet stabs into the pad of my thumb, and I cry out again and drop the flower, which is my only defense against the intruder who's come into Sir Chills.

"It's just me," Tahlia says, holding up both hands. "No need to start throwing things." She smiles at me, and she's wearing a pretty blouse in pink and white, along with a pair of navy slacks. She's obviously just come from one of her summer school meetings, and I move over and hug her.

"Oh," she says as I grab onto her and hold tight. "Are you okay, Em?"

"I miss you," I say with a sniffle. "I miss everyone."

"You've just been working a lot," she says. She steps back, and I reach up to tighten my ponytail.

I take a breath and survey my flowers. Listen to Sir Chills complain about me constantly letting in the heat from out front. "Yeah."

"Well, I just wanted you to know that my teacher friends and I went by the park, and we watered your plants and flowers for you this afternoon." She beams at me with so much sunshine, I almost burst into tears.

"You did?" My voice pitches up, and yes, I'm the most emotional roommate in the Big House. When I first bought this shop, I found myself getting overwhelmed constantly, and my friends and roommates would come help me get caught up, usually while I sniffled through my emotions.

"Oh, thank you so much." I hug Tahlia again, so glad for amazing friends and watering miracles.

"Not only that, but Hillary took the afternoon off, and she's almost here with iced coffees." Tahlia pulls over a stool and sits. "Keep working, Em. And then you can tell us what you need us to do once we've had our four o'clock caffeine."

We both survey my workbench, which looks like a floral tornado blew through. I know what this chaos is, though, so I pick up where I left off before she came in and I got thorned.

Tahlia lets me sniffle into the silence for a few minutes, and then she asks, "How are things going with Aaron?"

I shrug one shoulder. "Good enough. We're still dating."

She doesn't say anything, and I throw her a look to find a puzzled expression on her face. "What?"

"Good enough? Is that what you want?"

"Of course not," I gripe at her as my chime rings out front again. "But we're so busy right now, and he'll introduce me to his parents when he's ready." I shoot her a death glare and go see who's here.

Thankfully, it's just Hillary, and she's brought Claudia and a whole tray of iced coffees. "Bless you," I say as I take the tray from her. "I'm in the cold room."

"This place looks so great, Em," Claudia says, and

earning a compliment from her is like winning the lottery.

"Thank you," I say, smiling at her. I have found my footing here at Pretty in Petals, and I hardly have any crying days anymore.

"Do you have anything for men?" Hillary asks. "Liam finished that major build at the Reed's, and I want to get him something."

"No wings?" Claudia asks, and I look at her.

"I agree with Claude. Seems like something you'd celebrate with food," I say. "Or a hat. Liam loves hats."

"Yeah," Hillary muses, but she still wanders over to the only masculine display I have in the shop.

"Where's Handyman Hottie?" Claudia smiles at me.

I groan and roll my eyes. "Please don't call him that."

"Why not?" Claudia asks, her grin wicked. "He is hot. And handy. A rare combination."

"He's also my boyfriend," I say, trying to sound firm, but my voice comes out softer than I'd like.

And no one can ever get anything past Claudia. She sobers and studies me. "Take your coffee," I say. "And come say hi to Tahlia."

She does, and I turn my back on her, so I don't have to explain anything. I don't even know what I'd say anyway. Aaron is sweet, but I feel like I'm using him to win twenty-five thousand dollars? He says he doesn't care, but he must?

I shake the troublesome thoughts from my head, because I don't have room for them.

"It's okay to date for a long time," Claudia says almost under her breath.

I glance over to her. I know she feels a little self-conscious about how long she and Beckett have been together, and that they're months behind Hillary and Ryanne in tying the knot.

"You want to be really sure with him," she says.

"Are you really sure about Beckett?"

"Yes," she says without a moment of hesitation. "Becks and I are solid. I just...you seem a little less-Emma lately when it comes to Aaron."

She's not wrong, and since I already told Tahlia, I might as well spill my fears and anxieties to everyone. I get back to work after a healthy swig of my iced coffee, and Claudia and Tahlia chitchat until Hillary comes in.

"Will Lizzie and Ry be upset if I tell you guys something?" I ask.

"We can catch them up," Tahlia says casually.

So I tell them I wish Aaron were ready to take me to meet his parents. "I mean, I sort of met them once, but I haven't really met them."

"Grams likes him," Tahlia says.

"Yeah." I position another gardenia in exactly the right spot. "I'm worried I'm using him in the park renovation."

"What?" Claudia asks. "That's ridiculous. You're working just as hard on that."

"Yeah, but he'll build everything," I say. "I planted some flowers, Claude. Let's not act like it's the same."

Not only that, but I have no idea when Aaron will actually be able to find the time to work on the park demo plot. He's still working on the addition at the Lindsey's, and he runs the entire hardware store. He definitely burns the candle at both ends, and I have the thought that I should take him one of my men's arrangements and let him know that I see how hard he's working.

Sometimes all we need is someone to *see* us.

"What else?" Hillary asks, oh-so-not-casually lifting her coffee to her lips.

"I'm afraid I'm falling too fast for him," I say, my attention so needed on the orchids in my hand. "Just like I did Tucker."

"Em, he is nothing like Tucker," Hillary says. "Tahlia, tell her."

"He's nothing like Tucker," Tahlia says. "And Em, I've never seen you so happy."

I nod, because she's right. My shop is humming along, despite Sir Chills's hiccups every now and then. I have a super-handsome boyfriend who has never once said he resents me for using him for his building skills in the park renovation.

My phone chimes, and it's Aaron's snap-crackle-and-pop. "Oh, boy," I say. "That's him."

"I've got it," Claudia says, and she picks up my phone and taps in my PIN. Then her gasp echoes through Sir Chills.

"What?" Tahlia, Hill, and I all ask.

She looks up, her dark eyes so bright and filled with so much wonder. "It's Aaron, and he just asked you when you could go to dinner at his parents' house."

CHAPTER TWENTY

AARON

I pull up to my parents' house, the familiar sight of the white two-story farmhouse settling something deep in me, even as my chest tightens with the weight of why I'm here. The place hasn't changed much since I was a kid—same wide porch, same rocking chairs that have seen major action since Dad retired. The flowerbeds along the front are still meticulously kept, a mix of roses and marigolds that Mom insists are "timeless," even if they're a little too perfect for my taste.

And Emma says marigolds are the stinkiest flowers out there. They may be pretty, but she doesn't like them much.

I look over to her as I park behind my dad's old Jeep. "They're going to love you. Everyone does."

She leans her head back against the rest as she turns it toward me. A soft smile graces her pretty face. She's tired, and I know it. Heck, I am too. "You're just saying that, because no one has ever cracked Fonda."

I grin back at her. "You have a special way with people."

"I haven't met anyone's parents in a long time," I say.

"You've met them."

"You shoved them out the front door before I even got their names." She looks toward the front door. "I feel like she's watching already."

"Oh, she is," I say, following her gaze. My nerves fire at me, and my mind races in a dozen different directions. "I'm almost done with the Lindsey addition." Why I brought that up, I'm not sure.

"Yep," she says, because I've told her that already. She reaches over and takes my hand in hers, grounding me and settling some of my frenzied thoughts. "Then you're going to start on the park bench."

"Right." I run my free hand through my hair. "Should we go in?"

"I think she might come out if we don't." Emma somehow gives me the reassuring smile, and she stays put so I can come open her door, kiss her quickly, and lead her up onto my parents' porch. My stomach buzzes like I've swallowed a hive of angry bees after evicting their queen.

"Jenny and Rawlins," Emma mutters under her breath. "Jenny and Rawlins."

I open the door and call, "We're here, Ma," though I

expect her to be hovering only inches from the door. To her credit, she's standing at the end of the couch, an embroidered dish towel in her hand. I smile at her, because, fine, I'm a momma's boy.

With the scent of coffee hanging in the evening air, I go to hug her. "Oh, my boy is home," she says fondly, squeezing me tightly. She releases me, her eyes already fixed on Emma. "And his lovely girlfriend." She opens both of her arms, and Emma smiles and eases into them.

Her eyes drift closed, something soft and vulnerable on her face. In that moment, I realize she hasn't hugged her mother in years. Decades. Something in my chest pinches, especially as she whispers something to my momma I can't hear.

When they part, Momma's already wiping her eyes, and I look from her to Emma and back. "Everyone okay?"

Emma nods, and migrates into my side, where I hold her in place securely against me. Momma sniffs and turns to go into the kitchen.

"Daddy's pulling the Dutch ovens off the fire. Anyone want coffee?"

I look down at Emma, but she shakes her head. "I'm too keyed up for more stimulants," I say to Momma. In a much quieter voice, I ask Emma, "Will you be okay here if I leave you with her?"

"You still haven't introduced us," she whispers. "Where are you going?"

"To get Thomas out of his room," I say, taking her hand and going into the kitchen just as Daddy comes in the back door. "Daddy, this is Emma. Emma, my father, Rawlins. My momma is Jenny."

"It's so great to meet you." Daddy wears the biggest smile I've ever seen and he shakes Emma's hand, hugs her, and sweeps a kiss along each of her cheeks. So old school.

She flushes, and I'm not sure why. It's a touch warm in the kitchen, but nothing too bad.

I meet her eye, and she nods. "I'll go get Thomas," I say, and it takes everything I have to turn my back on my gorgeous girlfriend and leave her in the kitchen alone with my parents.

Momma's already talking to her as I enter the hall, and I remind myself that Emma is really good with people.

Thomas's bedroom door is open, which means he heard me call out my arrival. He's got a bright desk lamp on, shining down on his hands as he paints a figurine. I knock lightly on his doorframe and wait for him to lift his head.

"Tommy," I say. "Em and I are here for dinner, and we want you to come out." I smile at him, because I do love my brother. I've just always had to meet him where he is, and there's always this touch of distance between us that I can never quite bridge.

He's six years younger than me and has always been

my opposite. Quiet, introverted, more comfortable in his own world than in ours. And I've always been on the other end of the spectrum—loud, active, constantly moving.

"You're looking good, brother," I say. His dark hair is longer than it was the last time I saw him, curling around his ears, and he's got a streak of blue paint on his cheek. His focus is intense, his hands steady as he works on a tiny, intricate piece of armor.

"What are you working on?" I walk over to the desk and look at his figurines.

"Space Marines," he says, his voice clipped. "Ultra-marines, specifically."

I nod like I know exactly what he's talking about. "They look cool. I really like that guy's shield."

"They're not just cool," he says, glancing up at me with a frown. "They're the finest warriors in the Imperium of Man. They're genetically enhanced super-soldiers."

"Right," I say, trying not to grin. He's always been like this—so passionate about his hobbies, so sure of himself when he's in his element. It's one of the things I admire about him, even if it also makes me feel like an outsider in my own family sometimes. "Sounds intense."

He stands up and hugs me, and I sink into it for a moment, finally feeling synced. "Is dinner ready?"

"I think so, yeah." I watch him for another moment, wishing I knew how to connect with him better. We've had the same conversation a hundred times—me asking about his hobbies, him either giving me short answers or going on and on about things I've never heard of. It's like we're speaking different languages.

"Let's go," Thomas says, and if there's one thing he doesn't kid about, it's dinner. I let him lead the way out into the kitchen, where we find Emma standing over a Dutch oven with a wooden spoon in her hand. I pause, because Daddy doesn't even let Momma touch his Dutch oven potatoes.

But Emma's stirring them up like she's the one who's been here for hours, peeling, dicing, layering in bacon, and babysitting the coals. She laughs, and of course she's already seamlessly integrated herself into my family.

How she does that, I'll never understand.

Hey, her grandmother liked you, I tell myself, but I still have a pinch in my gut that tells me that Em's better at being a Stansfield than I am. And I don't know why that bothers me, only that it does.

"Get over here, boys," Momma says in her no-nonsense voice. She had to use it constantly on both of us growing up. If she didn't, I actually wouldn't hear her, and Thomas takes his time with everything—unless Momma speaks in that voice.

We both go into the kitchen, and I sweep my arm around Emma and nod to my brother. "Em, this is Thomas, my younger brother. Tommy, this is my girlfriend, Emma."

"Hello," Thomas says. He shakes Emma's hand, and she practically vibrates with energy.

"It's so great to meet you, Thomas," she says, glancing at me. "Aaron tells me you like *Lord of the Rings*."

"They're my favorite movies and books," he says.

"I've just started them."

"For the first time?" he asks. "How old are you?"

"Thomas," Momma says gently. "Not everyone likes to read, remember?"

"And girls don't always like *Lord of the Rings*," he says.

"I'm sure lots of girls do," Daddy says easily.

"He uses a lot of words," Emma says.

"I didn't know you had time to read," I say, giving Emma a look.

She gives me a semi-heated glare. Or maybe it's ice-cold. It's hard to tell in the split second she looks at me. "I listen to the audiobook on the way to the shop and home again."

"Listening to books isn't reading," Thomas says.

"What?" Emma scoffs and pushes one palm against Thomas's shoulder. "That's the most ridiculous thing I've ever heard. Listening to audiobooks is *exactly* like reading a book."

Momma smiles as she puts a big bowl of frog eye salad on the table. "Thomas, not everyone has to agree with you."

"I know," he says. "I didn't even argue back about the audiobooks." He smiles at Emma. "I have an Aragorn costume, and Aaron dresses up as Legolas."

"Is he the elf?" Emma asks.

"Yep."

"Yes, I've seen that costume," Emma says, giving me a warm look now. Listening to her interact with my brother in an easy, natural rhythm has me falling head over heels in love with her, and I have to find a way to catch myself.

"All right," Daddy says. "We're not talking about orcs and elves all night. Tommy, ask Emma something about herself."

A healthy pause fills the kitchen while Momma pulls a huge roasting pan covered in aluminum foil out of the oven.

"What do you do for a living?" Tommy asks.

Emma grins and grins. "You know what? Let me show you." She exchanges a glance with me and adds, "Did we leave that out in the truck?"

"I forgot about it," I admit.

"I'll be right back."

"We're eating," Momma says, but I give her a look that tells her this is important. She presses her lips together as Emma jogs lightly out of the house, leaving the door ajar. "She is just lovely," Momma gushes. "No wonder we haven't seen you or heard from you much."

I tear my eyes from the front door and look at her

and Daddy. "I've been around and communicative the normal amount."

Daddy shakes his head, and Momma swats me with her handmade tea towel. "Not true, Mister."

"Well, I have a big build right now," I say, my voice wounded.

"And a pretty girlfriend," Tommy says.

Momma gasps, and I even look at Tommy with my jaw dropping open. Then I start to chuckle. "You think she's pretty, Tommy?"

"She is," he says matter-of-factly. "Maybe I could ask Melinda out. She's pretty too."

"You should," Momma says, and I nod along.

"Do you think I'm too focused on her?" I ask, my eyes drifting back to the doorway. I don't want Emma to overhear this, though I've told her how I hyper-focus. I'm just not sure she really understands what it means, how it dominates my life sometimes.

Before Momma can answer, Emma comes barreling back inside, her Lord of the Rings inspired arrangement in her hands. "Okay, got it," she says, breathlessly. It doesn't matter if Momma answers or not, and I wouldn't believe her even if she told me no, I'm not too focused on Emma.

I know I am, and I don't know how not to be.

Emma arrives and holds up the arrangement, which looks really poky to me. "It's mostly thistle and eucalyptus," she says. "With some very pretty calla lilies, and orchids, and roses."

All of the flowers are white, creating a nearly mono-chromatic vibe with the dusty green leaves.

"Very long-lasting, like the fires of Mordor." She hands it to Tommy, who looks at it like he's been presented with the One Ring to Rule Them All. "I named it *Gondor's Glory*."

I stiffen, because Tommy has strong feelings about Gondor.

"This is a gift worthy of the elves," he says, finally looking up. "Thank you, Emma." He sets down the arrangement and steps over to her to hug her.

"Wow," Daddy whispers, and Momma's pressing one hand to her heart as her eyes fill with tears.

And I know that I'm not the only one falling in love with Emma Newberry.

CHAPTER TWENTY-ONE

EMMA

I'm standing in the Stansfields' kitchen, and it feels like I've been plucked straight out of my life and dropped into someone else's. Someone who has their act together. Someone who doesn't have a mountain of orders to fill, a grumpy fridge to placate, and a looming park project that's become more of a pressure cooker than I'd like.

Someone who fits here, in this cozy country kitchen, with its warm yellow walls and the smell of bacony potatoes curling through the air.

But I don't fit. Not really. Not yet, anyway.

Jenny's got a literal buffet of food on the counter, and I know I'm going to eat way too much. She's the kind of woman who seems like she could churn her own butter, sew a quilt, and still have time to check on all of her friends and loved ones before breakfast.

She wears an apron covered in little sunflowers, and when she smiles at me, it's with the same warmth as a summer day. It's so genuine, it makes me feel guilty for every ounce of self-doubt creeping through me.

"Emma, honey, thanks for the help with the potatoes," Jenny says as she now stirs them. "These are a family favorite."

"It smells amazing," I say, my voice a little too high-pitched to sound natural. I clasp my hands together to keep from fidgeting and glance at Aaron, who's standing there, staring at me. The same way his brother and father are, almost as if they've never seen a blonde woman before.

His eyes finally come to mine, and he gives me that easy smile of his—the one that makes me feel like I can do anything. Like I belong here.

I want to believe him. I do. But there's a voice in my head whispering, *You're just playing house. You don't really fit here. You're pretending.*

Rawlins claps his hands together, and I jump. "All right, let's get this show on the road. I'm starving."

Thomas gazes down at Gondor's Glory with fondness streaming from him, almost like he's holding the crown of the kingdom itself. He sets it on the sideboard, then glances at me with a small smile.

"Thank you again for this," he says quietly.

"You're welcome, Thomas," I say, touched by the sincerity in his voice. "I'm glad you like it."

"I love it," he says, and his words are so earnest, they make my insecurities feel a little smaller. Just a little.

We all gather around the island again, which is laden with Dutch oven potatoes, roast chicken, those green beans people make at Thanksgiving, and a loaf of bread that has herbs and seeds in it.

Grams would love that, and in fact, Grams would love being here with the Stansfields. It's the kind of meal that feels like a hug in food form, and it's hard not to feel a little lighter as I slide my hand into Aaron's while his mother says, "Let's say grace. Rawlins?"

"Thomas?" He lifts his eyebrows, and I look at Thomas, expecting him to say no.

But he folds his arms, bows his head, squinches his eyes shut, and starts to pray. He doesn't wait for any of us to get ready, and I quickly drop my chin toward my chest as I grip Aaron's hand. Thomas isn't a man of many words, and he finishes only a couple of sentences after he starts.

"Amen," Aaron booms throughout the house, and Jenny flies into motion.

She picks up a plate and hands it to me, gently guiding Thomas back with her elbow. "Do you cook, Emma?"

"Oh, well, my grandmother tried to teach me," I say. The truth is, my cooking skills are limited to pancakes, popcorn, and the occasional one-pot pasta. "I like eating what my roommates make." I pile cheesy potatoes and bacon on my plate. "Aaron's a good cook."

"Is he?"

I glance at him. "I think so." I shrug as I move down and pick up some dark meat from the platter of roast chicken. "I like what he's made for me."

"Oh, is he cooking for you a lot?" Jenny asks, her voice pitching up toward the rafters.

"Abort," Aaron coughs from his spot at my side. "Abort."

"Just sometimes," I say. "Then he works on his house, and I do my online flower orders while he sands or paints or whatever."

"I thought the house was done," Rawlins says.

"It's livable," Aaron says. "That's different than done, Daddy."

I take some of everything and look over to the dining room table. I don't want to sit down first, because I don't know the assigned spots the Stansfields might have.

"Aaron—" I turn to ask him where I should sit—and ram right into him. I shriek as if I've just seen a wraith from my Lord of the Rings books, and Aaron grunts as he backs up.

My plate has been knocked askew, and I fight with everything I have not to drop it. Quickly, I balance it with both hands, but some of the cheesy goodness of the potatoes has definitely slid off the side.

"I'm behind you," he says needlessly.

I look up just in time to see a chunk of potato fall from his shirt to the floor. *Plunk.* It lands near a puddle of Dutch oven potato sauciness I really wanted to eat.

Horror and embarrassment make a bitter cocktail in my stomach, and I'm not quite sure what to do.

Aaron takes my plate and nods. "Go sit," he commands in his Doberman voice. "It's fine, sweetheart. This floor has had worse things on it."

"What's happening?" Jenny asks, and before I can stop her, she moves around Aaron, her foot destined for that slippery, cheese puddle of sauce.

"Wait!" I throw up both hands, causing Aaron to grunt and back up again, this time lifting both of our plates high above his head.

"Emma," he yells.

"Don't step there." I throw myself over the goo on the floor, so his mother won't step in it, slip, and break a hip. I'll never be able to show my face again if that happens.

She goes, "Oh, my," but she stops. And she doesn't slip. She blinks at me rapidly. "What's going on?"

"I just spilled," I say, pointing at the ground. "I don't want anyone to slip and fall."

Jenny flies into domestic mother mode, setting down her plate of food in favor of the washrag. She gets the floor spick-and-span, and we all manage to sit down to eat. Aaron comes over last, and he puts my plate in front of me like I'm an errant toddler and he'll fasten a bib around my neck before giving me any silverware.

He does give me a look I can't quite read before he says, "So, Thomas, how's your budgeting class going?"

"I hate it," his brother says. "But Momma won't let me quit."

"Everyone needs to know how to manage their finances," Jenny says with a bit of self-importance in her tone. "You don't hate it that bad."

"Ask him how he liked fishing," Rawlins says with a chuckle, and both Aaron and I look at him.

"I'm *not* doing that again," Thomas says, shaking his head. "They're so slippery—and kind of creepy."

I grin at him. "I couldn't agree more. Fish are creepy."

"Tell her about your fishing disaster, Daddy," Aaron says, and all of the things I imagined about families are true. They do know each other enough to set up stories and jokes. They talk to each other without yelling, and they sit down for meals made for a crowd.

No, they aren't perfect, and sometimes people smash potatoes into their boyfriend's torsos, but there's laughter and ribbing and serious conversations too.

For a moment, I forget about everything waiting for me back in the real world. For a moment, I feel like I could belong here. For a moment, I am part of a family bigger than two.

"So, Aaron tells us you're working on the park competition together," Jenny says after the fishing disaster story wraps up and we all stop laughing about Rawlins losing the nine fish he caught because he thought he saw an alligator and nearly capsized the boat.

I nod, my stomach tightening, as I glance over to him. "That's right."

"It's such a wonderful opportunity," she says, and I'm not sure how much Aaron has told her. "And such an important project for the community. I'm sure you've heard how much the town council is hoping this will revitalize the area."

"Yeah," I say, my voice a little too quiet. "We've heard."

"And with your flower shop being so new," she adds, her tone still kind. "I imagine winning would really help establish your reputation in town."

I freeze, my fork halfway to my mouth. It's not an accusatory statement. It's not even remotely mean. But it feels like a spotlight has just been turned on me, exposing every single one of my fears.

"It would." I force a smile. "It's a great opportunity for everyone in the small business group." After all, everyone will have a sign in front of their demonstration plot, with their company names.

"She's already done so much," Aaron says, his voice cutting through the tense moment. "She's planted all the flowers, and they look incredible. And don't forget, she made the plans for the layout. I just do the building."

He says it like it's no big deal, like I'm the one doing all the heavy lifting. But the truth is, without Aaron, I wouldn't have a chance at winning this competition.

Flowers? They're going to give me twenty-five grand because I can plant some *flowers*?

I almost scoff right out loud.

He's the one who can make the designs come to life. *He's* the one who knows how—and has the materials—to build the benches and pergolas and all the other elements that will make our plot stand out. Without him, I'd just be a florist with a thousand square feet of water-less dirt.

Jenny smiles at Aaron, then at me. "Well, I think it's wonderful that you're working together. And I have no doubt you'll do an amazing job."

"Thanks," I say, but the word sounds hollow. My chest is so tight, and my brain is suddenly a whirlwind of thoughts. What if we don't win? What if Aaron starts to resent me for dragging him into this? What if people in town think I'm using him? What if *he* thinks I'm using him?

"Emma?" Aaron's voice pulls me back to the present. He's looking at me, concern etching his handsome face. "You okay?"

"Yeah," I say quickly, plastering on a smile. "I'm fine. Just thinking about all the work we still have to do."

"You've got plenty of time," Rawlins says, his tone easy and reassuring. "It's only May."

"And you've got Aaron," Jenny adds. "He's always been the most reliable one in the family."

"Thanks, Momma." Aaron rolls his eyes even as he smiles. "No pressure or anything."

The conversation continues, with Thomas asking Aaron if he's going to put a porch swing in the backyard of his house and Rawlins going on about growing up in that house and the things that used to be there.

I keep eating, keep smiling, but Aaron flicks his gaze over to me more often, and I see his growing concern. The meal finishes, and I jump up to help clean up, but Jenny waves me off.

"You're our guest," she says. "Go relax on our back deck." She smiles. "Then you'll see what Aaron wants to do at his place."

Aaron doesn't have to be told twice, and he takes my hand and leads me out the sliding glass door to an enormous deck that spans the width of the house. "Wow," I say. "Look at this."

"My dad built it," he says, sweeping his arm across the whole backyard. "For my mom. She loves to grill, so she has a place to do that. He likes to cook in the Dutch oven, so there's a fire pit for that."

"And there's a whole living room of furniture out here." I lead him over to the loveseat and let him sit down first so I can curl into him.

"It's so peaceful," I say, drinking in the green grass and the trimmed bushes on the side of the yard. Two big trees stand proudly about two-thirds of the way back, providing shade for most of the yard at this time of evening.

His thumb brushes gently over the back of my hand, and I really enjoy the sensation. The evening air is warm and soft, with a hint of honeysuckle on the breeze. The crickets are already chirping, their song filling the quiet between us as we sit there.

"Something happened in there," he finally says, his voice low and careful.

I avoid his gaze. "Yeah, something did."

"Are you going to tell me about it?" he asks.

I close my eyes, exhaling slowly. I don't quite know how to put my thoughts and feelings into words. They feel rational in some moments and completely bananas in others. "You'd tell me if you didn't have time or didn't want to do the park project, right?"

"I—" He cuts off. "Where is that coming from? Of course I want to do it. It's a lot of money."

"That we have to split."

"Still a lot of money."

"And you're doing all the work." There. I've said it.

Aaron gives me the courtesy of staying quiet. I'm not sure what he's thinking, but that mind of his is buzzing away, I'm sure. "You think I'm getting the short end of the stick."

"You are."

"You think you're...using me?"

I pull in a slow breath, because it sounds so much worse when he says it. "Maybe. Yes? I don't know."

"Emma-honey."

I really love it when he connects my name like that, making it one word, as if perhaps my mother meant to name me that and simply forgot the last part.

He kneads me closer, his grip on my bicep tight. "You're not using me," he says in his firm, barky, Doberman voice.

"You'd tell me if you felt like that, though, right?"

"Yes," he says, and I sincerely hope he's telling me the truth. "I'd tell you. When have I ever been able to hide anything from you?"

I snort, then start to giggle. "You're right. You're terrible at hiding how you feel about stuff."

"Hey, now," he says.

"Really," I say. "You think you're hiding it, but you're not."

"Oh, you mean like you just did during dinner?" He scoffs and shakes his head. "You're not great at hiding how you feel either, honeybee."

"Two peas in a pod," I say.

He presses a kiss to the corner of my eye. "Yeah, I like the sound of that."

I look up, and Aaron—my hot, honest, cinnamon roll

handyman—doesn't waste any time touching his mouth to mine and kissing me.

And while my worries have been placated for now, I can't help but wonder if Aaron will feel the same once he's the one who'll have to be out in the summer heat, building a covered bench for our park demo.

CHAPTER TWENTY-TWO

AARON

THE SUN STARTS TO COME UP AS I ARRIVE AT THE park. I'm the only one here, and I get out, lower the tailgate, and look at the tool belt and lumber I brought with me. I figure I can build a bench in under a half hour, and to add a cover is just a couple of pillars and a pitched roof.

I've done races with my dad for a ten-minute door, and I can put long, straight pieces of wood together quick-quick. I smile to myself as I put on my belt, wishing Emma was here to dare me to make this bench in less than an hour.

She's not, so I have to issue the dare to myself silently.

That done, I head for our plot, more silent talking to myself happening. I'm glad our plot isn't super deep in the park, because I'm going to have to bring all of that lumber down here. I have to make cuts at the truck, haul it in, and put it together on the plot. With a bench made of cypress wood—a tree native to South Carolina—and the half-barrel, white oak end tables I'm planning to put on each end, the covered bench should make an impressive showpiece for our demo plot.

"Wow," I say as I approach our plot. Yes, I'd told my parents that Emma's flowers looked amazing, but I haven't been here in a couple of weeks. We're not the only team to have planted something in our plot, but Emma's flowers are twice as big as anyone else's.

Ten times as colorful. A hundred times better.

I set down the barrel I reclaimed from a plantation down the road a little bit and separate the halves I've already cut. White oak is also native to South Carolina, and my vision for the bench is to provide a place for people to sit and eat lunch. So of course, they need somewhere to put their drinks, their phones, anything else they want to set down for a few minutes while they sit themselves down for a few minutes.

The cypress pillars will come out of the middle of the barrels to support the roof over the bench, and I can't wait to see this come together. I survey our plot, the sketches Emma and I have gone over right there in my mind.

She's got sculpted beds along the left side of our plot, and our vision was to have the bench be in the center. As I'm standing there, I'm not sure how a bench and a bunch of blooms will win us twenty-five thousand dollars, but I can't build a gazebo, benches, picnic tables, and a pavilion all in one spot, even if it is one thousand square feet.

I return to the truck and make my initial cuts for the seat and back of the bench. I carry them to the plot four at a time, and within twenty minutes, I have the bench built. I use my jigsaw to cut out the square holes I need for the pillars, and back to the truck I go to get those cut.

The thing about building—about woodworking specifically—is that it's like meditation for me. The noise of the saw, the smell of the wood, the feel of the power tools in my hands—it all shuts out the chaos in my brain. I can focus, really focus, in a way I struggle to do with almost anything else. It's just me and the project, and everything else—the deadlines, the expectations, the what-ifs—fades into the background.

This bench is going to be beautiful. Solid. The kind of thing people will sit on for years, maybe even decades. A place where couples might hold hands, where kids might climb and laugh. A place that lasts.

I cut the lumber for the roof too, and I make a few trips back and forth, sweating like nobody's business as I do. I screw the half barrels to the bench, then thread the pillars into them and make those solid with three-inch screws.

"This would benefit from cement," I say to myself and the lightly waving flowers. Then, I could hide the unfinished ends of the barrels and have the pillar down into something super supportive. I don't want to pour concrete right here on our plot, because our demo can't be permanent. We'll be disqualified.

I make a mental note to tell our artist that we're envisioning the benches on a pad of cement, and I keep working.

I lose track of time. I know I do. It's one of those things I've always struggled with—"time blindness," my momma calls it. It's not like I don't know time is passing. It's just that once I'm locked into a task, the minutes blur together, and the rest of the world doesn't seem to exist.

The roof goes up quickly as well, and I stand on the ladder and take in the gardens surrounding me. "Stop drooping, Daisy," I mutter under my breath, mimicking Emma's voice in my head as I climb down to the ground. "This is a team effort."

I chuckle to myself, imagining how she'd roll her eyes at me for butchering her flower pep talks. She's probably at the shop right now, talking to her floral fridge like it's a grumpy roommate. The thought makes me smile, but it also makes me wish she were here.

That's when I hear someone catcall. I twist back toward the parking area, my heartbeat throbbing in my throat.

Emma comes to a stop next to me, one hand on her hip and the other holding a watering can. "You're moving that, right?" She pants out the words, and I take the heavy watering can from her, because she has to haul in the water.

"Moving it?" I look back at the bench. It's utterly fantastic, and I don't think I could move it myself even if I wanted to. "No, I wasn't going to move it."

"Well, it's in the wrong place."

My pulse misfires. "No, it isn't. It's our showpiece."

"I deliberately left a gap in my garden right there." Emma sweeps her hand toward the bank of bushes and flowers on her right. "For the bench. It was part of the design. Now it's just, like, stuck out there in the middle of the dirt."

I don't know what to say. We've been over the designs so many times. My brain blitzes out, and I can't remember anything. "I thought it was the showpiece."

"It is, but it should still be part of the design." She adjusts her sunglasses and sighs. "We have to move it."

I can see the half-barrels nestled among her flowers and grasses, and she's right. I shouldn't have built it out in the middle of nothing.

She moves away from me, displeasure radiating off her like heat waves. "What is this made of?"

"Cypress," I say. "I got it for free from a plantation and upcycled it. It's great." I put my hand on the pillar. "Natural resistance to rot and insects, and it does really well outside in hot and humid climates."

"You sound like an infomercial for cypress wood."

She rolls her eyes. "What are these?" She runs her fingers along the top rim of the end table barrel.

"It's a recycled white oak barrel," I say, the words scraping my throat. "It's used all over the south for whiskey or wine. Also local to our South Carolina forests." I know people like reclaiming items and reusing them, and I'm fully intending to put that in our copy that people can read as they walk the park and take in each plot.

"It's an end table," I say.

"People aren't going to sit here and watch TV."

"No, I know." Frustration builds through me. "I showed up at dawn to get this done," I say. "Why don't you like it?"

"Because it's not what we discussed."

"It so is," I say. "It's a covered bench that shows the kind of work I can do. We'll have the artist mock up gazebos and picnic tables and a pavilion."

"Actually..."

I look at her, trying to figure out what she's going to say before she says it. "Actually?"

"I was hoping you could build one of the picnic tables." She turns and points to the corner where she's got some bigger bushes and plants. "And put it there. Otherwise, it's some flowers with a bench."

"The flowers are amazing," I say.

"I'm going to do some raised beds," she says. "To add some variety."

"Em, I don't think you need to do that."

"I do." She won't look at me, and I don't like that. "I like the barrels on the end, but we have to move it to this spot."

"I'll have Jake come help me," I say, trying not to bark out the words. "You know, it would be nice if you'd acknowledge that this is an amazing bench."

Her lips press into a thin line, the tension in her shoulders stinging my lungs.

"Never mind," I say as I turn around. "If it's that hard for you to say, don't say it."

"Aaron." She catches up to me quickly, because I only move a few feet to start watering her flowers. "I didn't know you were going to go rogue and start building without me."

"I told you I was building this morning."

"The roof is double-sided."

"Yep."

"The drawing had a single sloped roof. You didn't do anything on our design."

I blink, taken aback by the sharpness in her tone. "Emma, it's a bench. It's not like I bulldozed the whole plot."

"Do you even know if this fits with the rest of the design?" she asks, gesturing to the flowers she's cared for over the past couple-few weeks. "Did you think about how much bigger it would be with those barrels? Or that roof that looks like a cabin almost? Or literally anything else we already talked about?"

"I—" I stop, realizing too late that I didn't think about any of that. I was so focused on the bench itself, on using the amazing reclaimed barrels and wood, on making it perfect, that I didn't consider how it fit into the bigger picture.

"I just wanted to make something amazing," I say, not sure how to explain.

"And it *is* amazing." She leans into me, gazing up into my face with earnestness in her expression. "Aaron, it's not hard to say: It's amazing. It's the most amazing bench in the whole wide world, and I can't wait to see it in your backyard after its done doing its job here."

My emotions coil tightly, and I swallow. My throat is too narrow to let words out, and I don't know what to say anyway. I look away, my fists clenching at my sides. I want to argue, to defend myself, but deep down, I know she's right. I've been so caught up in my own head, in my own way of doing things, that I didn't stop to think about how it might affect what she's been doing here.

"But, baby," she says. "I have to make some adjustments in the gardens now."

"I know that now," I say. "I'm sorry. I'll fix it." That's all I want to do—fix things for her. I'd do anything to fix everything for her.

"Aaron," she says.

I look at her, and she smiles. "There you are." She

takes my face in her hands, and I let my eyes drift closed. I don't know what she's looking for or what she sees, but I just like the way her delicate fingers feel against my skin.

"I want you to just move the bench into the spot we talked about, okay?"

I nod.

"I don't need you to *fix* everything," she says, her voice breaking. "I know you like doing that, and I promise I'm going to let you come fix Sir Chills-a-Lot every time he breaks down."

I smile and open my eyes. "But?"

"But for this, baby, I just need you to realize I might have good ideas too." She drops her hands and steps back.

"I know that. I just—I get excited about wood." I sigh when I realize how that sounds. "When I took over the hardware store, that was a non-negotiable with my daddy and me. With my employees and me. I have to be able to still have build projects."

"Okay."

"And I just get a little focused on upcycling this gorgeous wood, and I want to do my best for this project." I swallow hard. "For you."

She grins. "So you can make me feel even more like I'm not doing enough here." She doesn't phrase it like a question, and I hear the teasing quality of her voice.

"I don't want you to feel like that," I say very seriously.

"I come haul water to these plants every day," she says, turning to be with her flowers.

"I know you do, sweetheart. You're killing it." I go with her and simply let her pick through her flowers, pet them, and prune them. "Talk to me about the picnic table, Em. I'll listen to all of your ideas, I swear."

"Then I want you to take me to breakfast." She grins at me as she walks backward for a few steps. "Doable?"

"I'll call Fonda," I say with a smile. "And no matter what, we can have breakfast for dinner tonight."

"All right." She reaches the back corner, where she's planted lilacs and a bleeding heart bush that thinks this ground is the most fertile place on the planet. "Remember, I'm doing that thing with my roommates this weekend. Will you be okay with the boys on Friday night?"

"Yes," he said.

"Beckett said something about a fake bachelor party? One tame enough for a government official to keep his job."

I scoff-snort. "Beckett's idea of a wild time is going running twice in one day."

Emma bursts out laughing, and I'm glad we made it to this point. She's also reached the corner, and she says, "Okay, so hear me out..."

"Poisoned pansies," I say.

She blinks at me, a slow smile filling her face. "I

think you meant Don't stop!" She strikes a pose. "Believin'!"

I tip my head back and fill the sky with laughter. "Sure, that works too."

"But really," Emma says. "I think we should do a cobblestone path through our plot, first to the bench, and then back to a picnic table. It wouldn't have to be huge. Six people—three on each side."

"Standard build?"

She blinks. "Yes?"

I can see the path in my head, and though it means more work for me—hauling stones, no less—I say, "Okay, honeybee. Now, let's see about that breakfast."

CHAPTER TWENTY-THREE

EMMA

The Big House smells like freshly baked cookies when I walk in on Friday evening, and for a second, I'm hit with an overwhelming sense of relief. There's something magical about the way this house always feels like a safe haven, like no matter how chaotic things get in my life, I can come back here and breathe again.

Tahlia loves to bake, and she gets off work before anyone else in the Big House, so I expect to find her triple-chocolate chip cookies on the table, ready for our girl's night in only another hour or so.

I'm so late, but I slide my crate onto the shelf at the back of the kitchen and step over to the dining room table where the cookies are cooling.

They're not Tahlia's triple-chocolate chip. They're Lizzie's peanut butter mini M&M delights.

Ry will love these, and now that they make mini peanut butter M&Ms, I'm not sure if I'm going to get chocolate on the first bite or double peanut butter.

"Lizzie?" I call, kicking off my sandals and shoving them partially under the shelving. The faint sound of music drifts from somewhere else in the house, some upbeat indie song that perfectly matches her vibe.

I pick up a cookie just as she says, "Those are hot." She pockets her phone as she approaches, her long, dark blonde hair tied up into a perfect French braid. She's wearing an off-the-right-shoulder oversized sweatshirt like it's the next runway-ready piece of clothing and a pair of black leggings. She always looks like a million bucks, even dressed down as she is.

"I need this," I say, lifting the cookie to my mouth.

"Rough day?"

"It's Friday." I take a bite of the soft peanut butter cookie, the edges perfectly crisp. The M&M shell breaks and I get piping hot chocolate on my tongue. I don't even care, because in this moment, everything is right in the world. "Mm." I moan and let my eyes roll back in my head. "Merciful marigolds, this is my favorite cookie."

Lizzie smiles at me and opens the oven to check the batch inside. She never uses a timer the way Tahlia does, but instead "eyeballs" it.

"How was your day?" I ask, leaning against the counter and letting the warmth of the cookie and the comfort of home settle over me.

Lizzie closes the oven and shrugs, but there's a small, secret smile tugging at her lips. "Not bad. Work was fine."

"Mm hm. And?"

Her smile grows. "Matt and I had lunch again."

My eyebrows go up. "Again? How many lunches is that now?"

She blushes, which is rare for Lizzie. She's usually so composed, so effortlessly calm, so perfectly put together.. "I don't know. Five? Six?" She takes a breath, and says in a rush, "It's not a big deal."

I turn away from her to get another cookie, simply so she can have a moment to collect herself. "It's so a big deal," I say. "Just admit it."

"The ones on the right are peanut butter M&Ms," she says.

I pick up one on the right and the left. "Are we having dinner tonight?"

"Yes," Lizzie says. "Claudia is bringing home the extra catering from their calendaring meeting today. She texted."

"I had no time to check texts." I turn back to her, and she takes out the cookies and sets them on the stovetop. "And don't think I'm not considering how many lunch dates it takes to make a relationship." I take a bite of the double peanut butter delight. "I think six," I add around a mouthful of deliciousness.

"It's not a relationship," she says as she shoots me a

glare as she moves over to the dining room table and starts transferring the cookies to the cooling rack. "We just...we talk. He's easy to talk to."

"And?" I finish my cookie, realizing the challenge in my voice. "Do you like him?"

She turns away from me, all the answer I need. "Of course I do," she says. "But he won't ask me out."

Lizzie is one of the toughest and most guarded people I know, and seeing her like this—soft, unsure, vulnerable—it makes me want to wrap her in a hug and never let go. "So you'll tell everyone tonight, and we'll help you figure it out."

She nods as she scoops another pan full of cookie dough and slides it into the oven. "Yeah, I don't want to have to say all of this twice."

"Incoming," someone calls from the front door, and I stuff the last of my cookie in my mouth and go see what Claudia needs.

And that's to stay out of the way as she quick-steps under the load of the catering she's brought home with her. Thankfully, Tahlia has a table set up in the living room already, and I spy the pink-painted mic sitting there as Claudia slides the box onto it.

"Phew." She wipes her dark hair out of her face. "Who knew club sandwiches were so heavy?" She's wearing wedged heels, and I'm sure that doesn't help.

"Anything else in the car?" Tahlia asks.

"Chips," Claudia says with a huff. "Packets for the sandwiches. Mayo and mustard and stuff."

"I'll go," I say, and Tahlia comes with me. We get everything out of Claudia's car as Hillary crosses the lawn toward us.

"Hey," she calls, and she radiates happiness now in a way I haven't seen from her in all the years I've known her. "Need help?"

I slam the trunk closed as Tahlia says, "We got it all."

Hill still comes toward us and gives Tahlia a hug and then me. "Hey, you," she says with a glinting note in her tone. "I just saw Aaron at my place."

I look that way. "Yeah, he's over there tonight."

"Beckett is the only one who hasn't arrived," Hillary said. "Ry just dropped off Elliott, and she's driving over so she doesn't have to walk back in the dark."

We all go into the Big House, where Ry has arrived. She's setting plates on the table and chatting easily with Claudia about something that happened at the office supply store where she works.

"Ry's got her M&Ms," Hillary says as she scoops up a handful. "What kind are these?"

"I'm surprise you can't tell by the shape of them," Ry says. She glows too, and I wonder if she'll have news tonight. She and Elliott have only been married for about a month, but Ry's told us they want to have a baby right away, so Elliott can experience and see as much of his life and family while he still can.

She won't say anything until we've eaten and Tahlia's explained the rules of our Mic Night, so I pick up a plate and say, "I'm starving."

"You ate three cookies only five minutes ago," Lizzie says in a deadpan.

"And lunch with Aaron was hours before that," I say, kicking open the door for the shenanigans to begin.

"Ooh, you did it," Hillary said, bumping me with her hip as I pick up a boxed lunch with a club sandwich and potato salad inside, according to the sticker on the outside. "You better start talking, lady. I want all the goods on my husband's best friend."

I think about our mini argument earlier this week and dinner with his family last week. I think of how he brings me the mint truffles I like for no reason at all, and all the simple weeknight meals he's made for me. I think of how I lay awake when I first crawl into bed, and he makes me smile with the things he's said and done that day.

"I think things are going really well for us," I say. "For the most part."

"Oh, those last four words concern me," Ry says.

I take my food over to one of the recliners and sit down with a sigh. "I feel like I'm using him for the park project, and because he's such an amazing builder, that we'll win—and all I did was plant flowers."

"Okay," Tahlia says, and I see her shoot looks to everyone else in the room. It works too, because they stay silent, which is just what I need. If they all start shouting things at me, my thoughts get derailed, and I just shut down.

"And he's just wonderful, you know." I rip open a mayo packet and realize I haven't even gotten out my sandwich yet. "A little scattered sometimes. A little anxious, but nothing he can't manage or that bothers me too much."

"Don't sound so happy that your boyfriend is wonderful," Claudia says.

"Yeah, what's with the 'for the most part' bit?" Ry asks as she sits on the end of the couch nearest me. She watches me with soulful eyes, and I don't know how to answer her.

I stay silent as I peel the plastic wrap off my sandwich and lift the lid so I can mayo and mustard it. Chatter picks up at the table as others get their food, and I listen to them chit and chat about this and that. No one forces me to say anything about Aaron, but as we finish eating, Tahlia reaches over the back of the couch and scrabbles around to find the pink mic.

"Emma," she says, but my phone has vibrated with a text from Aaron.

> I'm sure you're having fun, but guy's night is not really my vibe.

> Really? Liam's your best friend and you like Beckett and Elliott.

> Sure, I like them. Food's great. I'd
> rather be watching a romantic comedy
> with you on my couch.

"Emma," Claudia barks, and she yanks my phone out of my hands. "It's time to talk, and you're first." She replaces my phone with the pink mic, which is just a paper towel tube that's been shortened and made into a cone at the bottom, with a tennis ball atop it. Tahlia repaints the whole thing bright pink every few months, and I hold it up to my mouth like I'm about to start a mega-concert in a super-arena.

"I'm worried that I'm too bossy," I say into the mic. "I'm worried that he's too good to be true. I'm worried that he sometimes gets so ultra-focused on projects that he forgets to include me, so that makes me wonder if I can trust him to do what we talked about doing."

I take a breath and look around at my adoring fans. Lizzie pops a chip in her mouth, as she's heard some of this before. "But I really like him," I say. "I worry that we're too busy to be together."

"You won't have three weddings in three months all the time," Tahlia says.

"And he's not Tucker," Lizzie adds.

I flinch at her words, but Hillary says, "Yeah, he's not even close to Tucker."

"He's not Tucker," Claudia says, and my gaze darts to hers.

"He's the opposite of Tucker," Tahlia says. "And

Em, you're going to have to figure that out, because everything else just seems like..." She looks around at everyone, then finishes with, "Nothing."

"She's right," Hillary says.

I extend the mic to Ryanne, who sits closest to me. "Okay," I say. "That's me."

He's not Tucker rings in my ears, and while I haven't thought about him since that day he showed up in my shop—and Aaron fake-kissed me as my fake-boyfriend—I can acknowledge that my relationship with Tucker has informed my decisions in the dating arena.

I hate that I've let him do that, especially for this long, but the fact is, I have. And blooming begonias, I don't know how to stop.

Ry smiles around at all of us. "I'm happy to report that Luna, Peppermint, Elliott, and I are adding another member of our family."

Tahlia sucks in a breath, and I refocus on the conversation. Ry giggles and says, "I'm getting a new sister-in-law in October, number one."

"Boo," Claudia says, cupping her hands around her mouth as she does.

"Yeah, that's mean," Hillary says.

"*And* we're getting chickens in a couple of weeks," Ry says, still grinning for all she's worth. "We've only been married for a month, and no, I'm not pregnant yet." She passes the mic to Lizzie, and I lean forward, my eyes on the only roommate I share the second floor with now that Ry is gone.

"I've had lunch with M—a man at work several times," Lizzie says. "I really like him, and I feel like I've been dropping *I'm-single* hints for a solid month now, and he still hasn't asked me out. I need ideas for what else I can do." She lets the mic fall to her lap as she looks around at us. In a hurry, she whips the mic back to her mouth. "And I don't want to ask him, so don't say that."

Hillary's shoulders go down, and Claudia, who always has something to say, glances around like she's lost.

"You're friends already?" Tahlia asks.

"Yes," Lizzie says. "It's friendly, not like Claude and Beckett."

"Well, if I had any success getting a man at work to ask me out," Tahlia says. "I wouldn't still be single. So."

I give her a sad smile, because Tahlia's not had the best luck with men, friends or enemies or anywhere in between. Claudia reaches over and pats her leg, because Tahlia herself looks so sullen.

"Does he have a girlfriend?" I ask.

Lizzie shakes her head. "He says no."

"Maybe he doesn't date," Hillary says. "Maybe he just got out of a bad break-up."

"Maybe," Lizzie says. "His mother lives here, and he's got a sister in Hilton Head. He's smart, and funny, and I don't know. I just think we'd have an amazing time together, and I don't know what he wants to see in me that he's not."

"You can't change who you are," Hillary says quietly.

"Yeah." Lizzie hands the mic to Tahlia, the third person on the couch.

"Wait," I say. "I think you should introduce—hear me out—a fake boyfriend. Just start talking about this hot guy you're going out with, and see if he gets jealous."

"Maybe he's not into women," Hillary says.

"He's talked about former girlfriends," Lizzie says.

"Wear the eggplant wrap dress," Claudia says, nodding over to me. "And talk about your hot date this weekend and see how he reacts to that."

Lizzie shakes her head, though her smile has appeared. "The eggplant wrap dress is a ballgown, Claudia. It has sequins and everything."

"Not ChemTech appropriate?" Claudia teases. "Weird."

I laugh with the others, and it feels good to do so. Tahlia wants to pass, and she gives the mic to Hillary.

"I have no news," she says. "Liam and I aren't in a hurry to have children, and I don't know. Things are settled and great."

The mic lands in Claudia's hand and she sighs. "I'm regretting my long engagement now," she says. "That's it. I don't want to talk about it more than this. I'm simply ready to be married."

"But I'll miss you so much." I get up and pile on her where she's sitting on the love seat, and that causes a flurry of activity as everyone vacates their spot and joins us amidst Claudia yelling and others laughing.

In the end, we're all giggling, though there are elbows where elbows should never be and I'm getting just as smashed as Claudia.

I don't care. I love these ladies, and I hate that some of them are moving on and moving out. At the same time, I'm wondering if *I'm* ready to do that...with Aaron.

CHAPTER TWENTY-FOUR

AARON

ANOTHER ONE BITES THE DUST. THE SONG LYRICS RUN through my mind as I solve yet another problem on this horrible Monday. As if coming back to work after a day off isn't hard enough, today feels like someone turned the irritate-Aaron knob all the way to eleven.

I'm so going to be the one biting the dust, especially if I can't find the Mellow Yellow paint Mrs. Pickering is coming to pick up in the next hour.

Or the lumber shipment that didn't arrive by noon today, the way I'd been told. There are people waiting on that lumber, and I hate that I can't meet their needs as promised.

The start to a new week is always a little crazy, because so many builders and general contractors rely on the hardware store for their projects. They need a ton of materials, from lumber, to screws, to paint, to flooring.

I'm grateful for them. I am. The construction and automotive needs of the community is what keeps me in business. They pay my bills, and I can't imagine my life being anything but the hardware store.

But sometimes, the moon must be in perfect alignment with Mars or something, and when that lands on Monday, it makes everything go wrong.

Things hum away in the front of the store, thanks to amazing employees—and Fonda. But the moment I step beyond the customer service desk that she usually mans, pure chaos takes over. I take a breath while two phones ring somewhere back here in the storage area of the store.

Andy, my loading and unloading manager, approaches. "Hey, Aaron, do you have a second?"

"So many," I say, though I just want to retreat to my office and try to figure out what I need to do next. When the store matches my frenzied mind, things tend to go bad.

Andy takes off his ballcap and wipes his hand through his hair. "I just sent Flint away without the lumber he needs."

"Yeah, I've been promised the shipment will be here tonight."

"I told him that, but he said he has to have it this afternoon, and he's going to the store over in Sugar Creek."

"Okay," I say, because there's nothing I can do about

that. "We never have a problem selling lumber." I turn and pick up the clipboard from the counter to see what Flint Sanders had ordered. He's one of my best customers, and he builds barns and sheds for people who are raising chickens and horses and goats. Semi-home-steaders, I call them.

"Why do you have my clipboard?" Fonda snatches it from my hands. "I leave for five minutes, and you're in my space."

She hasn't had a great day either, and that's the only reason I don't bark back at her. "Did we find that paint?"

"Have *you* found it?"

"No, ma'am." I give her a smile. "I can focus on that." I look over to Andy. "And you need me to..."

"Get that lumber here before Jenkins gets wind that it's not in-stock." He wears concern on his face. "And maybe disconnect my line?"

I chuckle and say, "Wouldn't that be nice?"

"Maybe we could close early," Fonda says.

I don't tell her there's no way that's happening. I've seen my daddy work through a hurricane, for crying out loud, just so he could be in the store when it passed and people showed up needing tools and supplies. Not only that, but I've been promised that lumber by eight p.m., and someone has to be here to receive it.

That someone is me.

Snapdragons, I think, mimicking a flower-swear I've heard Emma use.

My brain is like a jigsaw puzzle with half the pieces missing, and it's all I can do to keep from panicking. "I'm going to go make a call," I say, only so I can get away from the customer service desk and my employees who are carrying so much of the load too.

"I'll let you know when Mrs. Pickering comes looking for that paint," Fonda says.

"And I'll keep you up-to-date with the lumber should I see it," Andy says.

"Thanks, guys," I manage to say before I retreat to my rat-packed mess. I close the door behind me, so many things tangling together in my brain. Paint. Screws. Shipments. Customers. Fonda. Andy. The phone. The clipboard. My scattered mind.

The pressure builds in my chest, a heavy, suffocating weight. I feel like I'm drowning, and no matter how hard I try, I can't seem to get my head above water.

"Just take it one step at a time," I say out loud to myself, and I move over to my computer. If I ordered the Mellow Yellow paint, I should have a record of it. And the Past-Me that can focus and get things done always makes sure Future-Me is taken care of. I have to believe I did that for this too.

A few clicks and search terms later, and I find the order. "Great, so it's coming from Walden's," I say, and I'll never forget that paint color and brand again. "So, where is it?"

We have systems here for when product arrives,

especially special-ordered product. And trust me, no one under the age of sixty-six would order Mellow Yellow paint. I'll have to ask Claudia what it could be used for, as Emma's told me Claudia knows a plethora of paint colors and where they'd be best utilized.

I find the email confirmation that says the paint has shipped, and the one that says it was delivered on Saturday. I lean back and try to get my mind to think, think, think.

"Saturday was only two days ago." I spent a lot of time over at the park plot, building the picnic table Emma wanted in the corner. That's done, except for the staining and sealing, and thankfully, there's been no rain. Double-thankfully, the park plot has to be finished by Thursday next week, and then it gets turned over to the public.

But once that project finishes, Emma has her third wedding to prep for, and I need to complete the build at the Lindsey's, so I can get paid and stop working out in the summer sun. How Liam does this year-round, I can't fathom.

"Aaron?" Fonda's voice cuts through the thoughts. "Mrs. Pickering is here."

"Right." I lean back into my computer. "This says the paint was delivered on Saturday, and that JP signed for it."

"Oh, that boy." Fonda rolls her eyes. "I know right where that paint is."

"Great." I jump to my feet. "Point me in the right direction, and I'll get it."

Fonda looks over her shoulder and brings the door closed. "Aaron."

I pause, because Fonda's gone through a transformation right in front of my eyes. "What is it?"

"You're not going to like it."

"I don't like not knowing where the supplies are either," I say. "Or that my lumber order got tied up in Tennessee." I fold my arms. "Just tell me."

"I think you're probably going to want to let JP go after you find out."

I sigh. "It's his girlfriend, isn't it?" I suddenly know where the paint is too. "That paint is sitting on the shelving across from the bathrooms, isn't it?"

"I'd bet my life on it."

I sigh with all the air in my lungs, a frustrated hissing sound coming out at the end. "You're right. I'm going to have to let him go." At the very least, I'm going to have to talk to him, and I'm not the greatest at being the boss.

I don't like having those hard conversations, but I also can't have special-order paint going on a Nothing Shelf, because the employee who signed for it was kissing his girlfriend.

"I'll go get the paint," I say. "Will you look and see when JP is working again?"

"Yes, sir." Fonda turns and leaves my office, and I follow her.

I see Mrs. Pickering, and I paste a smile on my face. "Mrs. Pickering." I lean in and give her a Southern kiss on the cheek. "I'm on my way to grab your paint. Give me two minutes."

"I've waited nine days, I suppose I can give you two more minutes."

My smile drops as I walk away, and I pray harder than I ever have on my way to the employee restrooms. Across from it, in the hall, is our Nothing Shelf. It's where we put things that I don't know what to do with. Sometimes I find things there I can use on a build, and sometimes I send materials home with someone if they see them and have a use for them.

I have Nothing Drawers and Nothing Cabinets in my house, and every once in a while, I go through them and clean them all out.

I arrive at the Nothing Shelf, my eyes flitting from a mismatched set of screwdrivers to an opened package of picture hanging nails. I don't see any paint cans, and my pulse throbs through my whole body. If they're not here, where else would they be?

Pulling out my phone, I quickly send a text to JP, hoping he's awake. His job here is his second job, and he works a graveyard shift at a salt-packing factory. *You received some yellow paint on Saturday, and the customer is here. Where is it?*

I hesitate to tell him he can't have his girlfriend here while he's working, though closing time is generally a super-slow time. Still, I need my most responsible people here, so the store is ready to open the next day, with paint where everyone and anyone can find it.

I stare at my phone, willing JP to text so my brain will stop buzzing. It's like there's a swarm of bees in my head, each one carrying a different thought, and they're all colliding into each other at once.

I can't focus. I can't think. I can't find that paint. I can't—

"Aaron?"

Everything freezes at the sound of Emma's voice.

I turn to see her standing at the corner, her honey-colored hair pulled back in a loose ponytail, her blue-green eyes scanning the hallway with concern. She's wearing a floral dress, her Pretty in Petals apron still tied around her waist, and she looks like she just stepped out of a picture-perfect small-town postcard.

"Hey," I say, my voice hoarse. "What are you doing here?"

"I came by for our breakfast-for-late-lunch date," she says, her tone light but her gaze sharp. "But Fonda said you were back here, so I thought I'd see if you needed help."

"Sorry," I mumble, running a hand through my hair. "I lost track of time."

She steps closer, her eyes narrowing as she studies my face. "Are you okay?"

"Yeah," I lie, turning back to the Nothing Shelf. "Just a busy day. Nothing I can't handle."

"Aaron," she says, her voice soft but firm. "Look at me."

I don't want to. I don't want her to see me like this—frazzled, overwhelmed, barely holding it together. But something in her tone leaves no room for argument, so I turn to face her, my shoulders slumping in defeat.

"I'm not okay," I admit, my voice barely above a whisper. "I've got late shipments, customers going to other stores because I don't have what they need, and missing paint in the ugliest color you can imagine."

I reach out and flip the stupid picture nails. "And my brain—it's just like, firing something new at me every half-second."

Her expression softens, and she reaches out to take my hand, her touch warm and steady. "Okay, what are we looking for?"

The way she steadies me, simply accepts me for this quivering mess I am, and tries to help makes me feel so many things at the same time. Guilt, because I shouldn't need her like this, and she's willing to give herself to me like this. Relief, because I need her like this, and she's willing to give herself to me like this.

"Paint," I manage to push out of my throat. "Mrs. Pickering needs her yellow paint."

She squeezes my hand. "Okay, paint. I at least know what that looks like."

Releasing her hand, I turn away from her. "I'm the forgetful one today, honeybee. I forgot you were coming with breakfast."

"It's okay," she says. "There's a lot going on here today. We can just have it for dinner tonight." She touches my shoulder, but I don't face her. "Are you okay?"

"I don't want you to see me like this," I admit, my throat tightening. "I don't want you to think I can't handle things."

"Aaron." She moves around me and stands right in front of me. "I don't think that. I've never thought that. You're one of the strongest, most capable people I know."

I shake my head, looking down at the floor. "It's not just today, Em. It's every day. I'm always losing track of time, getting overwhelmed. I feel like I'm always one step behind everyone else. And I hate it. I hate feeling like I'm not enough."

Her grip on my hand tightens, and she reaches up to cup my cheek, forcing me to meet her gaze. "Aaron, listen to me. You are more than enough. And I don't care if you lose track of time or get overwhelmed. I care about you. All of you. The good, the bad, the messy." She scoffs and lowers her hand. "Heck, I set four alarms for our breakfast-lunch today, and I still almost missed it."

I smile at her. "But you're here."

"I'm here."

"Thanks, honeybee," I whisper, pulling her into a hug. The frenzy in my mind quiets, and my phone rings. I step back and take a breath as I check my device. Then I swipe on the call. "JP. Four cans of Mellow Yellow paint. Tell me you know where it is."

"Uh," JP says. "I do remember getting it, but I'm not sure where I set it down."

"It was a special order," I say, turning away from the Nothing Shelf. "Did you put it out on the floor?" It would've been delivered near closing-time, and perhaps he shelved it and moved on with his night. Maybe he wasn't making out with his girlfriend.

"I think I gave it to Belinda to put on the shelf, yes," he says.

I give my heavy hiss-sigh again, heading for the paint aisle. We're closed on Sunday, and we've only been open for eight hours today. No one would ever buy that paint —that's why I had to order it for Mrs. Pickering in the first place.

"Listen, man," I say. "Belinda can't be here during your working hours."

"I know," JP says in a resigned voice. "I'm sorry."

"If I can't find this paint..." I let the threat hang there as I enter the paint aisle. Of course, now there are dozens and dozens of paint cans, and I've gone way past the two minutes I said it would take to find Mrs. Pickering's paint. "Did she at least put it with the other yellows?"

"I texted her, and she said she did it alphabetically."

"Mellow Yellow," I mutter when I really want to bust out "We're not gonna take it!" but I swallow the Twisted Sister scream.

After all, only Emma will get it, and that fact makes me smile.

But nothing makes me happier than spotting the four cans of Mellow Yellow paint. "I got it," I say, and JP's sigh of relief on the other end of the line comes through loud and clear. Mine matches his, and I add, "No more Belinda, buddy, or I'm gonna have to let you go."

"I need this job," JP says. "No more Belinda."

I can't carry all four cans of paint and stay on the phone. "I have to go, JP. You're awesome, okay?"

The call ends, and I gather all four gallons and head for the customer service desk. When I see Emma standing there chatting it up with Fonda and Mrs. Pickering, all of them smiling, a twinge of guilt pinches through me. So I can have my girlfriend here, but JP can't?

Yes, I tell myself. Because I'm not making out with her when I should be working.

"Mrs. Pickering," I practically bellow, drawing the attention of all three women there. I hold up the heavy paint with a wide smile on my face. "I've got your paint."

"That was way more than two minutes, young man," she says.

I grin at her and then over to Emma, and she takes a

couple of the gallons from me. "Let's get you out of here, Mrs. Pickering," she says. "I'll go with you, so you can finish telling me about your grandson."

I hand the other two gallons of paint to a worker and nod after them, then I stand there and watch my pretty girlfriend charm the pants off prickly Mrs. Pickering, thinking, *Maybe we can still have our breakfast-for-late-lunch date after all.*

CHAPTER TWENTY-FIVE

EMMA

THE SCENT OF FRESHLY BAKED BROWNIES FILLS THE Big House, mingling with the tangy aroma of Tahlia's lemon bars and the buttery-salty goodness of popcorn that Claudia is busy tossing in a big, oversized bowl. It's one of those rare nights when all of us are working in the kitchen for tonight's party, and the energy feels electric.

"Are these brownies for the party or just for me?" Lizzie asks, leaning over the counter to swipe a finger along the edge of the pan.

"Party," Tahlia says sternly, smacking her hand away with the spatula. "You'll survive."

Lizzie pouts, but the gleam in her eye says she's not giving up. I duck out of the kitchen and head to the living room, where I need to lay out plates and napkins. Tonight is supposed to be a celebration—our mock-up is done, the park project is nearly ready for presentation, and all of our men are coming to join us.

The thought of Aaron sends a ripple of warmth through me, but it's quickly followed by a pang of anxiety.

"Emma, can you come grab this sparkling cider?" Tahlia calls from behind me.

"Sure thing," I call back. I head to the fridge, trying to shake off the unease curling in my stomach. This is supposed to be a fun night, but the weight of everything —this project, my feelings for Aaron, the fear that a bunch of flowers and a bench is nowhere near enough to win twenty-five thousand dollars—is pressing down on me.

I am so bad at operating under pressure. How Claudia works as a major government figure is a complete mystery to me. I just want to fade into the background and make beautiful things, so doing a very public park project that literally thousands of people are going to walk by, look at, judge, and vote on?

I swallow, so I don't throw up, then grab the sparkling cider from the fridge.

"Hey-o!" someone calls from the front of the house, and I drop the bottle of apple-grape. It explodes with a deafening *pop!* and I scream. Claudia shrieks as purply fizzy drink sprays all over her ankles, and I hold very still as if I've been turned into a statue.

Tahlia yelps and jumps up onto a kitchen chair, and

Lizzie slides herself up onto the counter while the whole place continues to get ciderized.

The bottle spins and spins as the last of the carbonated liquid drains out, finally coming to a rest with the open top pointing to the doorway leading into the kitchen, where Aaron now stands.

He's carrying a tray of something I asked him to bring. I can't remember what off the top of my head, and I can't wait to hear what Claudia will say about his Army green camouflage shirt with the word STANS-FIELD on the front in blocky white letters.

I love it with my whole soul, and as I stand there in a complete soda mess of my own making, I realize I'm in love with him.

Pure fear grips my heart, and an extremely loud voice blares in my head, yelling, *It's too fast! Slow down! You can't trust him!*

"Hey," he says, his smile as warm and familiar as a summer sunrise. "Looks like you have a problem."

"There are towels in the laundry room," Tahlia says. "Can you grab us a couple? It's just behind the stairs."

"Sure thing." He turns, does something with the tray he brought, and returns a few seconds later with towels. He spreads them on the floor and uses his big, booted feet to swish them around and clean up the soda. He chuckles as he gets closer to me, frozen in front of the fridge. "Hey, honeybee." He leans in and kisses me quickly, just right in front of everyone. "I'm always fixing things around you."

"Hey," I say, half saying hi to him and half protesting that he's always fixing things around me. But he kind of is. He kind of fixes *me*.

"Here's a washrag," Claudia says, wringing one out. She tosses it on the floor and Aaron starts wiping up the stickiness now that most of the wetness is gone.

Tahlia gets down and takes the sopping towels into the laundry room while Lizzie eats a brownie in the background. Claudia excuses herself to go change her shoes and pants, which have been sprayed with soda, and I'll have to go do the same.

But I stay right where I am and let my handsome boyfriend "fix" things around me. Then I say, "I have to go change too."

"I brought my momma's deviled eggs," he says. "Should I put them in the fridge?"

"Yes," Tahlia says. "We're about a half-hour out still." She takes the tray from Aaron, and I give him one look that speaks volumes, and he ducks upstairs with me.

My heart hammers out of control, and tears prick my eyes. I duck into my room and leave the door open for Aaron. He follows, but stays over by the door while I pace to the window. "Is this not a good night for the party?" he asks. "I thought you'd had a good day at the shop."

I turn to face him, not sure how to hide what I'm

feeling but also not ready to say it out loud. "I did," I say. "Did you see my arrangement out there?"

He comes toward me, his gaze singularly on me. "I sure did." He takes me into his arms. "It was half tools and half blooms."

"I'm trying to decide what to name it."

"What are your ideas?"

"Uh, let's see." I had a whole bunch in my head, but they've all flown out with that vision of Aaron standing in the doorway, that dark green shirt with his name plastered on the front of it. "Wrenches and Roses. Hammers and Hibiscus. Petal Power Tools."

"I think you know what I'll choose."

"Wrenches and Roses," I say. "Because it sounds like one of your eighties bands."

He grins down at me, his smile staying for a few moments before it fades. "Something besides that cider spill happened in the kitchen."

"We should've waited to have this party until after our presentation," I say. "I'm so nervous about that." I have to close the flower shop for a couple of hours tomorrow while we do our presentation for the Community Council and other government leaders. Then, our rendition and designer notes will be erected, and the park on Sweetbriar and Salty Dog will be open to anyone who cares enough to come walk through it.

Voting will be done online, with a QR code on every sign at every plot.

"You are *so* good with people, Em. It's going to be great."

"Should I bring Wrenches and Roses?"

"Of course." He grins down at me. "You're the only person Fonda has ever spoken to with respect." He leans down and touches his mouth to mine. "You're exceptional, and this is a party with all of our friends. I'm not even anxious, so it's weird that you are."

Below us, the doorbell chimes, and I take a deep breath. "You're right. This is popcorn and brownies and all of our friends."

"And sparkling cider," he says. "And my momma's deviled eggs."

My heart finds a little bit of courage, and I smile at him. "I want the whole tray of those."

"Let's go snack it up." He falls back a step and takes my hand. He squeezes and says, "I'll wait for you to change outside."

I quickly strip out of my jeans and step into a pair of puddle sweats that make me seem partly dressed up but sort of dressed down too.

Outside in the hall, Aaron takes my hand again before leading me downstairs, where Elliott and Beckett have both arrived. Luna, Elliott's dog, stays right at his side, even with new people in the room and plates of food coming into the living room.

Aaron separates himself from me to say hello to Beckett, who pulls him in to a half-man-hug. Claudia approaches them, and says, "You should wear this green color all the time, Aaron." She give him a quick hug. "It's by far your hottest color."

"What color is it, sweetheart?" Beckett asks, pulling Claudia to his side.

"Hmm." She gives Aaron another up-down-up look as I join them. She smiles at me, and she's changed into a pair of skinny jeans in black, making her that sophisticated cat she is. "Evergreen Fog, I think."

Aaron chuckles and shakes his head. Everyone's here except for Liam and Hillary, and Tahlia says, "Let's get food, because Liam's late on a build, and he and Hill are going to be another little bit."

"I'll get my eggs," Aaron says, and he darts into the kitchen to do that.

"You okay?" Ry asks me, and I lean into her side-hug.

Lizzie flanks me on my other side and says almost under her breath, "I saw him go upstairs with you."

"Yeah, and we came right back down," I say in my defense.

"Why are you wearing this face that says you're expecting a bomb to drop?" Ry asks.

I take a breath and glance at those chatting in line, loading their plates with shrimp skewers and snacks and desserts. "I think I'm in love with Aaron, and I'm scared out of my mind."

"Deviled eggs," Aaron says as he goes right in front of the three of us. "I've got deviled eggs here."

Tahlia lifts a flute of sparkling cider. "To Emma and Aaron and their amazing park plot."

"Hear, hear," Claudia says, lifting her lemon bar. "And to these lemon bars, which are the best dessert Tahlia makes." She grins over to the mom of our group, and I'm filled with the same fondness I see on Lizzie's face, and Ry's, and Claudia's.

I so want Tahlia to have everything, and I know having all of her bestie's boyfriends here is amazing for her—and also difficult. She owns the Big House, and she gave all of us the perfect place to be.

The line continues, and I give Ry and Lizzie a *don't-you-say-a-word* glare and move away to get something to eat. Aaron's laughing at something Elliott said, and he says, "I'm just her carpenter. She's definitely my boss."

A knot lands in my chest. Am I bossy?

Of course you are.

I know I've been a little bossy with Aaron on the park project. As I pick up a paper plate and take a cup of popcorn, all I can think about is all the things I made him do. *Move the bench over there. Fix the stones so that corner isn't poking out over there. I want a picnic table to go by these lilac bushes.*

"You okay?" Aaron asks. "There's lots of eggs still."

"Yes." I jump into motion and tong a couple of deviled eggs onto my plate. They're slippery little things, and my third one slides right across my plate and over the lip of it. "Dang dahlias," I swear as Aaron's perfect egg splats on the table.

I want to throw my whole plate, scream, and escape upstairs. I straighten away from the table set up along the back of the couch, completely paused.

Aaron takes my plate and says, "I got you, honey." He takes the tongs from me, picks up the fallen egg and replaces it on my plate, and moves down the line to get me the exact desserts I'd have gotten for myself. I follow him over to a pair of kitchen chairs we've brought into the living room and set up in a circle.

We're sort of out of the way, and he waits until I sit before he hands me my food. Pure light and warmth comes from him as he settles beside me. I take a breath and try to center myself. "Thank you," I tell him.

"Anytime, Em." He leans closer; so close, the scent of his cologne lingers in my nose. "And after our presentation tomorrow, you'll tell me the real reason why you're so keyed up."

———

THE NEXT MORNING, Aaron and I stand side-by-side at our park plot, our mock-up gleaming in the sunlight, with the yards of flowers and bushes and plants behind us. "I just want to walk through it one last time," I say, and I step away from him while I still have a few minutes.

Aaron's handiwork with the cobblestones laid over the grass is impressive, with every one spaced exactly right. They lead through the flowers and grass—which has come back due to my unending energy in watering our plot—to the covered bench. As I arrive there, I sit on it for the first time.

And it's perfect. It slopes just right against my back and along my legs, and I can reach out and set my phone beside me on the reclaimed oak barrel. The scent of roses and honeysuckle tickle my nose, and I get up and wander along the path back to the picnic table. I've concealed the blemishes of the park with taller lilac bushes and bleeding hearts, and it's glorious and beautiful.

I run my fingertips along the top of the picnic table, which Aaron stained a nice dark honey, and then sealed. I can't wait to see it in his backyard.

Then I go around the back of the middle clump of plants and the bench, and complete my circle back to Aaron. He takes my hand again and says, "You barely made it," out of the corner of his mouth.

Jean Hygrove walks toward us with a clipboard, her sharp eyes taking in every detail, from my floral sundress to Aaron's hardware store shirt to seemingly everything in the plot behind us.

A small crowd comes with her, and everyone is watching, judging, critiquing. I know they said the plots would be open for public voting, but I have to believe these people have a heavy voice in who wins this money.

Aaron stands tall next to me, his broad shoulders squared, but I sense the tension in him. He's gripping my hand a little too tightly, and his jaw is clenched just a bit too hard.

He's supposed to start with a welcome, a greeting, something besides just stupefied silence. I pull my hand away, because surely not all the other plot partners are romantically involved.

When Aaron stays silent, I look up at him. He's got a great smile painted on his face, but he's nowhere near speaking.

"Welcome," I say, practically bellow-blurting the word out. I tell myself to calm down, and I slip into my customer service personality, the one I use when people walk through the front door of my flower shop. "Good morning. It's so great to see you. I'm Emma Newberry." I touch my hand to my heart. "I own Pretty in Petals, an amazing flower shop on Main Street. And this handsome guy is my neighbor on the street, as well as my partner in life and crime, Aaron Stansfield. He owns the hardware store and can build literally anything you want him to build."

Several of the council members are smiling now, praise all the stars in the sky. I grin at them and half-turn toward our plot. "Come walk with me, as I take you down a path of what this park could be." I gesture for them to follow me, and they do.

"So I've planted native plants and flowers and bushes here in our plot," I say. "If there'd been enough time for a tree to grow, I'd have done that, and whether I win or not, I can consult with the park development team for the types of trees and landscaping that would thrive here."

"How did you get all of this to grow?" Jean asks.

"I brought water in several times each day," I say as if it was as easy as breathing.

"While running your shop?"

"Yes, ma'am." We arrive at the bench. "This marvelous piece was constructed by Aaron, with a pitched roof so there's shade in both directions. The wood is all locally sourced from a plantation down the road in Goose Creek, and it's South Carolina cypress. The barrel is an upcycled white oak barrel from a whiskey distillery on the outskirts of town."

I survey the crowd. "Who wants to take a seat and tell us how comfortable it is?"

"What's this stained with?" someone asks as a couple of women move forward and sit on Aaron's bench in their skirt suits and heels.

I look over to Aaron, who's herded the group this way and stands at the back of it. I raise my eyebrows, and he says, "Oh, uh, it's a walnut color that brings out the natural highlights in the wood."

Hey, I got a sentence out of him. I wait for him to tell more about the bench, the pillars, something. He was supposed to do the pitch on the pieces he built. He says nothing and benignly tucks his hands in his front pockets.

Okay, then.

"Let's move along to our back garden." I step along the path as several people start talking in low voices. "Now, of course, we can't plant flowers and bushes in every part of this twenty-four-acre space. Our rendition is back here by the picnic table, also done by the masterful hands of Aaron, and we've envisioned pickle-ball courts, a pavilion full of multi-use picnic tables, with grills, facilities, and running water. We've created space for a sunken amphitheater with our artist."

I indicate the six-foot tall sign with our rendition on it. "As you can see, the land in the back corner has sunk a bit, and due to Aaron's amazing architectural mind, he claimed that corner for a place that people can rent for performances, weddings, and more."

I smile around to all of them, starting to feel like plastic that's been left out too long in the hot sun. "We truly envision this as a multi-use space, from impromptu soccer games, to family picnics, to sporty pickleball games, to big private parties, and even community shows."

I indicate our sign and then walk past it. "Any questions?" I ask as I circle back around to the front of the plot, stepping carefully so I don't twist an ankle off the side of the cobblestone.

A few people ask questions about the types of flowers I've planted, and some linger at the picnic table with Aaron. I see his mouth moving, thank goodness, and he comes to my side as the Community Council continues to the next plot.

I feel like Thank You Barbie until every last one of them is yards and yards away, and then I turn away from them and let my face fall.

"Whew," Aaron says. "I'm glad that's over."

I round on him. "*You're* glad that's over? You completely spaced on me, Aaron."

CHAPTER TWENTY-SIX

AARON

THE SUN IS TOO BRIGHT, CAUSING ME TO BLINK AND blink and blink. Emma's words don't help. No, not her words.

Her accusation.

"Say something!" She throws her hands up in the air and spins away from me with a semi-roar. "Freaking forget-me-nots!"

She stomps away, and nothing but pure guilt guts me. The morning started with so much hope—Emma's floral sundress, her confidence in leading the council through our vision, the way she effortlessly charmed everyone.

But she's right—I froze. I let her down. She had to step in and carry us both. Again.

I was supposed to talk about the bench and the picnic table. I was supposed to welcome everyone. I groan as I look up into the sky. "Why am I so bad with people?"

I stood there like a frozen lump of a man, and Emma had performed effortlessly. Just like she is now.

I kick myself into gear and go after her. "Emma, wait."

She turns back to me and plants her hands on her hips, clearly waiting for an explanation.

My mind was a jumbled mess—it still is—with too many thoughts colliding at once. I couldn't grab hold of a single one, and I still can't. The council's eyes felt like lasers, and my brain just stopped.

But I can't tell Emma that. Not right now. Not when she's looking at me like I've personally sabotaged everything she's worked for.

"I'm sorry," I manage, my voice low. "I didn't mean to—"

"You didn't mean to?" she cuts me off, her tone rising. "Aaron, this isn't just about *you*. This project is my business, my reputation, as well. We were a partnership."

Her words hit me like a hammer, each one driving deeper into my chest. I take a step back, trying to put some distance between us. "You think I don't care about this project? About you?"

"I don't know what to think." She turns around and starts for the parking lot again. "I have to get back to the shop. Some of us don't have dozens of employees to keep our shops running when we have something like this."

"I said I was sorry, and I told you to do the whole presentation anyway." I catch her and match my stride to hers. Wow, when she's angry, she can *move*. "You're the one who can speak so effortlessly."

"I wanted you to talk about your pieces," she says. "I don't know anything about them."

"You handled it fine." I suck at the air. "It went fine."

"If you say *fine* one more time..." She glares at me, and I give it right back to her.

My frustration feels like it's at a boiling point. "It was more than fine. It went perfectly. The pieces, the flowers, the speech, all of it."

"No thanks to you."

I stop completely. "No thanks to me?"

She keeps on walking, and I let her go. She throws me one final death glare as she gets in her car and leaves the parking area, but her words have rooted me to the spot. "No thanks to me."

I only built the two pieces in our plot. I laid all of the cobblestone—with all materials donated from my hardware store. I spent hours with the proposal while she prepped boutonnieres and bouquets for her friends' weddings.

I met with the artist doing our rendition, and the amphitheater was *my* idea. I may not have been very vocal during the presentation, but I deserve a lot of thanks.

"She doesn't trust me." The words tumble out before I can truly think about them. But I know they're true. And to be completely fair, I went mute on her when I should've had a perfectly prepared speech ready for the Community Council.

She doesn't trust me and she has to have things her way. Every step of this project, she's second-guessed me, bossed me around, nitpicked the color of the stain, all of it, as if I've never stained a piece of furniture before.

I stomp over to my truck and slam the door behind me. She's unleashed the Doberman, and there's no way I can go back to the hardware store without massive repercussions. I'll say or do something awful to the people I need on my side, so I can't go there.

I also don't want to go home, and I simply drive around town for a few minutes, then find myself pulling into the park behind the hardware store, and I walk over to the leaking gazebo where Emma and I took shelter in that spring rainstorm a few months ago.

The day after she kissed me. The day after we found out about the park renovation and contest.

The day I told her I wanted to be more than friends.

I step up and into the gazebo, the wooden floor creaking under my weight, and sit on one of the benches. The roof above me is warped and weathered, and I lean forward, resting my elbows on my knees, and let out a long, heavy sigh.

I look over to my hardware store, with the huge loading docks in the back. Right next door is Emma's shop, and her car sits in its usual spot. So she's there. My pulse skips a beat when I think of walking down the fence and to the back door of her shop.

I'm a handyman, and I've literally been hired to fix everything from a plumbing issue to a doorknob to adding a whole new level to someone's house.

But I'm not sure I can fix this break between Emma and I. "Last night," I muse, and I wonder what was really in her head. She claimed to be nervous about today's presentation, but I know there's something more there. I just don't know what, and I didn't want to push her to tell me in front of all of her friends.

"They're your friends too," I mutter to myself. If Emma and I break-up, I'll lose all of them—except maybe Liam. We were friends before, so I'll probably still be able to convince him to meet me at the sports bar to watch rodeo reruns.

I get to my feet, determined to find out what's really in Emma's head. Something happened last night, and I need to know what if we're going to keep moving forward. Every step toward Pretty in Petals screams, *Maybe Emma deserves better.*

And maybe she does. Maybe she deserves a man who doesn't get overwhelmed by a simple presentation.

Who can organize his thoughts. Someone who can give her everything she needs without making a fool of himself.

The thoughts settle in my chest like a stone, heavy and unmovable. Maybe I've been deluding myself, thinking that we can work, that I can somehow be The One for her, that we can make each other happy.

Maybe that's all just wishful thinking, and maybe the best thing I can do for her is to let her go.

I arrive at the back door of the flower shop, somewhere I've been at least a hundred times. I usually just go in, but today, I knock and ring the delivery buzzer.

She'll be annoyed at the interruption, especially after having to open late. I know that, but I'm unprepared for the storm that accompanies her when she finally opens the door. "Why didn't you just come in?" She turns and walks away, leaving the door open. "I'm busy, Aaron."

As if I'm not.

I follow her to the cusp of her walk-in refrigerator. "I wanted to say I'm sorry and have you hear it."

"I heard you," she says, throwing me a daggered look.

"I wanted to—I'm not sure we're meant to be."

She pauses with a bright orange daisy in her hand, her long eyelashes blinking fast.

"You don't trust me," I say. "You're just waiting for me to mess up the way Tucker did, so that you can be vindicated in your reasons for holding me at arm's length."

"I do not hold you at arm's length."

"You don't let me close," I say. "I just feel—I—no matter what I do, it's not going to be good enough for you. And that's fine. It is. You deserve the world, and a man who can give it to you, and I just don't think that's me. So."

She wears a flustered expression, her cheeks pink and her eyes wide, and for a brief moment, I consider turning around and walking away.

Her mouth opens, then closes, and for a moment, there's nothing but silence between us. The kind of silence that feels thick and heavy, pressing down on my chest like a weight I can't lift.

All I can think is, *Three months. I still can't keep a girlfriend for longer than three months.*

And I say, "So...I think we should take a minute and see how we feel. See if we really think this can work, because right now, I'm not convinced it can."

She doesn't contradict me. She doesn't say anything.

So I lift my hand in a lame wave and say, "I'll get out of your hair." And with that, I turn and walk away, somewhat stunned and completely heartbroken that the events of this morning have led me here, leaving my now-ex-girlfriend's flower shop.

CHAPTER TWENTY-SEVEN

EMMA

"All right," I tell Grams as I set my coffee cup in the sink at her house. "I'm headed back to the Big House after work tonight."

"Okay," she says in her weathered, gravelly voice.

She hasn't asked me why I've been coming to stay with her every weekend for the past couple of weeks, and I'm grateful for that. She did wonder if Aaron would come to dinner last night, and I told her he was busy. For all I know, he is.

I haven't spoken to him much since he showed up at the back door of the flower shop and told me I deserved someone better than him. I don't even know what that means because Aaron is a great guy. He's by far the best boyfriend I've had in years.

Every time I think about the park plot presentation, a string of guilt pulls my stomach tighter. Yes, I'd been frustrated with him. That didn't mean I wanted to break up with him.

I've been able to make it through evenings at the Big House because Claudia is super busy with her end-of-year tasks as the city planner, as well as her wedding. Ry and Hillary have moved out, so it's just Lizzie and Tahlia. Both of them know Aaron broke up with me— and that I don't want to talk much about it.

Every time I replay what happened at the park, I realize I was a little too angry, a little too irritated, and a little too frustrated. But I also realize I didn't call Aaron any names, I didn't accuse him of anything, and I have no idea what's going on in his frazzled mind that makes him think I don't want to be with him because of one little thing.

Then I think, if we can't make it through a little spat, how are we going to make it through life? Certainly, we'll get more curveballs and fastballs and wild pitches than him clamming up at a park presentation.

And then I spiral because I think, *of course you will, and look how you went off on him.*

I know I'm a little bossy. I know I like being in charge, and I know I like having a plan. Last time I checked, I couldn't be arrested for any of those things.

I sweep a kiss across Grams's cheek and head out the door. I have so much to do for Claudia's wedding this Friday. In fact, wedding season is in full force, and hers is not the only one I have on my calendar.

The flowers make me happy, even if the reason I'm creating the gorgeous bouquets and perfect boutonnieres is for a reason that makes me sad. *Sad isn't even the right word*, I tell myself as I get behind the wheel and start the quick drive over to the flower shop.

No, it's something much deeper than sadness. It's a yawning inside my soul, a yearning for something that other people seem to find, and I can't. I know Lizzie and Tahlia feel the same way, which is why it's okay to be there with them on weeknights.

But on the weekends, when Hillary and Liam come over, and Ry and Elliott stop by for Sunday breakfast before church, I just can't be around them. It's a little too fresh and a little too raw. I'm hoping whatever excuses Tahlia and Lizzie have made for me will last a few more weeks—just to get through the wedding and the announcement of the winner at the park.

I've walked through all the park plots—something Aaron and I were going to do together—and I think we have as great a shot at winning as anyone else. I've wanted to text him and tell him that so many times.

I want the two of us to be huddled over his desk, looking at the pictures he's taken on his phone of the other plots, trying to figure out if we'll win or not. I want to be able to text him with my two a.m. worries over whether what we did in the plot was enough and maybe theorize about some other things we could have done.

I want to hold his hand as we wander the Summer

Faire together, because I decided I didn't have time to sign up. He did, though, because he always does, and that's only made him even busier than he was before.

Thus, I've stayed quiet and away.

Now that I've had some time to gain clarity and do more thinking, I know none of that would really accomplish anything. The plot is what it is. But it's a seething need inside me to talk about it, and I'm sure Lizzie and Tahlia are sick of it.

Grams seems to have an unending well of patience for me to say the same things over and over to her, but I'm pretty sure if I try to stay at her house for another weekend, she'll demand answers. And I'll have to tell her that I ruined the best thing that's happened to me in a long time.

The problem is, I ruined it by being *me*, and I don't know how to not be me. I don't know how to be someone else. I don't even want to be someone else. I want someone to love me for who I am, even if I'm bossy, even if I get too upset over a presentation, and even if I'm highly irritable. It's not like I'm like that all the time. I had a bad few minutes after a very good presentation.

I sigh as I key my way into the back of my shop, my crate digging into my chest and stomach as I use it to push open the door. Inside, I flip on the lights and greet Sir Chills-a-Lot. "Good morning, Sir Chills-a-Lot. I hope you're ready to be extra cold today because we've got a lot of work to do."

I have a lot of pickups for a Monday as well, because there's a funeral I flowered happening this morning and a rehearsal dinner for a wedding tomorrow with orders that need to be picked up this afternoon. I'll be in and out of the walk-in cooler all day, fulfilling orders, making arrangements, and taking care of customers.

It's exactly what I need after a slow Sabbath day of stewing over Aaron, sighing over Aaron, and trying to figure out how I can talk to Aaron.

I have no need to go next door to the hardware store, and he never has a need to come get flowers. He's only ever come to the shop when I've asked him to help me, but I can't see myself doing that now. He did it before because we were friends, and then because he was my boyfriend. Now, he's neither of those things.

My chest tightens, and the emotion moving through me can only be described as grief. I sniffle as I mourn the loss of him in my life, letting tears track down my face as I realize how big of a hole he's left behind.

I work all day, making beautiful masterpieces, Aaron never far from my thoughts. I'm going to have to break the silence between us at some point. I simply don't know how yet.

Later that night, after all of Monday's promised arrangements have been picked up and delivered, my shelves are stocked for Tuesday, my orders are filed into their correct color folders, and my crate is sitting on the shelf in the kitchen at the Big House, I pull a box of pancakes out of the freezer. My plan is to hide in my room with something playing on my tablet and plenty of blueberry pancakes with lots of butter.

Before I can escape upstairs, Tahlia gestures to me from across the living room. "Can I talk to you for a second?"

I look up the stairs, then set down the box of pancakes on the bottom step and go to see what she needs. She has the master suite on this side of the house, the only bedroom on the main floor. There's a half bath off the kitchen, a full bath at the back of the living room, and Tahlia has a full bath in her suite as well.

Her room smells like tangerines and flowers, the scent of her favorite perfume that she special-orders from the Dominican Republic after she visited there once and bought it. I shouldn't be surprised to see her bed neatly made, the lamp on in the corner of her reading nook where she has a double-wide recliner, an ottoman, and a bookshelf stuffed with pretty pastel novels. I'm not.

But I am surprised to see Lizzie chilling on the bed. She puts her phone down and looks at me as I enter the bedroom and freeze. I know immediately what's happening. Somehow, Tahlia moves me out of the way and closes the bedroom door.

"I don't need an intervention," I say.

"Yes, you do," Lizzie says back.

Tahlia nudges me, and as Lizzie scoots over, I climb

onto the foot of it and crawl up to the pillows. I lay down in the middle with a sigh, and Lizzie curls into me from behind while Tahlia lays on her other, normal side. She looks at me with soulful eyes.

"You've told us almost nothing," Tahlia says. "And you're not even sleeping here on the weekends. My heart hurts, and I just want to help you."

She reaches out and tucks a lock of my messy ponytail behind my ear.

"I know," I say. "It just hurts." I close my eyes, and I can feel Tahlia and Lizzie exchanging a glance over my shoulder.

"You've fallen in love with him," Lizzie says. "Maybe it'll hurt less if you just admit it. Tell us what happened and let us help you."

"It's not going to help," I whisper.

"Sure it will," she says back. "I'm a really great brainstormer, and I'm sure we can come up with something you can do to get him back."

She puts her arm around my waist, and I clasp my hand with hers.

I still don't say I'm in love with Aaron, though I probably am. I've never admitted that, not even to myself, but none of my other breakups have ever hurt this much. They hurt, don't get me wrong, but in a totally different way. They hurt my pride and made me feel stupid, like I couldn't see Tucker for who he was.

Like I couldn't tell that Chris had another girlfriend in another town.

I've been embarrassed that I wasted so much time on Ethan—time that I'll never get back. With each breakup, it's taken me longer to get back into the dating pool. And with Aaron, I don't even want to, because if I can't have him, "I don't want anyone else," I whisper out loud.

"We know you don't," Tahlia says. "You're in a bad way. You have to let us help you."

I'm definitely the weepiest roommate, and I let myself cry in the soft solace of Tahlia's bedroom.

"Maybe I'm in love with him," I say. "And maybe he messed up at the park presentation. He just stood there. We had everything rehearsed, and he just stood there. I had to do it all, and I was frustrated and irritated, even though it went really well."

"Yes," Lizzie says. "You said it went really well."

"It did go really well," I say. "But because of me. He just froze."

"Okay," Tahlia says. "That's happened to me before when I'm presenting in front of the faculty."

"There's just so much emotion tied up in the park project," I say. "My flower shop could really use that twenty-five thousand dollars, and I know Aaron doesn't need it at all. So then I feel guilty that I made him build this amazing bench and picnic table and do the whole project with me when he probably didn't even want to."

"Are you putting words in his mouth?" Lizzie asks.

"Yes," I admit quietly. Because he's never told me that he didn't want to do the park project. In fact, he's the one who did the proposal when I was too busy with Ry's wedding.

"So we fought at the park," I say. "And I hate that I let that monster out of myself. But you know, I have a right to be frustrated sometimes too. The fact is, you guys, he broke up with me because of *me*. He broke up with me because he doesn't like me that much—because I was irritable and angry, and I said mean things to him."

I wipe my eyes because I hate the hot feeling in my face when I cry. "I don't know how to say I'm sorry, because I made him feel bad about himself when he's the most wonderful, thoughtful, kind, hardworking man I've ever been out with. He's got some..."

I trail off because it's not my place to say the things Aaron struggles with. "He has some issues of his own that he's dealing with," I say. "And I compounded them. Basically, all the bad things he thinks about himself, I confirmed for him. And he doesn't want to be with me."

"Did he say that?" Tahlia asks softly but earnestly. "Did he say, 'Emma, I don't want to be with you'?"

I give myself a few moments to think about it, my tears drying up. "No," I say. "He said he wishes he could be the man that I deserve."

Lizzie and Tahlia let a few minutes pass, not brainstorming for how I can get Aaron back. The silence is both comforting and stifling.

"It's okay," I say finally. "I'll figure it out eventually. I've got to get through this wedding and one next week, and then the announcement for the park is the week after that. Maybe I can show up in his office with breakfast sandwiches for lunch, and he'll forgive me."

"I'm sure he's beating himself up the most," Tahlia says. "He doesn't need to forgive you. He thinks you need to forgive him."

"It was just a bad few moments," I say. "Everyone's allowed to have a bad few moments, aren't they?"

"Of course, sweetie," Lizzie says.

"Maybe you can just start by texting him something easy," Tahlia suggests.

"Like that you saw the Lindsey build and that he finished it," Lizzie adds.

I've been stalking Aaron on social media, and Lizzie caught me the other day looking at his feed. I even commented that he'd finished the Lindsey addition before I realized Aaron and I weren't together anymore.

"Maybe," I say, though I can't see myself just texting him out of nowhere. I take a deep breath and continue with, "The reason I stay at Grams' is because it's really hard for me here on the weekends when everyone comes over, and they're all happy-happy in love. I know you guys feel like that all the time, so I'm just a huge jerk that I can't handle it. But right now, it just hurts too much. At Grams', I don't have to deal with any of that."

"I think Lizzie is right," Tahlia says. "You should text

Aaron friendly things, like you did before when you were friends. Get through your weddings, get through the park announcement, and then you can decide what to do after that."

I nod and let my eyes drift closed again, because I'm so, so tired. The only time I'm not thinking about Aaron is when I'm asleep. And mercifully, Lizzie and Tahlia let me drift off right there in Tahlia's bed. My dreams, however, are not as kind.

I wake up with the stark realization that Aaron and I have been paired to walk down the aisle together at Claudia's wedding. And I haven't told her yet that we're not together anymore.

CHAPTER TWENTY-EIGHT

BECKETT

"I don't know about this." I brush my hands down the front of my suit shorts as I look at myself in the full-length mirror. Yep, you read that right.

My wedding day tuxedo came with shorts.

First, I want to point out that Claudia chose to get married the second week of July in South Carolina. It's hotter than Hades right now, with a humidity index near one hundred.

Two, I've always been on the cutting edge of fashion, and apparently, these tuxedo short sets are all the rage. Mine happens to be the color of charcoal, and I like the dark gray. It's got a vest and a jacket, which is short-sleeved as well, and a bow tie. It looks like I'm dressed up, but I can't decide if it's for my wedding or a clown party.

My aunt comes to my side, and our eyes meet in the mirror. "So?"

"I think you look handsome," Aunt Jill says.

"But will Claudia?" I ask, because Claudia is the only thing that matters. I've never been married, but I'm smart enough to know that.

Liv arrives at my side, and my sister scans me from my shiny shoes back up to my face. "What's the holdup?" she asks. "You literally have five minutes before you have to be at the altar."

"I'm not sure this is the right thing to wear," I say.

"Not the right thing to wear?" Liv screeches. "Beckett, you've been engaged for ages. What you're wearing while your bride comes down the aisle should've been worked out *months* ago." Her level of frustration and disdain comes through loud and clear.

"Do you think she'll like it?" I ask, not sure why I'm so insecure all of a sudden.

"Becks." Liv grabs onto my shoulders and turns me toward her. "Claudia is in love with you, and she knows who you are. If she doesn't, then this is a problem way bigger than you wearing a pair of shorts for your wedding." She says all of this in a saccharine-sweet, honey voice, which means I'd better get my butt down the aisle to the altar.

"You're right," I say.

"Of course I'm right." She smiles at me. "Now, it's time to get married."

I turn toward the door where the wedding planner is waiting. "What do I need to do?" I ask as I walk toward her.

She straightens my bow tie and makes sure the snowy white flower is magnetized perfectly in place, which, of course, it is. "We need you at the altar."

"Yes, ma'am," I say, heading down the hall made of tent flaps and toward the exit that leads to the outdoor wedding Claudia has been planning for months. We both used to work for the city of Cider Cove, and we did a lot of work in the parks department. In fact, I cleaned up this park as one of my major projects, and Claudia and I ran into each other while walking our dogs here. That set our romantic spark to ultra-hot and started our relationship.

The park is free, and anyone can use it at any time, even if there are tents and chairs set up for a wedding. Everyone's left this area clear, though, and holy cow, a five p.m. wedding in the middle of July should be a criminal act. The heat's been trapped all day in the ground, and it radiates into the air as I step onto the grass.

I make it to the aisle under the second tent with my sister and aunt, and we pause for a moment. Guests mill about, most of them in their seats, but some standing and chatting. I don't care at all because this is not my show.

I walk down the aisle with my family and take my position at the altar. I hug my aunt and let Liv cry over me for a few seconds before she kisses her kids and grabs her husband's hand. They have to go join the wedding party now that I've been parked at the altar.

So I face the tent again, where the aisle is marked with clear glass pillars at the end of every row, with a puff of flowers on top, and vines and petals spilling over the sides. Lights and flowers hang in the rafters of the tent as well, where a speaker system has also been threaded. Right now, fancy-frilly elevator music plays as everyone anticipates Claudia's arrival.

I've asked to see her wedding dress a thousand times, and she's denied me over and over. I brush my hands down the front of my tuxedo again, this time to make sure my palms aren't too sweaty for when Claudia arrives.

Liam and Hillary begin their trek down the aisle, their faces shining with happiness and love. Hillary's deep red dress also screams Claudia, and I'm not surprised by the color choice or the satiny gown.

Liam's wearing a matching tie, with a white rose on his lapel. He grabs me in a hug, laughing as he slaps me on the back. "You made it here," he says.

"I sure did," I say, though I wish Claudia stood at my side.

Ryanne and Elliott come next, with Luna carrying a basket on her back with tons of red rose petals spilling out with every step she takes. I grin at the trio of them, give hugs all around, and face the aisle again.

Emma and Aaron come next, and while they look

like a million bucks in their matching clothes as the other couples, there's some serious—*serious*—tension between them. Emma smiles at me and hugs me, and Aaron leans in and taps his shoulder to mine before they separate.

My sister and her husband come next, and I grin and grin at them. Matt is my best man, and I laugh as he embraces me and his wife at the same time. Then they go to sit by their kids, and Aunt Jill leads Lizzie and Tahlia down the aisle, both of my dogs with her.

Duke and Rocky both wear tuxedos, and I crouch down to hug them when they arrive, panting so hard, it's hard to hear the music. I straighten and hold my aunt, because she's my lifeline in so many ways.

But I'm not going to cry. Not before I see my almost-wife.

Everyone moves to their places, and the whole crowd faces the top of the aisle, waiting. I feel like I've been standing there for half a year before the music twinkles into silence. The crowd murmurs as if they've sighted a celebrity. I swallow, my throat dry.

Though I've been waiting for this day for many long months, my nerves rattle. Claudia will move out of the Big House and in with me once we get back from our honeymoon. Then we'll both have a commute to our jobs —hers about the same, just on different roads. I'm so excited to have her in my life, in my house, and in my bed.

I don't see her, though, and I have the best view

straight down the aisle. My feet shift. I clear my throat as if I'll make an announcement that there won't be a wedding today. A gasp comes up from the guests in the back row. I see movement there, and while Claudia isn't short, she's also not tall. I can't see her past the standing rows of people.

Her brother appears at the end of the aisle first, smiling with pure love toward someone walking along the left-hand side of the congregation. Then Claudia appears.

Her gown is unlike anything I've ever seen before in my life. One look at it, and pure laughter flows from my throat. Joy explodes through me, and I know she won't be mad about my tuxedo shorts.

Because her dress is black.

She'd probably call it Bohemian Black or Black Magic.

I think the color of it should be Black Beauty, because she's simply stunning.

Every thread and every piece of fabric fits precisely to her body, her curves.

The dress has no sleeves and a scalloped bust line that gives way to what looks like feathers. If I could see them in full sunlight, I'm confident they'd shimmer with rainbow colors like gasoline. As it is, the fairy lights in the tent make the dress flicker in different colors—pink, yellow, green.

I can't erase my smile as she links her arm through her brother's and starts toward me.

She's carrying an all-white bouquet with billowy flowers and plenty of greenery. The monochromatic color scheme simply suits her. She's my favorite person on Earth, and I'm so glad I get to spend the rest of my life loving her.

She reaches me, her smile somewhat subdued. She sweeps a kiss along her brother's cheek and then looks at me fully. "What do you think?"

"I think you're the most gorgeous woman in the world," I tell her. "With the most beautiful wedding dress I've ever seen."

She ducks her head and smiles, and then we turn toward Winslow Harvey. He used to be our boss, and he retired at the end of last year. Claudia got his job, and I moved to the planning and zoning committee in Beaufort. Apparently, Winslow has the power to marry people.

He grins at us like he raised us from birth and says, "If there's a more gorgeous couple anywhere, I'll eat my hat."

We laugh, and I tuck Claudia closer to me simply because I can.

CHAPTER TWENTY-NINE

LIZZIE

I'VE NEVER SEEN CLAUDIA LOOK BETTER, AND I WISH I had the guts to wear a black wedding dress. Heck, I wish I had the guts to take Matt's hand in mine and ask him if he'll dance with me. I did ask him to be my date for the wedding, and he agreed. He even came to the Big House and picked me up.

I staged it so that I would be the only one home, which wasn't that hard because Ry and Hillary don't live there anymore, and Emma has been flitting around with the flowers since this morning.

Claudia, of course, has been here for hours, and Tahlia came to help her get ready since neither of her parents came for the wedding.

I took a half day off work and went home to do my hair and makeup and shimmy into this beautiful red dress that Claudia bought for each of us. Matt stopped by on his way home from work. I know because his white shirt and tie are the same ones I saw this morning when I double-checked with him to make sure he was still good to come with me tonight.

I don't know how much longer I can sit at this table with this Etch-a-Sketch smile on my face, like everything is okay. The problem is, dessert has barely been served, and then there's going to be a whole cake cutting and then dancing, and then who-knows-what-else Claudia has planned.

Oh, wait, I do, because she's gone over every detail with those of us still living in the Big House at least a dozen times.

I try not to have bitter feelings, and I really don't. I'm super thrilled for Claudia and Beckett because, while they didn't get along for the first few years of their relationship, they really are made for each other.

Maybe I get along too well with Matt. No matter what, if this red dress—with all of its lace, its form-fitting curves, and the bit of cleavage peeking out—doesn't alert him to the fact that I'm a single woman, nothing will.

"Are you done?" I ask him and stand up as if I'm about to bus the table. I reach for my plate, pure foolishness moving through me.

He looks up at me, surprise etched on his features. "I mean—"

I put my plate back down, and it still holds half of

my slice of strawberry cheesecake. "I need some air," I say, turning away from the table of my friends, where Emma's eyes have locked nervously on me.

"I'll come," she chirps and gets to her feet too.

I simply walk away from the table, adding an extra sway to my hips as if Matt will be watching me. Of course, he won't be. He barely seems to know I'm alive. Familiar frustration froths through me, and I might have to do something drastic, like spell out for him that I want him to ask me out on a date.

Maybe I just need to ask him if he's straight or not. Or I could ask if he's been hurt in the past and simply doesn't want to date right now. Something would be better than not knowing and torturing myself with the unknown day and night.

I expect Emma to catch me quickly, but she doesn't. Another warm body comes up beside mine, and it's decidedly not female because of the clean, crisp, pine-scented cologne.

Matt.

"Hey," Matt says almost breathlessly, like we've just run into each other at the grocery store and he's in a hurry to checkout and get home.

"Hey," I say back, because what else am I supposed to say?

"There's going to be dancing later," he says. "At least according to Liam."

"Yep," I say. "There is dancing later."

I push out of the Grand Hall, where Beckett and Claudia are having their wedding luncheon. Thankfully, Claudia only wanted to get married in the park, and that ceremony only took about twenty minutes, so we didn't have to sweat to death or have makeup running down our faces. In the last hour, we've eaten, toasted, and celebrated the amazingness of their love.

"I kind of have two left feet," Matt says. "But would you dance with me anyway?"

I look over to him. "You want to dance with me?"

"Well, we came to the wedding together," he says.

I stop and fold my arms, cocking out my hip in what my brother calls my Danger Pose. "Well, I don't want to do it, if the only reason you're asking is because we came to the wedding together," I bite out.

Matt pauses too, staring at me like I've morphed into a giant, human-sized ogre. When he doesn't say anything, I sigh and turn away from him, pushing myself to go faster in my heels. But there's no way I can outstep a man like Matt. He was probably born in shoes like that, and he has the body of a runner. Now, whether he runs or not, I don't know, as we've never gone out on a date so I could ask him personal questions.

Even my thoughts are sharp and demanding, and I remind myself of the mess Emma has found herself in for letting her tongue become too pointed.

Matt falls in step with me again, and I don't know

where I'm going. I just know I needed to get away from the table with Hillary and Liam, Ryanne and Elliott, then me, Emma, Tahlia, and Matt.

"Listen," I say as I approach the front door of the hall, realizing I'm going to have to turn around and go back the way I came, because I certainly don't want to go outside. "Do you not date?"

"Do I not date?" he asks, clear confusion in his voice.

"Yeah," I say. "I've been throwing myself at you ever since I got the promotion, and you barely act like you know my name."

"I know your name," he says, plenty of defense in his voice. "I didn't hesitate to come to this wedding with you, did I?"

"No," I say. "But only after I fell all over myself to make sure you knew it was just a friend thing."

I reach the door and put my hand on the bar like I'll push it open and go outside. I don't dare look at Matt, even though he comes to stand right beside me, and I can sort of see our reflections in the glass. He's looking at me, and I'm pretending not to look at him.

"Do you know anyone who dates at ChemTech?" he asks.

That gets me to look at him. I search his face for the answer—and I find it. "No."

"That's because ChemTech has one of the most rigorous employee dating policies in the world," he says.

"In the world?"

"It's *very* rigorous," he says. "In fact, because I came to this wedding with you, I had to get a *packet* from HR."

"A packet?"

He nods. "I didn't fill it out," he says, turning his attention back out the window. "I'll probably get a reprimand or something, or I'll just have to lie and tell them I didn't come."

"Just to come to a wedding with a friend?" I ask.

"Yep," he says. "And dating for real, Lizzie?" He shakes his head. "It's a whole three-ring circus."

He reaches out and takes my hand off the bar, threading his fingers through mine. "You're not gonna actually go outside, are you?"

"No," I murmur as fireworks and pops zing through my body from where his skin touches mine.

He works in an office, and his hands feel like they're made from vanilla-honeyed cream cheese—soft, silky, and smooth. I look down at my hand just to make sure that it's really being held by his, and my eyes confirm it.

"If there's anyone I would go through the red tape of paperwork for," he says quietly. "It would be you, Elizabeth."

"Lizzie," someone calls, and I turn away from the door. Matt drops my hand like it's been covered in fire ants, and he steps away from me at the same time. Emma looks at him, then at me, gesturing for me to come with her. "They're doing the cake, and you won't want to miss it."

She's right. I don't want to miss that, so I hurry to follow her, Matt at my side. I don't know what to say to him on the way back, so I simply stay quiet.

Inside the Grand Hall, Claudia has changed from her black wedding dress into a little black party dress that is somehow ten times as fantastic as her gown. She and Beckett are already standing next to the five-tier wedding cake at the back of the room, right where I've entered with Emma and Matt.

It feels like every eye zeroes in on me, like they all know Matt touched me. Heat fills my face as I try to duck out of the way, but my foot catches on something.

This can't be happening, I think as I fall to one knee, my heel dragging the microphone cord with it. Thankfully, Beckett and Claudia haven't picked up the mic yet, but the stand still teeters, sways, and falls. I watch it even as Matt comes to my side.

"Are you okay?" he asks.

The microphone hits the ground with an ear-splitting electrical screech that causes the whole crowd to cry out and groan as the awful reverberations slice through the air.

I've only gone to one knee, and I put my hand in Matt's as I stand. "I'm fine," I huff. I kick off my shoe, which is still tangled in the microphone cord, as Beckett steps over and picks up the mic.

"Whoopsie," he says into it, which is such a Beckett thing to say. He looks over at me, and that only draws more attention to where Matt and I stand close together.

"Now that everyone's here," Beckett says, which only shoots another round of humiliation through my bloodstream. "We'll cut the cake, and anyone who wants second dessert can come get some." He grins out at everyone who's come to their wedding dinner. "It's double chocolate, which is Claudia's favorite."

She's already holding the slicing spatula, and Beckett puts his hand over the top of hers. Together, they cut down through the bottom tier of cake to raucous applause. I put my hands together for them too, a smile on my face despite everything that's gone on in the past ten minutes.

"Do you want some cake?" Matt asks.

I nod, just because I need a breath that isn't filled with the essence of Matt. He nods and smiles, then dashes away from me in the same golden retriever style he's always had.

Emma takes his spot and asks, "What is going on with you two?"

"Nothing," I say, watching him until he moves into the crowd, and I can't see him anymore.

"I saw you holding his hand," Emma says.

"Yes, well, apparently ChemTech has a massive amount of paperwork we have to do if we date other employees."

"So he likes you," Emma says.

"I don't know," I say, though I do. The skin on my palm and between all of my fingers sizzles, telling me a different story, but I ignore it.

What if I'm not worth a mountain of paperwork? What if Matt takes me out a couple of times, realizes that, and everything at work gets awkward between us? Maybe dating a coworker would be a fiasco.

I link my arm through Emma's and say, "Well, you made it down the aisle with Aaron. How was it?"

"Just fine," she says. "He's already left."

If they'd still been dating, I feel certain Aaron would've been at the table with us. But since he wasn't, and a group of eight made the table full, he'd been seated somewhere else for dinner. I don't even know if he stayed for that, and I don't want to hurt Emma further by asking, so I simply say, "I'm sorry, sweetie."

She swipes at her eyes and says, "It's fine. I should have talked to him before today."

I don't have any other advice for her, and I can't make her send Aaron a text about anything. I can't make her go next door to the hardware store and tell him she loves him. I can't make her apologize, and I can't make him change either.

If there's anything I've learned in the past five years —from my job experience, dealing with my parents, and my disasters with men—it's that I can't change other people. I can only work on myself.

And as I catch sight of Matt again, joining the line to get double chocolate cake for both of us, I realize I'm at an even greater loss as to what to do about him now than I was before.

Because I was wrong: Knowing something is definitely not better than knowing nothing.

CHAPTER THIRTY

AARON

"Come sit down, my boy," Momma says, and I want to tell her that I'm thirty-four years old and not a boy. Instead, I drain the last of my milk, put the glass in the sink, and brush the cookie crumbs from my beard before I go sit down at the dining room table with her.

Yes, I've gone to my mother's after work for cookies and milk. It's not a crime, and it makes her happy. It makes me happy too, and I could definitely use a dose of joy in my life right now.

"Tell me why we haven't seen Emma again," Momma says.

"You know why, Momma," I say.

"You broke up with her," she says, not asking.

"Why do you think I broke up with her? She could have broken up with me."

Momma scoffs and adds a laugh to the end of it. "I highly doubt that, son."

"Why?" I ask. "Plenty of women have broken up with me."

"Yeah, but I saw the way she looked at you," Momma says. "There was something there between you two."

"Yeah." I sigh in one of those long, drawn-out ways that I've been doing lately. "There was, Momma. But in the end, I think I frustrate her too much."

"You?" she asks. "How is that even possible?"

I grin, because Momma's always made me feel so good about myself. "There are people who don't like me, Momma. You have to accept that fact."

"I will not," she says, with plenty of haughtiness in her tone. "You and Emma were so cute together."

"You have to be more than cute together to stay together," I say.

"You worked so well on that project together," she says.

"Yeah, well, until we didn't."

"What does that mean?" she asks. "Aaron, you tell me right now what happened."

I've been over it so many times in my head, I can recite it word for word. I give her the Cliff Notes version so that she won't have to know everything. Then I say, "I'm just not good enough for her, Momma."

"Oh, pish posh," Momma says, and she actually gets

up and stalks over to the kitchen sink. "You both—you and Thomas—have such a problem. I don't know where you got it from. You're a handsome man, Aaron, and any woman on this planet would be lucky to have you."

"Thanks, Momma," I say.

"You're successful." She starts washing dishes, something she does when she gets stressed and upset. "You own your own business—a thriving business, I might add. You don't hurt for money. You can fix anything."

"Okay, Momma," I say, because if she gets going, I'll never get her to stop.

"You deserve someone just as good as you are," she says. "And she's not better than you, son."

I get up and go over to the sink, covering my mom's sudsy hands with mine. "Okay, Momma," I say.

She stalls and looks at me. "I don't know why you don't believe it."

I take the glass from her and finish rinsing it. "I don't know why either, Momma. It's just how my brain works."

"Our brains can play tricks on us, you know."

"I know, Momma." This is not the first time my mother has told me this. "What do you mean about Thomas? He doesn't seem to have a self-esteem problem."

"No, but he's got some girlfriend issues right now too."

"Wait, wait, wait," I say, feeling even worse about

myself now for some reason. "Are you telling me Thomas is dating someone?"

Momma takes the glass back from me and starts rinsing it, even though I've already done it. "Where have you been the last few weeks?" she demands. "Yes, he started dating that woman who works down at the ice cream store."

Where have I been the past few weeks? Brooding and sighing and missing Emma. That's where I've been. "I haven't been to the ice cream store since I was ten, Momma. Who is it?"

"Her name is Claire," Momma says. "Or Clancy, or Kristen. I don't know, something that starts with that hard-C sound."

I still don't know who it is, and I'm actually shocked that Thomas has met someone at all. He's not exactly social, even with his own gender, and I've never known him to have a girlfriend in all thirty years of his life.

"Wow," I say, genuinely dumbstruck. "Good for him."

"It wouldn't kill you to give him a few pointers," Momma says. "I caught him trying to leave the house to go pick her up in his corgi sweats."

"Oh boy," I say with a chuckle. "I don't know, Momma. Thomas and I don't really talk about dating."

"Well, you *should*." She slaps the dishcloth against my chest. "And we need to figure out how you're going to march next door to the flower shop, tell Emma you're in love with her, and get her back into your life. Because I'm not dealing with this broody, middle-aged man anymore."

"Middle-aged man?" I demand. "Momma, I am *not* middle-aged."

"Well, you're no spring chicken." She marches away from me and back to the table, where she grabs a notebook from the center of it and starts scribbling something —surely ideas for how I'm going to win Emma back.

I look out the window above the sink, wondering what my options are. I can fake a text detailing an emergency at the store and rush out. I can be an adult and tell Momma I don't want to talk about this and go home, but I don't want to be at the store, and I certainly don't want to be home by myself.

Emma used to come over every night after work. I'd make us fun dinners, we'd put on movies, and she'd lay in my arms on the couch. Everything in the world was quiet and still and perfect. She hasn't been by in weeks now, and I feel like someone is turning me inside out one inch of skin at a time.

"Did you apologize for freezing at the park presentation?" Momma looks up, her eyebrows sky-high.

"Yes," I say. "Several times."

"So she was just mad for a few minutes," Momma says. "You Stansfield men, you're always blowing everything out of proportion."

I sigh as I sink down into the chair where I ate my

chocolate chip cookies and drank my milk. "If you knew this was a problem with my genes, Momma, why didn't you tell me?"

"I thought you knew," she says, her voice growing in intensity. "Your dad did the same thing when we were dating and for the first several years of marriage, I'll have you know." She stabs the pen toward me like it's my fault.

Maybe I did overreact. Maybe I let myself get too far in my head. Maybe my self-loathing took over too much.

With some distance from the situation and time without Emma, I know all of the above maybes are absolutely true. She had a bad few minutes, and so did I. And I hate that a half-hour of my life has caused so much misery for the past several weeks.

"I have to get her back," I say.

"Yes, you do," Momma says. "So how are you going to do that?"

I look up, hope streaming through me, but pure helplessness holding it at bay. "If I knew, Momma, I would have done it already."

"Well, you've got the park announcement coming up," she says matter-of-factly. "Maybe that would be a good time."

My mouth drops open. "In front of other people?"

"Yes, Mister Stansfield," she says. "Emma seems like she would enjoy that. She'd like to see you apologizing and begging for her hand back in front of a great many people." She scribbles something down on the pad quickly. "You can buy a bunch of flowers from her shop to do it."

She drops the pen like it's a mic, and she leans back in her chair, a self-satisfied smile on her face.

"That's it. That's all you need. A few minutes with that mic on that stage in front of everyone in town declaring your undying love for the girl next door, with all of her flower arrangements around her. It's perfect."

"Momma," I say, pure disbelief in my voice. "The park thing is five days away. I can't plan that in five days."

"Plan what?" Momma rips the paper off the pad and pushes it toward me. "I wrote down everything you need to say right there."

I pick up the paper, but I can't read any of the words. Momma's penmanship is not that great, and she writes in cursive with a slant that makes it hard to read. I don't have the attention span to do this right now, and I slap my palm down over the paper.

"I'm not just gonna get up in front of everything and read something that my mommy wrote."

"It'll be better than anything you can come up with," she says, and she marches away from the table again. "I don't care what you do, Aaron," she says from the kitchen sink. "But the moping has to stop. And the best way to do that is to get that lovely girl back into your life."

"She's not a girl, Momma," I say wearily. "Just like I'm not a boy."

I look down at the paper, my thoughts racing. How hard would it be to ask Jean for a few minutes before things begin? How hard would it be to send spies next door to Emma's shop to buy up the flower arrangements she's made? I have over two dozen employees at the hardware store, and even if Emma catches on that they all work there, they can simply say it's their mother's birthday or their grandparents' anniversary or their girl-friend's something.

How hard would it really be?

And a little voice in the back of my head starts screaming, growing louder and louder with every passing moment.

It won't be that hard, Aaron. Just get it done.

CHAPTER THIRTY-ONE

EMMA

I LEAN MY HEAD AGAINST THE COOL WINDOWPANE IN Grams's sunroom, the faint chirps of crickets serenading the warm South Carolina evening. The sun has already dipped below the horizon, leaving streaks of pink and orange to fade into the deep indigo of night. I've always loved this view, the way Grams's backyard stretches out with wildflowers and billowy willow trees, like a secret garden that refuses to be tamed. It's comforting, in a way, like her—a little chaotic, a little messy, but full of life.

I don't feel full of life right now. Hollowness stretches through me, like someone reached inside me and scooped out all the petals and greenery, leaving behind nothing but brittle stems and barren earth. I thought coming here to Grams's house would help me clear my head before the park project announcement, but all it's done is give me more time to think about Aaron.

About the way he said, "I can't fix us, Emma," and then walked away like I wasn't worth fighting for.

I still haven't texted him. He hasn't reached out to me either. We made it down the aisle at Claudia's wedding, and I've never held my head so high. Then he left in the middle of dinner, and I haven't seen or heard from him since.

I close my eyes and wish I could turn off my thoughts too. It's not fair to put all the blame on him. I know that. I'm the one who let my fears get in the way, who doubted him and pushed him away without even realizing it. But knowing that doesn't make it hurt any less.

"Emma, sweetheart, you're going to smudge the window with all that brooding."

Grams's voice cuts through the quiet, soft but firm, the way she's always been. I turn to find her standing in the doorway, her gray hair pulled back loosely, her floral apron dusted with flour. She's holding a plate of jammed toast, my absolute favorite thing in the world.

"I'm not brooding," I mumble, even though we both know I am. I move toward her and sink into the wicker chair beside the door as she sets the plate on the small table beside me.

"Mm-hmm," she says, settling into the chair beside me. Her sharp blue eyes—so much like mine—study me, and I know there's no escaping her interrogation. Grams has a way of seeing right through me, peeling back the layers I don't even want to admit are there.

And she brought me strawberry-jammy toast the day my mother moved to Michigan. So this is so not going to be a good conversation.

"You've been moping around this house for weeks now," she says, folding her hands in her lap. "And I know it's not just because you're worried about the park competition."

I pick up a slice of toast and take a big bite, avoiding her gaze. I have no excuses or explanations, and I can't even deny it.

"You haven't named a single flower arrangement since you got here," she says pointedly. "If that's not moping, I don't know what is."

I can't help the small smile that tugs at my lips. "I don't know if I can go to the announcement ceremony."

"Of course you can." She makes this *tsk*-ing sound that grates against my nerves. "And you'll talk to Aaron this time, and you'll see that it's always better to get things out into the open."

My stomach twists at the mention of Aaron. He's everywhere—in the way the sunlight dances just beyond the windows the way it did in his kitchen, in the way the wind rustles the trees like it did that day at the park when he went around and watered my flowers for me. He's in the scent of sawdust and the sound of off-key humming that still echoes in my mind.

Grams doesn't say anything for a moment, letting the silence stretch between us. Then she reaches over and takes my hand, her grip warm and steady. "Your parents broke, because they wouldn't talk to each other."

I pull in a breath, because we each have a different version of my parents in our heads, and Grams sees things so differently than I do. I was only fifteen when my mother moved, and my daddy had been gone for a few months before that.

"And they broke so much for you too," Grams continues. "I know that sometimes still haunts you, but baby, you can be better than them."

Her words knock the air out of me. I stare at her, my heart pounding in my chest. I can—and should—be better than my parents. I never, ever want to do to another human being what they did to me.

"I know you're in love with him," Grams says next.

"I think I am," I whisper, following her gaze. "But what if love is not enough? What if he leaves me, just like everyone else?"

After all, love didn't hold my parents here.

Grams squeezes my hand. "Oh, Emma. Love isn't about guarantees. It's about taking a chance, even when you're scared. *Especially* when you're scared."

Her words settle over me like a warm blanket, wrapping around the cold, empty parts of me. I've spent so much time trying to protect myself, to avoid getting hurt, that I never stopped to think about what I might be missing.

"I don't even know if he'll take me back." I hate that my voice trembles, but my whole life has been on shaky ground for the past month.

"There's only one way to find out," Grams says with a small smile. "But you can't let fear hold you back, sweetheart. You're stronger than that."

I nod, the weight in my chest loosening just a little. Maybe she's right. Maybe it's time to stop running from my feelings and face them head-on.

———

THE MORNING of the park competition announcement dawns bright and warm, the kind of day that feels like it was made for fresh starts. I dress in a simple sundress—soft blue with tiny white flowers—and pull my hair back into a loose braid. It's not fancy, but it feels like me, and that's enough.

"I have to be enough," I whisper to my reflection.

I meet Grams in the kitchen, and she is dressed in her Southern best—a cotton dress in red, orange, and yellow plaid. She loves autumn with her whole heart, and she's obviously broken out her fall collection early.

She's perched a hat with a bright orange flower along the brim on her head, and she's already got her purse looped over her forearm.

"Wow," I say, grinning from ear-to-ear. "Look at you."

"I might have my picture in the paper," she says, patting the back of her perfectly set hair.

I tip my head back and laugh. "Grams," I say between giggles. "People don't read the paper anymore."

"Oh, they do too." She frowns at me, but her eyes sparkle with energy. "I read the paper every morning."

"On your giant tablet." I pour coffee into my thermos, though it's a million degrees outside. I'll need some form of caffeine, and I leave a third for ice. With my iced coffee ready, I turn back to Grams. "So we have to go, don't we?"

"Yes, we do," she says matter-of-factly. "I wouldn't miss this for the world."

I help her down the stairs and into my car, and then the drive to Sweetbriar and Salty Dog only takes a few minutes. Grams's house is only a few minutes from literally everywhere in Cider Cove. My heartbeat hammers out of control, and a sip of iced coffee doesn't help much.

A crowd has already arrived, and I get out and look at them. The air buzzes with anticipation, and mine gets added to it as I see my fellow small business owners among all the people. We've all worked so hard for this, and even if I don't win, I still might be asked to help with the park.

The City Council has set up a stage right in the middle of the two rows of plots, decorated with balloons and banners that read "We love our small businesses in Cider Cove!"

All of the park renditions are displayed along the back of the chairs, and I reach for Grams as she comes to my side. "Even if I don't win," I say. "I'll be okay."

"Yes, you will," Grams says.

I like the sense of peace and contentment running through me as we slowly make our way up the slope to the flatter ground where the plots and stage are.

I scan the crowd, my heart skipping a beat and then two and then ten when I spot Aaron near the back. Holy hydrangeas, he's so good-looking. And he's more than a pretty man in a pretty picture. He's kind and funny and hard-working, and I am so in love with him.

He's wearing one of his tool-themed T-shirts, this one with a hammer and the words "Nailed It" across the chest. His dark hair is slightly messy, and his beard is neatly trimmed, but it's the look in his eyes that catches me off guard.

He looks tired. Sad. Like he's been carrying the same weight I have.

I turn away quickly, my pulse racing. I want to run to him, but my feet seem to have grown roots. Jean

Hygrove steps up to the microphone and taps it a few times, calling the crowd to attention.

I look around for Claudia and Tahlia and Hillary, all of whom should be here. Lizzie said she *might* be able to make it, and I didn't check my phone this morning to find out.

"Thank you all for coming today," Jean says, her voice clear and authoritative, just as Grams and I arrive at the chairs. "Can everyone find a seat? Do we need more chairs?" She shields her eyes and peers out into the crowd.

I make sure Grams is settled next to Tahlia, and she squeezes my hand. "Go stand by Aaron," she whispers.

I nod, and I take a moment to hug Claudia. "You don't know who won, do you?" I ask.

She shakes her head, her dark eyes glittering like dark diamonds. "But it has to be you and Aaron," she says. "Your plot is spectacular."

I've spent the month watering the flowers and bushes by hand so the plot would stay as beautiful as possible throughout the showing. I move to the end of the aisle and start toward the back, where the other small business owners are standing. I don't see Aaron among them, and my chest feels like a giant rubber band is getting tightened around my ribs.

"Before we begin, I'm going to turn the time over to Aaron Stansfield," Jean says.

I gasp as I spin around, and I haven't quite reached

the back of the rows of chairs yet. But I can't move as I watch Aaron trot up the steps, all smiles and Cheerios now. He takes the mic from Jean, and all I can think is *Why? Why is he up on the stage?*

"He's going to be our Small Business President this next year," Jean says with a flirty, fond smile on her face, though she's at least twenty years older than Aaron. "And he requested a few minutes today."

"Thank you, Jean," he says, his gaze locked on hers. She takes a step back, and Aaron turns his attention out to the crowd.

He's the Small Business Association president?

A pinch like I've never known fills my throat, because I should've known that. I would've thrown him a party and a big chocolate cake and been at his side.

I can't swallow, and when Aaron's eyes land on mine, I swear the sky starts to fall. He blurs behind my tears, and I become very aware that I'm standing in the middle aisle all alone.

His dark eyes search mine, and they refuse to let go. "I love you," he says into the mic, and my eyes widen. I have no idea what's going on inside his head, but I can guarantee that he didn't mean to lead with *that*.

"I miss you," he says next. "And I conned Jean into letting me have the mic, so I could tell you how sorry I am that I've been such a fool."

By the time he finishes that sentence, everyone has turned to stare at me. I want to move. Duck and hide.

Something. But my hands hang like lumps of clay at the ends of my arms, and I can barely breathe.

He clears his throat, and I blink back my tears. I want to see him right now, not a blurred version of him. "You told me once that love isn't about the big things, but the little things we do everyday. And you were right. My little moments all day long are bleak and black without you."

Aaron steps closer to the edge of the stage, never breaking eye contact. "But I have to do something big to get you back, so here I am. Because sometimes, love deserves to be shouted from the rooftops—or in this case, from a stage in front of our entire town."

As tears flood my eyes again, I blink them back rapidly, not wanting to miss a single expression on his face. His eyes shine with an intensity I've never seen before.

"You're the first person I want to share my victories with," Aaron continues. "And the only one I want around when life knocks me down. You're the only person I'd drop everything for, and you're my home, honeybee. My heart. My everything."

My breath catches in my throat. I want to run to him, but I'm stuck hanging on his every word.

He takes a deep breath, and I find myself holding mine. "I promise to love you in the big moments and the small ones. To cherish every second we have together. Because a lifetime with you still wouldn't be enough."

The world around us rushes back in, and I become acutely aware of every eye on me. But all I can see is Aaron, his heart laid bare before me and the entire town.

Someone comes to my side, and Lizzie links her arm through mine. "Well, that was pretty dang perfect, wasn't it?"

"Yes," I murmur without moving my mouth.

"Maybe you should get up there and put that man out of his misery."

I sob as I take off toward the stage. The crowd starts to whoop and clap, the loudest voice among them Hillary's. She probably got everyone going, but it all blurs as Aaron hands the mic back to Jean, jumps down from the stage, and catches me as I throw myself into his arms.

"I'm sorry," I say agains this chest. "I'm so sorry. I was just mad for like, two minutes."

He smoothes his hands over my hair and says, "I know. It's okay. We're okay."

We're not, but I know we can be.

"Okay," Jean says in a crisp voice, nowhere near the flirt-fest she'd used before. "We're all gathered here for something specific. The park renovation competition has been a wonderful opportunity to showcase the creativity and dedication of our community, from our local talent inside our Cider Cove small businesses. Every team has put in so much hard work, and we're thrilled to announce the winner today."

Aaron moves us to the side, and starts to lead me toward the back, where the other contestants wait. Tahlia's wiping her eyes as I go by, and Claudia lifts both fists into the air in a victory move.

Meanwhile, the crowd claps politely for Jean, the tension thick in the air. I glance at Grams, who gives me an encouraging nod, and then back at Aaron. He leads me to the back, where we stop and face the stage. Then he watches Jean, his jaw tight, his hands shoved into his pockets.

My heart goes back to being shoved into a tight box, where it struggles to beat properly.

"And the winner of the Cider Cove Park Competition is…" Jean pauses for dramatic effect, her smile widening. "Team EmRon!"

The crowd erupts into applause, and I freeze, the words barely registering. We won. We actually won. Beside me, Aaron yells like he's just won the Superbowl, and he turns into me, pure joy on his face. He lifts me right up off my feet while those around us laugh.

"We'd like to invite Emma Newberry, who owns Pretty in Petals, and Aaron Stansfield, who owns Stansfield Hardware, up to the stage." Jean claps politely, her eagle-eyes locked onto us.

The moment Aaron sets me on my feet, I take a big breath and start the journey back to the stage, my heart pounding.

We have to go in front of the crowd along the length

of the stage to get to the steps, and I go first, trying to ignore all the eyes on me. Behind me, Aaron gallops along, raising the roof. The small-town crowd responds too, their roar of congratulations filling the sky.

Which totally hasn't fallen.

CHAPTER THIRTY-TWO

AARON

MY HEART POUNDS AS I STAND OUTSIDE PRETTY IN Petals, a bag of takeout from Emma's favorite deli clutched in one hand. The events of the morning—my public declaration, our win as "Team EmRon"—still feel surreal. But this moment, right here, feels more important than any of that.

I take a deep breath, steeling myself before I knock on the back door. No answer. I try the buzzer next, hearing its cheerful *zzzz!* echo inside. Still nothing. Worry creeps in, but I push it aside. Her car's here; she has to be inside.

"Emma?" I call out, turning the doorknob. It's unlocked, so I step inside, the familiar scent of flowers enveloping me. "It's just me. I brought lunch."

I hear rustling from the front of the shop, then Emma's voice. "I'm up here! Come on in."

Relief washes over me as I make my way through the back room, past buckets of freshly cut flowers and the humming of Sir Chills-a-Lot. I find Emma at the front counter, misting a bouquet of sunflowers and daisies. She looks up as I approach, and my breath catches.

She's beautiful, her blue eyes bright, a few stray wisps of hair escaping her braid. There's a smudge of dirt on her cheek, and all I want to do is brush it away with my thumb before I kiss her, kiss her, kiss her.

I still haven't kissed her, and I'm dying a little more with every moment that goes by.

"Hey," I say, suddenly feeling shy despite everything that's happened today.

"Hey," she says back, a small smile playing at the corners of her mouth. "Is that from Sal's?"

I nod, holding up the bag. "Turkey club for you, pastrami on rye for me. And that sour cream potato salad you love."

Her smile widens. "You remembered."

"Of course I did." I set the bag on the counter, my eyes never leaving hers. "Can I kiss you now?"

A blush creeps up her cheeks, and she looks down at the flowers she's arranging. Then she sets down the mister, and I sweep her into my arms. She giggles, and as she fists her fingers in my collar, I lower my mouth to hers and kiss her.

Oh, yeah. I've missed this so much, and this connection between us is so much more than physical. She completes me in a way I didn't know wasn't whole.

I know now, and I know I need Emma in my life.

She pulls away. "Aaron, about what happened at the park—"

"Mm?" I love the shape of her next to me. I love the warmth from her body, and the way her perfume mingles with that of the lilies and roses and dahlias surrounding us. "You closed today. All day?"

"All day," she says. "I just wanted a day to myself."

I back up a little. "I can leave you to eat."

"Don't you dare." She gives me a mock glare and picks up the bag from Sal's. "Let's go eat on my consultation couch." She leads me to the back of the shop, where she locks the door there and then goes into a tiny room between her office and Sir Chills.

I've never been in this room, and I smile at it from the doorway. Emma's put a beautiful flower arrangement on a tiny table beside a single loveseat. Across from that, a credenza stands against the wall, where a binder rests. A mirror hangs above that, making the narrow room seem bigger.

She sighs as she settles onto the couch and opens the bag. "Pastrami on rye for you." She holds out the sandwich and looks up to me. "I couldn't say it at the park, but I'm in love with you too."

I take the two steps to the other half of the loveseat

and sit beside her. As I take the sandwich and unwrap it, her words move through me, then circle back and start to sink in.

"You're in love with me," I say.

"That's right." She beams at me. "I swear I was going to talk to you today. Maybe not from the stage, with a mic, as the Small Business Association president..." She cocks her eyebrow at me and sinks her teeth into her sandwich, clearly asking me how I came to be the SBA president. But that's another story for another day.

"I'm sorry," I blurt out, because I can't eat until the words come out. "I'm so sorry, Emma. I never should have walked away from you."

She blinks, surprise evident on her face. "You're not the one who needs to apologize."

"I acted too rashly," I say. "My mother says it's in the Stansfield genes, and I should've waited until I'd calmed down."

"I'm sorry too," she says sincerely. "I let my fears get the best of me. I pushed you away without even realizing it, and I was so mean that day in the park." Tears fill her eyes as she takes my hand in hers. "I'm sorry. I was just frustrated. I didn't want to end things with you."

"My mind runs a million miles a minute sometimes."

She nods, but she doesn't go on. She's quiet for a moment, her gaze dropping to our intertwined hands. "I was afraid of getting hurt," she admits. "Of loving you so much that it would destroy me if you left."

My heart clenches at her words. "Because of your parents?"

She looks up at me, her eyes shimmering with unshed tears. "I have a hard time trusting people, but I trust you, Aaron. I do."

I thread my fingers through hers. "I know you do."

"I love you too, Aaron, and it scares me a little bit."

I press a kiss to her forehead. "Being scared is okay," I say. "I'm terrified I'm going to let you down again. I'm not perfect, Emma. I'm going to mess up sometimes. But I promise you, I will always fight for us."

A tear slips down her cheek, and I brush it away with my thumb. "I promise too," she whispers. "No more running away. No more letting fear win."

I lean in, pressing my forehead against hers. "I missed you so much."

"I missed you too." Her breath brushes against my skin. "Every day. Every minute. Every second of every minute of every day." I pull back slightly, meeting her gaze. Then I close the distance between us, capturing her lips with mine. The kiss is soft at first, tentative, but it quickly deepens. I pour everything I feel for her into it —all the love, the longing, the promise of a future together.

When we finally break apart, we're both breathless. Emma's cheeks are flushed, her eyes bright, and I've never seen anything more beautiful.

"Wow," she says, a grin spreading across her face.

"Yeah," I agree, unable to stop smiling. "Wow."

She tugs on my hand, pulling me to my feet. "Come on," she says. "I want to show you something."

Curious, I follow her out of the consultation office and into the main part of the shop. She leads me to the front corner opposite of where I found her, where a small table is set up with various tools and flowers.

"What's all this?" I ask.

"Your next dare." Emma picks up a potted plant—a succulent—and hands it to me. "This is going to be your section of the shop. A male perspective for what male customers would like to get for anniversaries, birthdays, landmark dates, whatever."

"A male perspective?" I take the succulent and look at it. "Honey, I gotta be honest, I don't think *any* male ever thinks, Gee, I wish my girlfriend would get me a bouquet of succulents."

"One," she says with a measure of spice in her voice. "You never make a *bouquet* of succulents. They exist on their own." She takes the plant back from me and sets it on the table. "Two, if you don't want to accept the dare, fine."

I look at her. "You think I'm going to back away from a dare?"

Her eyes shine like sapphire stars, and she cocks her hip, clearly daring me to accept—or reject—her dare.

I pick up the screwdriver sitting on the table. "Where did you get this?"

"Aisle five," she says matter-of-factly.

"That did not come from my store," I say.

"Yes, it did."

I grin at her and sweep her back into my arms. "I accept your dare, Miss Newberry, but I have one for you too."

"Do tell, Mister Stansfield."

"I need you to come into my office and make it look like that consultation room."

A look of horror crosses her face, and I start laughing. "I mean, if you don't want to accept the dare..."

"How dare you?" She gives me a little shove, and I take an extra-large step backward, laughing again.

She joins me, the combined sound echoing through the shop. It feels good to laugh with her like this, to be silly and carefree and together.

As our laughter subsides, I take her hands in mine. "In all seriousness, though," I say. "I don't want any more misunderstandings between us. I want us to talk to each other, even when it's hard."

Emma nods, her expression turning serious. "Me too. I promise to be more open with you, to tell you when I'm feeling scared or insecure."

"And I promise to listen," I say. "To really hear you, not just try to fix everything."

She smiles, reaching up to touch my face. "That goes both ways, you know. I want to hear about your fears and doubts too."

I lean into her touch, closing my eyes for a moment. "Okay," I agree. "No more holding back."

When I open my eyes, Emma is looking at me with such love and tenderness that it takes my breath away. "So," she says. "What happens now?"

I grin, pulling her closer. "Well, I was thinking we could start by finishing our lunch. Then maybe we could take a walk through the park—our park now, I guess."

"I like the sound of that," she says. "*Our* park."

"And after that," I continue. "I thought maybe we could head over to my place. I've been looking at Sir Chills's user manual, and I think I can make him stop humming so aggressively."

Emma's eyes light up. Her eyes scan my face. "Sir Chills?"

"If we're going to be together long-term, I thought I better figure out how to get along with your fridge."

"You can start by not calling him a fridge." She gives me a fake glare, but I'm just so happy to be here with her.

"I'll make you dinner," I say, hoping that will entice her to come back to my house and fill it with life again.

"Grilled cheese and tomato soup?"

"Yes."

Emma grins, linking her arm through mine as we head back to her consultation couch. "Sounds perfect to me."

As we finish eating and start cleaning up, Emma looks at me with a mischievous glint in her eye. "So, Mr. Small Business Association President," she says. "When were you planning on telling me about that little development?"

Heat creeps up my neck. "Ah, yeah. About that..."

She laughs and leans into me. "I'm so proud of you, Aaron. You're going to be amazing at it."

I pull her close, marveling at how perfectly she fits against me. "Thank you," I say softly. "I can't do anything without you. You make me want to be better, to do more."

Emma looks up at me, her eyes shining. "That goes both ways. You inspire me every day."

I lean down, capturing her lips in a soft kiss. When we part, I rest my forehead against hers. "I love you, Emma Newberry."

"I love you too, Aaron Stansfield." She sighs. "Now, how about that walk in our park?"

I grin, stand up, and take her hand in mine. "Lead the way, honeybee."

———

Oh, boy, I think Aaron and his fake bad boy vibes - and the way he and Emma can trade jabs - is my new favorite thing! I hope you liked them too!

Read on for a couple of sneak peak chapters at the next book in the Cider Cove series - **A VERY FRIENDLY FIASCO** - and move into fall with Lizzie and Matt in Cider Cove as they try out a "friends-only" relationship...

Get new free stuff every month, access to live events, special members-only deals, and more when you join the Feel-Good Fiction newsletter. You'll get instant access to the Member's Only area on my new site, where all the goodies are located, so join by scanning the QR code below.

SNEAK PEEK! A VERY FRIENDLY FIASCO CHAPTER ONE: LIZZIE

I sink into the salon chair and meet Morgan's eyes. "I think a little darker."

She runs her fingers through my hair, eyeing it in that way she has. "Darker? Are you sure?" She looks up, and I see the lightning-idea in her eyes.

"What are *you* thinking?"

She flops my hair over the back of the chair, sweeping the sides off my face. "I think you'd be an amazing redhead. And we've got your blonde to the point where we can do it." Joy rides on her face, and there's nothing Morgan likes more than reaching for new hair colors.

"A redhead?" I finger the ends of my hair. "Not orange, though, right?"

"Nowhere near orange," Morgan says. "Let's do it." She claps her hands together. "Please?"

I grin at her, and since I need a fresh start in so many ways, I might as well begin with my hair. "Let's do it."

Morgan squeals, bounces on the balls of her feet, and says, "I'll go mix up your color. Need a water? Diet Coke?"

"Water's fine," I say, though I'll get a giant soda pop on the way to work this afternoon. I'll need it to go over forms I need to turn in by Friday. My job is a blight on my existence, and I'm considering a big change in the New Year.

Or I was, until I got promoted a few months ago. I'm still settling into a leadership role. I'm still learning the ropes in the Department Head hall, especially with Matthew Giles just down the hall.

Fine, he's right next door, and the man dominates my thoughts even when I'm not at work. Like right now.

His cologne sits in my nose, though ChemTech is about as far from the salon as I can get and still be in a suburb of Charleston.

A knotted ball of unhappiness sits in my gut, though I laugh and smile with Morgan, tell her all about Claudia's wedding, which has happened since I came in last time. She and Beckett have been married for about three months now, and fall has started to fall here in South Carolina.

What hasn't happened is anything between me and Matt, though he said if there was any woman he'd go through a packet of red-tape paperwork to date, it was me.

I'm so sick of men saying one thing and doing another.

A couple of hours later, Morgan has me sitting with my back to the mirror, and she's called over four of her co-workers at the salon. They all have their phones out, and Morgan grins at me. "Are you ready for the reveal?"

"So ready," I say in a deadpan.

She ignores my sarcasm, because she's so used to it. It does take a moment—or a day or a week—to get used to my style of humor. Morgan turns me around and her assistant fluffs out my hair, letting it fall over my shoulders.

There's nothing sarcastic about the gasp that cuts through my throat. "Morgan," I breathe. I reach up and touch my hair, just to make sure it's attached to my head. It is, and it's glorious.

"You're a queen," Morgan says. "With a crown of hair on fire."

My hair is red, but not the orangey-red I was worried about. This is a soft brownish-red with plenty of shine and ruby-ness to it. "I love this," I say. Who knew I was a redhead?

Morgan giggles and unsnaps the drape around my neck. "I'm so glad."

I stand and hug her, and she says, "Mm, I love you."

She beams at me when she steps back. "Thanks for trusting me with your hair."

"It's amazing," I say. "You're amazing."

I check out, make my next appointment, as keeping up this new hair color will require regular visits, and head out to my car. Things had lightened there for a couple of hours, but now I have to go to work.

I drive through a sandwich shop and get lunch—and my giant Diet Coke with cherry and vanilla—and head west toward ChemTech.

"Do you really think you can quit?" I ask myself as I leave the city behind. I like talking things out, and sometimes I just need to hear myself say something before it makes sense. I look left as a car passes me. "Why not?" I ask. "We have a ton of savings, so we wouldn't have to work for a few months, at least."

And then what? I ask myself as I glance right.

"Then, we find something that makes us happy, the way Em quit her job and bought the flower shop. She pursued something she's passionate about, and we could too."

And what are you passionate about, Elizabeth? That question flows through my mind in my daddy's voice. He always calls me Elizabeth and not Lizzie, and I pick up my phone and tap the microphone icon. "Call your daddy tonight and see if you can go to dinner this weekend."

My daddy is my hero, and because he lives an hour

away, I don't see him as often as I'd like. Or as often as I should. My momma died over a decade ago, and Daddy's found a way to live alone, something I still haven't mastered.

I reset my phone in my cupholder and get back to thinking about what I'm passionate about. I love fashion, but I don't want to design or sew my own clothes. I love the modeling I do, and perhaps I could do that on a more full-time basis if I wasn't at ChemTech.

I love animals, and one of my favorite things about going home to see my daddy is that I get to walk through his five acres with his dogs, cats, goats, chickens, and donkeys. Maybe I should buy some land out in the middle of nowhere and try my hand at homesteading.

But that would require me to be alone...and I'm not super good at that.

My thinking always circles like this, because the real problem is, I don't know what I'm passionate about and want to spend my whole life—years and years—doing. I was good at math and chemistry in high school, and it felt natural to continue on that path in college and life.

I'm the Regulatory Affairs Department Chair at a chemical company that does everything from research, to development, to sales, to manufacturing. I have a lot of responsibilities, but today, I need to get the paperwork done for a state-required regulation of toxic materials.

Sounds exciting, right?

Trust me, the only bright spot in my day is knowing

that Matt is working on something equally as boring next door. And the lunches we share on a near-daily basis.

Today, though I eat as I drive, and I pull in the employee parking lot and move to the closest row, where I now have a dedicated parking space. I sigh as I park and reach for my bag. I refuse to carry a brown or black briefcase bag, but I do have a bright teal bag for my folders and documents to travel back and forth in. It doesn't always match my outfit, but it's the cutest bag I've found that still looks professional.

I get out with my bag and find my balance before I duck back down inside to get my soda cup. From there, I click in my heels down the sidewalk to the entrance of ChemTech. I press my badge to the elevator scanner, and I ride up to the fifth floor, where all the Department Chair offices are.

It's past lunch, and I work with all men. Routined men, so they'll be out of the lounge and onto their afternoon meetings and tasks. Thankfully. Because I can guarantee that the first man I see will ask me where I was this morning. Then he'll look at me like he knows there's something different about me, but he can't figure out what.

I brush my amazing hair over my shoulder as I step onto the fifth floor and turn toward my office. As predicted, things are calm and quiet, with literally a printer hum hanging in the air. So normal. Mundane. Sleep-inducing.

Someone's on the phone in one office, with another Department Head clacking away on his keyboard in another. I steadfastly refuse to take a peek in Matt's office as I mince my way by, and I turn into my space right next door.

Blast Matt to the moon, because his cologne is stuck in the air in here, and I frown up at the ceiling for its lack of a fan.

"There you are."

I yelp and do the only thing that makes sense in that moment—I throw my forty-four-ounce soda pop in the direction of the voice.

Unfortunately, I do this before I realize Matt has parked himself in front of my desk. "Toledo," I say as the cup hits his calf and explodes all over the floor. At least it didn't do that at a higher elevation and get all over my desk and laptop.

"What was that?" Matt looks down at his pant leg, which is drenched in Diet Coke. He looks at me with plenty of teasing in his eyes, and oh, how I wish he wouldn't. He bursts out laughing in the next moment, and through his gasping wheezes, he says, "You threw... your Coke...at me."

At least he's laughing and not marching down to HR for a complaint form.

I enter my office fully, my pulse settling back to its normal beat. "Why are you loitering in my office?"

He sobers quickly as I put my teal bag on my swooping, curly, two-sided desk. "Loitering?" He presses one palm to his heart like he's going to start reciting the Pledge of Allegiance. "A man of my stature does not *loiter*, Lizzie."

I sit down, my chair squeaking in a way that says it doth protest to my size-sixteen flop into it. I ignore it and meet his gaze. *Mistake*, screeches through my soul, and I look away. "Well, you're here when you surely have something to do in your own office."

Matt clears his throat and says, "Your hair looks amazing."

That draws my eyes back to his. "Thank you," ghosts out of my mouth. *Biloxi*—a US city swear—streams through my mind. Matt has the most beautiful eyes in the world. They're hazel, so this unique color of brown mixed with green, and I swear every fleck is different than another.

He gets up and closes my door, which makes my pulse start to pound like a big, bass drum. I played the flute in the marching band growing up, and I dated a drummer. I know beats and rhythms, and this one currently throbbing through my chest is no bueno.

Matt turns to face me, pressing his hands behind his back as he leans into the solid door. I want to ask him what he's doing, but my voice has gone on vacation.

"I wanted to talk to you about something," he says. He doesn't seem to have a problem getting his vocal cords to work, but he sure doesn't come over and re-take his seat in front of me.

Okay, I say, but only in my mind. I manage to nod curtly one time, and Matt stands up fully and tucks his hands in his pockets.

"They're doing concerts in the park until Thanksgiving," he says. "I went to one last weekend by myself, and I can't do that again."

"Okay," comes out of my mouth, because I don't know where this is going.

"I was thinking of taking a friend." His eyebrows go up.

Every cell in my body rebels at his words. He knows I want to go out with him. I said it right out loud at Claudia's wedding. The man standing ten feet from me held my hand, and my fingers vibrate with the memory—and the desperation to do it again.

"Are you asking me out?"

Matt grins and shakes his head. "No, because if I ask you out, I have to go get another packet from HR and fill it out."

"*Another* packet?"

"That's what you heard?"

"What happened to the first packet?"

Matt shrugs and advances toward me. He bends and picks up my leaky soda cup and drops it into the trash-can. "I threw it out." He sits back down and smile-stares at me. "I was thinking we could go as friends."

I want to throw something else at him, and I look around my desk for the right object as he adds, "At least for all outward appearances."

My chin lifts instantly. "Outward appearances? What does that mean?"

"I'd love to go to dinner first," he says almost nonchalantly. "Those concerts last a couple of hours, and they only have popcorn and candy and soda there."

Dinner and a concert in the park. A couple of hours each. On a weekend.

"That sounds like a date."

"Only if that's the label we give it." His eyes turn a tiny bit hard. "I'm asking you to go with me as a fake-friend, so we can circumvent the fraternizing rules here at work."

"A fake-friend?" I'm going to start swearing with that instead of US cities. "That sounds..." I don't know how to finish the sentence.

Dangerous to my health, I think.

A fiasco runs through my mind too.

"Like a way to get past HR and still go out together," Matt supplies. "Is what it sounds like to me. So what do you think?"

SNEAK PEEK! A VERY FRIENDLY FIASCO CHAPTER TWO: MATT

LIZZIE'S TEAL BAG PERCHES ON THE CORNER OF HER desk like it might come to life and attack me. Honestly, that would be better than the suffocating silence that's followed my offer for a weekend non-date. Her new hair —the soft, rich auburn—catches the fluorescent light, and I can't stop staring. I've never seen her look more radiant, more beautiful, or more intimidating.

I'm trying to play it cool, but every second she doesn't respond feels like I've asked her to move to Mars with me instead of to dinner and a concert. My heart is doing this ridiculous staccato rhythm, and I swear, if I lean forward just a little, it'll spill out of my chest.

Lizzie leans back in her chair and crosses her arms. I can't tell if she's amused, suspicious, or plotting my demise. Probably a mix of all three. "So, let me get this straight," she starts, her voice carrying that razor-sharp edge of skepticism I both fear and admire. "You want me to go to dinner and a concert with you. As your *fake friend*."

"That's right." I nod, trying to keep my tone light. Casual. Like this isn't the most important negotiation of my life. "Just two friends enjoying a nice evening out. Totally platonic. No HR forms required."

Her eyebrow arches. "Totally platonic, huh?"

"Completely," I say, my voice cracking just a little on the word. I clear my throat and press on. "It's the perfect solution. We get to spend time together without breaking any rules, and no one at ChemTech has to know."

She tilts her head, studying me like I'm some kind of complex equation she's trying to solve. "Don't you have *real friends* for this?"

"Byron doesn't like Indie music," I say coolly. My throat is full of sawdust, but I refuse to clear it again.

"Why me?"

Because I've been hopelessly in love with you for months and I'm too much of a coward to just say it out loud. The thought barrels through my mind, but I shove it into the deepest corner of my brain and lock it up tight. No way I'm admitting that. Not yet.

"Do I really have to spell it out for you?" I lean forward like we're sharing some big secret. "Last weekend, I went by myself, and it was depressing. I ate an entire bag of kettle corn just to keep from looking like a total loser."

"Kettle corn is a solid choice," she says, her lips twitching into the faintest hint of a smile. "But I'm not sure how that translates into me accompanying you."

I shrug, forcing a grin. "You're fun. You make everything better. And, honestly, I can't think of anyone I'd rather spend a Saturday night with."

Her arms drop, and for a second, I think I've won. But then she narrows her eyes, and I realize I've underestimated her. Again.

"Would you come pick me up?" she asks, her voice as smooth and lethal as a freshly sharpened blade.

"Sure. Friends pick friends up for events they're attending."

Her lips press together, and I can't tell if she's holding back a laugh or if she's about to muscle me out of her office. Either way, I'm sweating bullets.

Finally, after what feels like an eternity, she sighs. "Fine. Dinner and a concert. As friends."

Relief crashes over me like a wave. "Yeah," I say, grinning like an idiot. "It's going to be so much fun, I promise."

"We'll see," she mutters, but there's a glimmer of something in her eyes—something that looks an awful lot like hope mingling with desire.

I stand, ready to make my escape before I can say or do

anything else to jeopardize this fragile agreement. "I'll pick you up at six. Wear something comfortable. It's an outdoor concert, so there'll be grass and twigs and bugs and things."

"You're not selling this," she says with a half-smile. "Now get out of my office, so I can get this paperwork filed."

I don't need to be told twice. I head for the door, my heart still racing, and throw her a quick wave over my shoulder. "See you later, Lizzie."

As I step into the hallway, I can't help but grin. I did it. I got her to say yes. Sure, it's as a *fake friend*, but it's a start. And maybe, just maybe, my plans to take our friendship into a secret relationship won't end in a complete disaster.

———

BY THE TIME I pull into my driveway, the adrenaline from my "fake friend" win has worn off, leaving me with nothing but nerves and a mild case of buyer's remorse. What if this backfires? What if Lizzie sees right through me? What if I accidentally call it a date and that somehow gets back to Angela in HR? You should see this woman; she has the perma-frown of a bald eagle and the sharp eyes to match.

"Stop overthinking," I mutter as I get out of my car and head for the front door. "It's just a friendly dinner and a concert. No big deal."

The moment I step inside, I'm greeted by the unmistakable sound of claws skittering across hardwood floors. A split second later, a blur of gray fur launches itself at my legs, with a slightly darker charcoal only a moment behind.

"Hey, fellas." I crouch down to scratch my felines, Purricell and Purroxide. They're brothers and Maine Coon cats with big personalities and even bigger appetites. Purricell is the most vocal of the pair, and he meows loudly, his tail swishing like he's scolding me for being late.

"I know, I know," I say, heading for the kitchen to fill the food bowls. "I had a long day too, buddy. And I may or may not have just made a complete fool of myself in front of the woman I'm trying to impress."

He meows again, hopping up onto the counter to watch me with those judgmental green eyes. "You remember Lizzie, right? She was wearing the sexiest dress on the planet today, and she took the morning off to get her hair done, and she's a redhead now, guys."

I open the can of food and mix it in with their dry kibble. Purricell yowls and glares, as if he doesn't care about Lizzie, which simply can't be true. Purroxide rubs against my calf, and I think of the Diet Coke Lizzie threw at me when I surprised her.

I grin like a fool, because her defense tactic wouldn't scare away a spider.

Purricell paws at my hand, and I startle back to the

present. "Don't look at me like that," I say, setting their bowls down on the floor. "It's not like you've ever had to navigate ChemTech's dating policy. Or ask the prettiest woman in the state to dinner without actually calling it a date."

The cats ignore me and dive into their food like they haven't eaten in weeks. I lean against the counter, watching them for a moment as fondness tugs through me.

And how pathetic is that?

The nerdy chemical engineer smiling sweetly at his cats, because they're so cute and amazing? "This is why you need a girlfriend," I tell myself as I open the fridge and pull out a can of lime sparkling water. The house is quiet, as I live alone, and all that punctures the humming of the refrigerator is Purroxide's enthusiastic crunching of kibble. It's peaceful, but also a little lonely.

Fine, a lot lonely. I'm lonely, and I can admit it to myself.

I make a drink with an orange-mango packet and the sparkling water and wander into the living room before collapsing onto the couch. My laptop sits on the coffee table, and I open it up, pulling up the ChemTech employee handbook for the second time this week. The dating policy stares back at me, mocking me with its endless rules and regulations.

"Why does everything have to be so complicated?" I ask Purroxide as he joins me, his dinner scarfed down.

He stretches out beside me, his tail flicking against my leg.

The truth is, it's not just the dating policy that's holding me back. It's me. My inability to just say what I'm feeling without turning it into a joke or a half-baked "fake friend" scheme.

I close the laptop, setting it aside, and run a hand through my hair. "You've got two days to figure this out, Matty," I tell myself, hearing it in my mother's voice. "And you can do anything in two days." She always told me that, and I wish she wasn't out in the middle of the Atlantic Ocean so I could call her.

Because if there's one thing I know for sure, it's that Lizzie Trenton is worth every ounce of effort. Every awkward conversation. Every nerve-wracking moment. She's the smartest, funniest, most incredible woman I've ever met. And I'd walk through fire—or a mountain of HR paperwork if it comes to that—just to see her smile.

Purricell meows, curling up against my side, and I can't help but smile. "You're right," I say, scratching behind his ears. "One step at a time."

I reach for my phone and call my sister. Chanel is the closest thing to my momma I can get right now. Thankfully, she knows to answer when I call, or I'll just pester her until she does.

"Matty," she says, calling me that childhood nickname I grew up with.

I smile as I lean back into the couch and stroke

Purroxide as he snuggles into my other side. "Guess what I did at work today?"

"Solved the energy crisis," Chanel says without missing a beat.

I laugh and shake my head. "No, silly. I'm a chemical engineer," I tell her for at least the fiftieth time. "I don't even work in energy."

"You ate a peanut butter and peach jam sandwich."

"Guilty, but I wouldn't call you about that."

"You finalized the chemical formula for a pill that will cure cancer."

"Now whatever I say will be super-lame."

"You told me to guess." Chanel carries a smile in her voice, and I'm not really upset.

"I talked to Lizzie."

"You talk to Lizzie every day."

"I asked her to go to the concert with me this weekend."

Chanel doesn't immediately fire back at me, and that's how I know what I've done is huge. "So you're going to fill out the paperwork?" she asks. On her end of the line, a baby cries, and it gets louder as she presumably goes to get her three-month-old daughter.

"No," I say, a keen sense of supreme satisfaction pulling through me. "We're going as friends."

"Friends." Chanel says the word like she doesn't know what it means. "But Matty, you don't want to be friends with Lizzie."

"But friends don't have to fill out sixteen sheafs of paperwork to go to a concert in the park."

"Oh, I see what's happening here. You're going to *pretend* to just be her friend in public while you secretly kiss her in private."

"We have a winner, Purricell." I laugh, and Chanel adds a giggle or two to my voice, but it doesn't last long.

"I worry this is going to turn into a friendly fiasco," she says.

"That's because you worry about everything."

"And you worry about nothing," she fires back. "Matty, you've liked this woman for months. What if this backfires on you?"

Part of me wants to laugh it off the way I do most things. I'd rather just look at life from a glass-half-full perspective than anything else, but what Chanel doesn't get is that a pit of anxiety lives in the bottom of my stomach at all times.

"I've thought through this for months," I say. "ChemTech makes one or both parties turn in a detailed write-up of *every* date. Every single one, Chanel. They have a word count requirement."

"You work for a weird company."

"Scientists are kind of weird," I say, because everyone teases us about that anyway. I might as well admit it.

"So tell me your plan, Doctor Weird," she says.

I do have a Ph.D, and Chanel likes to poke fun at me

about it. "Well, obviously," I say. "I'm going to do a few friendly things with a good friend of mine from work, and I'm going to pour some gasoline onto the sparks between us, and hope that something hot happens."

"Oh, yeah," Chanel teases. "This is going to be a *very* friendly fiasco."

We laugh together, but I'm hoping for exactly that, because my life is as dull as watching paint dry, and I can definitely use something, or rather, some*one*, to liven it up.

And I'm okay if there are elements of it that aren't exactly perfect, as long as there's a lot of me getting to kiss Lizzie.

My phone beeps at me, and I pull it away from my ear. "Oh," I say, surprise and fear rushing through my bloodstream and spiking my adrenaline. "Lizzie's calling, Chanel. I have to go."

"Yep, go," my sister says. "Tell her—"

But I swipe to connect Lizzie's call, because she's never called me after work before, and I'm suddenly dying to know what she has to say.

———

MATT CAN'T BE SERIOUS, right? How is THIS going to work? I think his sister might be right, and this is going to be **A VERY FRIENDLY FIASCO. Read** now by scanning the **QR** code with your phone.

Just His Secretary, Book 1: She's just his secretary...until he needs someone on his arm to convince his mother that he can take over the family business. Then Callie becomes Dawson's girlfriend —but just in his text messages...but maybe she'll start to worm her way into his shriveled heart too.

Just His Boss, Book 2: She's just his boss, especially since Tara just barely hired Alec. But when things heat up in the kitchen, Tara will have to decide where Alec is needed more—on her arm or behind the stove.

Just His Assistant, Book 3: She's just his assistant, which is exactly how this Southern belle wants it. No spotlight. Not anymore. But as she struggles to learn her new role in his office—especially because Lance is the surliest boss imaginable—Jessie might just have to open her heart to show him everyone has a past they're running from.

Just His Partner, Book 4: She's just his partner, because she's seen the number of women he parades through his life. No amount of charm and good looks is worth being played...until Sabra witnesses Jason take the blame for someone else at the law office where they both work.

Just His Barista, Book 5: She's just his barista...until she buys into Legacy Brew as a co-owner. Then she's Coy's business partner *and* the source of his five-year-long crush. But after they share a kiss one night, Macie's seriously considering mixing business and pleasure.

———

Bonus for newsletter subscribers! Just His Neighbor, Prequel: She's just his neighbor...until his dog—oops, his brother's dog—adopts her.

Get this book by joining my newsletter here: https://readerlinks. com/l/3887964 **or scan the QR code below.**

BOOKS IN THE CIDER COVE SWEET
SOUTHERN ROMCOM SERIES

**A Very Terrible Text, Book 1:
Sometimes the thumbs slip...**

She's finally joined the dating app everyone in Cider Cove is raving about...when she accidentally sends a message about wanting to meet up for a first date to her enemy.

A Very Bad Bet, Book 2:
Sometimes a wager only makes things more fun...

She's got seniority over the obnoxious grump next door, and she's determined to beat him out for the top job in their charming home-town. But a bold bet spins their

rivalry into a flirty attraction that could change everything.

———

A Very Merry Mess, Book 3: *Sometimes the holidays are messy...*

Christmas is the season of joy, mistletoe, and, unfortunately for Ryanne, the pressure of bringing home a date. When she vents to Elliott, her best friend and co-manager at the small-town office supply store, he impulsively grabs her phone and texts her mother that they're dating.

Date. Ing.

A Very Disastrous Dare, Book 4: *Sometimes a person speaks before thinking...*

She's just bought the flower shop and he's taken over the hardware store for his dad. Sounds peachy, right? Sure, until they both want an assistance grant from the city...and now Emma and Aaron are rivals *and* neighbors.

A Very Friendly Fiasco, Book 5: *Sometimes the friend zone is breached...*

Sometimes the friend zone is breached...

He's her office crush, and she's the colleague he can't stop thinking about. But with HR's no-fraternization policy breathing down their necks, Lizzie and Matt have to get creative if they want to explore what's brewing between them—starting with a "fake-friend" date to a concert in the park.

ABOUT ELANA

Elana Johnson is a USA Today bestselling and Kindle All-Star author of dozens of clean and wholesome contemporary romance novels. She lives in Utah, where she mothers two fur babies, works with her husband full-time, and eats a lot of veggies while writing. Find her on her website at feelgoodfictionbooks.com.

www.ingramcontent.com/pod-product-compliance
Lightning Source LLC
Chambersburg PA
CBHW050504110726
47899CB00005B/1323